SAFE

The most electrifying crime thriller of the summer

JANE ADAMS

JOFFE
BOOKS

First published 2020
Joffe Books, London
www.joffebooks.com

**Please join our mailing list for free Kindle
books and new releases.**

We love to hear from our readers! Please email any
feedback you have to: feedback@joffebooks.com

ISBN 978-1-78931-453-3

CHAPTER 1

Blood on her hands, blood on her face, on her clothes. Blood everywhere.

She hammered on the window, knowing that the window was locked and she couldn't open it and that there was no one to hear. And anyway, she realized, forcing herself to think clearly, she didn't want anyone to hear, not really. If they heard then they'd find out what she'd done and she'd be dead too.

She ran to the door. He'd locked it when he came in but still she tried the handle again. What had he done with the key? He'd taken it, laughing at her, and put it into his pocket before throwing his jacket onto the bed. Was the key in the jacket now? She hoped so. She couldn't bear the thought that she might have to go over to him, over to his body lying on the floor, blood all over it, blood all over her, and search through his pockets. She imagined doing it and her stomach turned over.

She leaped over to the bed and searched his jacket. A wallet, car keys, handkerchief, but no key.

He must have it on him, then. Breathe, you can do this. Just breathe.

She approached him slowly, reluctantly, scared that he might suddenly wake up. Scared that he might just be

1

playing dead, even though she knew he wasn't. She poked him with her toe and then asked herself what the hell she was doing and knelt down. They would be back soon and she had to get away. Her father would never forgive this.

She slid her hand into a trouser pocket. Nothing. She pushed her hand into the other pocket and her fingers felt the hard shape of the key. Relief washed over her and she stumbled to the door, inserted the key and turned it. She pulled the door open and listened. No, the house was still empty. They weren't back yet. Her head told her she would have heard the cars if her father and his entourage had returned, but her heart was beating so hard and so rapidly she could hardly hear her own thoughts.

She took a deep breath, steadying herself. She *had* to be sensible, had to think carefully. If she was going to survive, she had to get away from here. Far away.

How?

Car keys, his car keys — they'd been in his jacket. She hadn't even passed her test yet, never driven an automatic before, and she knew that's what he drove. But how hard could it be? She had to at least try. She picked up the keys and then saw the wallet lying on the bed. She'd need money. She knew where her father kept a stash downstairs but . . .

She opened the wallet. Charlie always carried a lot of cash. She shoved the wallet into the pocket of her cardigan and raced down the stairs. She paused outside her father's study. He kept money and other things there, too, and she knew how to unlock the drawers, where he kept the keys. Did she have time? Retrieving the key from the little box on the sideboard, she fumbled with the lock on the drawer. It opened. She grabbed money and then, on impulse, the gun he always kept beside it, snatched her coat from the peg on her way through the hall and then halted. Could she hear cars?

Were they coming back?

Her father always travelled with an entourage. When he'd left, there'd been two more cars and at least a half-dozen men with him.

2

Over the sound of the pouring rain, she heard a car horn in the distance.

Fuck. Was that them?

Lauren hurtled outside, leaving the front door wide open and the rain falling on the hall carpet.

Charlie's car was parked out front and she was desperately grateful that the horseshoe driveway meant she didn't have to reverse. It would be bad enough making the damn thing go forward.

When it came to it, driving was easier than she'd expected. She had watched him many times, just like she watched everyone and everything, learning, studying, taking it all in until the time she might need it. Now it paid off as she started the ignition and stamped down on the accelerator.

At the end of the drive, she looked both ways. Which way were they likely to come back? If they spotted his car—

Left. No, right. No, left. God, she couldn't dither like this. What was it her father was always saying? Hesitation gets people killed. She indicated right, even though there was no one to see. *Mirror, signal, manoeuvre.* Then she took off into the night, certain that they were behind her as she put her foot down and raced away as fast as she could.

CHAPTER 2

Harry had fallen asleep in his chair. He woke to a hammering on the door and the sound of rain pelting against his window. Puzzled and wary, he checked the CCTV camera outside the front door and frowned. What was she doing here?

She must've guessed that he'd look at the camera first because she was staring into the lens. *Harry, help me.* He could see the words she was mouthing and that there seemed to be something on her face.

She almost fell against him as he opened the door.

"Fuck's sake, Lauren, are you hurt?"

"It's not my blood."

"Then whose?" Harry assessed the situation. "Does your father know?"

"I don't know if they're back yet. I took off in Charlie's car, but I thought I heard them coming. Harry, I didn't know what else to do."

"He'll guess you'd come to me."

This had obviously not occurred to her. She looked both contrite and scared.

"Harry, I'm sorry, I should never—"

"Bit late for that, girl. Go upstairs, get yourself tidied up. You left some clothes here last time you stayed over. I'll get

4

some stuff together and we'll go." *And hope for Chrissake, we've got a little bit of a head start*, he thought.

Five minutes later, they were in Harry's car. He had not bothered to hide the vehicle that she had arrived in, what was the point? Who else would she have run to?

She looked calmer now she'd washed the blood off her face. Curled in the front seat in jeans and a hooded sweatshirt decorated with a longneck cat, and snuggled beneath a blanket, she looked even more like the child who had climbed onto Uncle Harry's lap, knowing he always had sweets in his pocket.

Seventeen now, Harry thought. *Still a schoolgirl but as far as her father is concerned, just another disposable asset.* She'd told Harry that she'd taken money from her father's study, admitted to taking the gun and the wallet. Harry had let her hang onto both because it seemed to give her some sense of comfort, but the rest of the cash he'd stowed in the bag that now sat on the back seat.

"He'll come after me, won't he? And now he'll come after you."

"He will. So we'll have to stay one step ahead, won't we?" He spoke with far more confidence than he felt. Her father's organization was massive and he was not a man to be crossed. Harry was one of the few who had managed to retire from the firm, and only because he'd been injured in the line of duty, protecting his boss. Harry still walked with a bad limp because of it. But he knew all too well that any previous favour would count for nothing, not now.

"How did you kill him?"

"I shot him. Used his own gun."

So she humiliated him as well, Harry thought. *Another strike against her, in her father's eyes.*

"And he was the one your dad wanted you to—"

"Didn't want to wait till he got a ring on my finger, did he? Said my dad wouldn't care."

Which is probably true, Harry thought.

"But I told him *I* cared. I told him I wasn't going to—"

5

Harry nodded. He could guess the rest. "You took the gun off him?" He was curious about that part.

"He had it in his jacket pocket. He threw his jacket on the bed. Then he threw me on the bed."

"Bad move," Harry said. So, how were they going to get out of this? Frankly, Harry couldn't see a way. He had no doubt about the danger she was in. Her father had no regard for anyone who crossed him. No mercy, no forgiveness, even for members of his own family. He'd proved that, hadn't he? So what could they do?

As though thinking the same thing, she said, "I could go to the police. They could protect us because I know things. If I threatened to go to the police, he might leave us alone."

"As far as your dad is concerned, you knowing things is just another reason to have you killed," Harry said. "You, girl, need to keep your mouth shut and your head down." They needed to get as far away as they possibly could from his now ex-employer. But where the hell was far enough? In coming to him, she had signed both their death warrants. It was just a question of when and where they would catch up with them.

CHAPTER 3

Kyle Sykes stood at the doorway to his daughter's bedroom and surveyed the mess. Charlie Perrin lay on the floor where he'd fallen. A good portion of his face and an even bigger portion of the back of his head was missing. The gun lay in the corner of the room where she had thrown it. It had taken only one shot, and it was evident to Kyle that Charlie Perrin had assumed that a seventeen-year-old girl was no match for him. He had clearly underestimated her. Kyle allowed himself a second or two of grudging admiration. Pity she hadn't been a boy. But the admiration faded and the anger surged. She had defied him, it was as simple as that. Lauren had known exactly what her father intended for her and giving her to Charlie Perrin was not something he'd decided on a whim. A proper marriage, two families united, and no more interference from the Perrins into Sykes's affairs because now they would be Perrin affairs, too. The little bint had gone and screwed it up.

Had she killed one of his lieutenants, just one of his rank and file, Kyle Sykes would have arranged for the body to be dumped in a canal somewhere, but Charlie Perrin was different. He'd have to be taken home to his family and apologies would have to be made, explanations given. Knowing that made Sykes incandescent. Even if he'd been prepared to forgive his child — which he was not — the Perrins certainly wouldn't be. Gus Perrin was as old school as Sykes himself, as Old Testament in his view of justice.

Sykes walked back down the stairs and out to his car. It was raining now and he didn't wait for his driver to catch up but took the wheel himself. Minutes later, he was swinging out onto the road with little regard to any oncoming traffic, two cars pulling in behind him, heading to Harry's place. The girl would go there, he knew that. Who else would be stupid enough to look after her?

Harry had served his purpose in the old days and had lived quietly since Sykes had let him go. Harry's wife had died, Harry himself had been hurt shortly after, defending Kyle — Sykes had to give him that — though he'd not been right in the head since Jean died. Sykes figured he'd had a death wish since then anyway. Helping the kid, that sort of proved it, didn't it? Well, if Harry wanted to commit suicide, he was going the right way about it.

Sykes got out of the car, leaving the engine running and the door open. He kicked in the front door, setting off the alarm. It amused him that Harry had stopped to set the alarm before he left. Did he really think the police would care if his place was broken into? No one would give a shit about the old lag that was Harry Prentice. Sykes marched into the house, knowing already that no one would be there.

He was aware that his men had followed him in, standing back out of the way of the boss's inevitable fury.

"Burn it down," he told them.

CHAPTER 4

"Where are we?" Lauren stretched and looked around. They had pulled into a motorway service station and she wondered how long she'd been asleep.

"We need food and we need petrol," Harry told her. He looked exhausted and she realized with a slight shock that it was getting light. Still raining, still grey but obviously after dawn. He must have driven all night.

"You all right, Harry?" *Stupid question, of course he isn't all right. Neither of us are.*

For a second or two on waking, she had forgotten all about Charlie Perrin. She'd forgotten the noise of the gun, she forgot running out through the rain and getting into Perrin's car and driving to Harry's place. Forgot what she'd done and what she'd brought down on both their heads. She could feel the tears start and she wiped her eyes. Now was not the time to cry. And Harry was right, she was hungry, surprisingly so. And she needed the loo, quite desperately, now she actually had time to think about it.

The car park at the services was still busy with people coming and going, even at this hour of the morning. Lauren pulled her coat tight around her and shivered. She'd been warm in the car, but there was a real chill in the air and that heavy November grey that her mother had always hated wrapped itself around her like damp wool.

She took her time in the bathroom, checking that she looked at least respectable. She was so glad there had been clean clothes at Harry's house. When Jean had been alive, she'd stayed most weekends. Harry and Jean had loved her mother and then loved her and they'd had no kids of their own to spoil. Lauren's father had tolerated this closeness because after all, if you cared about someone, that bred loyalty. Kyle Sykes was fully aware that *he* could never breed *that* kind of loyalty. He was quite happy to be feared, but that didn't mean he was unable to see the value of emotional attachment when it could be manipulated.

Harry was waiting for her when she came out of the ladies and he nodded approval that she'd washed her face and combed her hair. He was, she realized, old enough to be her grandfather, and she decided that was what people would see when they looked at the pair of them. It was a game she'd played all her life, deciding what it was that people were going to see when they looked at her and then acting the part. She was surprisingly good at it — or maybe not so surprisingly, considering how she'd been brought up. At school, she was the daughter of a businessman, at home, the child of a crime lord. She rarely saw friends outside of school, but when she did, or when she took part in after-school activities, it was most often Harry who picked her up. Uncle Harry had been accepted as her guardian, even though he'd been a little old for that role. Most families, it seemed, had an honorary Uncle Harry somewhere about.

They took trays and queued up at self-service. "You hungry?" Harry asked.

"Absolutely starving. Is that normal?"

"I think we're beyond normal, love. But it's good that you're hungry. You need fuel to keep going. Me, I think I'm going to have the full English, hash browns and beans, the lot. And maybe some toast and marmalade to follow, and a nice big pot of tea."

She laughed. She couldn't help herself. Harry smiled approval and gave her a hug. A grandfatherly kind of hug.

Neither of them said much while they were eating. But after, when Lauren pushed aside her plate with a deep sigh and Harry poured her yet more tea, she asked him where they were heading.

"There's a cottage on the coast. It's a holiday let, but I know the owner and where they hide the spare key. There'll be nobody there, it will be shut at this time of year. It's really isolated and we stand some chance of defending it. Or at least getting some warning. There's a clear view all around. It's as good a place as any."

Reality crashed down again and the food she had devoured so eagerly now weighed heavy in her belly. "What are we going to do, Harry?"

"I don't know, girl. I really don't. But we'll get to the cottage, and then we'll sit down and figure it out."

"He's going to kill us both, isn't he?"

"He's going to do his damnedest, that's for sure."

CHAPTER 5

The fire service were still damping down the site when DI Toby Clarke arrived. He'd had a late night, grabbed three or four hours sleep and then been woken by the telephone at five o'clock with the news that Harry Prentice's house had been torched, and the fire chief suspected arson.

He knew what the house had looked like before, being familiar with Harry Prentice and very familiar with Harry Prentice's boss, and it was hard to believe that a five-bedroom, Georgian-style mansion had stood there only a few hours before. The house was now reduced to a pile of ash and smouldering timber, nothing stood more than a metre high on the entire site.

Two uniformed officers sat in a police car at the entrance to the horseshoe drive. The fire chief was parked up on the other side. Clarke passed the police officers and parked just beyond them. By the time he'd got out, both the uniformed men and the fire chief were heading in his direction.

"So, what happened?"

The fire chief spoke first. "The whole place went up fast, and even from what we can see before we send the investigators in, it's pretty clear that it was arson. There are three or maybe four points of ignition. Whoever set the fires wanted this place to go up fast, for combustion to be, well, pretty much complete."

"Anyone inside?"

"Not as far as we can tell. As you can see, the crew are still damping down. It'll be midday before we can make a proper survey. We've spoken to the crime scene manager and we'll work the scene in tandem."

Clarke nodded and turned to the two officers. "And you've been here since . . . ?"

"The house alarm was set off at twenty past midnight. Security company phoned us. We got the call about twelve thirty. We arrived about twelve forty-five a.m., spotted a couple of cars driving off, which looked as if they'd just come out of the drive, so we started to follow them, and then — boom."

"Boom?"

"Well, OK, not exactly 'boom.' It was like you'd imagine it would look if there *had* been a boom. Flames everywhere, spotted them in the rear-view, so we turned around and came back. We called in the registration number of one of the cars we were following. By the time we got back, the whole place was ablaze. Went up in no time at all."

Clarke glanced at the fire chief, who nodded. "You can still smell the petrol," he pointed out. "Even after the fire. Initial impressions are that someone went in and drenched the place. It took a full two hours to get it under anything like control. At one point, we had three tenders on site."

"Any luck on the car registration?"

"Vehicle is registered to one Michael Hoban."

"We all know who he works for. But of course, he'll have been tucked up in bed, and have no idea at all who was using his car last night."

One of the uniformed officers was looking at Clarke. "We heard over the radio that Charlie Perrin's dead. I mean, that's one hell of a night, now Harry Prentice's place is torched. What's going on, boss?"

Clarke had heard the news about Charlie Perrin's death on his way over but had no more details than uniform did. "You tell me," he said.

He walked over towards what was left of the house. The gravel of the drive was blackened by soot and debris mixed with water from the hoses, leaving dark puddles that would stain anything and everything it came into contact with. Clarke avoided these as best he could. The fire chief walked with him and pointed out areas where they believed combustion had begun. Kitchen, living room, hallway and, he figured, probably one of the bedrooms upstairs. It was hard to be certain, but there were areas where the burning had been more intense. "Certainly more than one seat of fire," he said. "It's going to take a bit of sorting out."

"What forensics should we be looking for on the arsonists?"

"Nothing that can't be destroyed by a shower and a trip to the dry cleaners."

And we don't have enough for an immediate warrant, Clarke thought. Except for Michael Hoban, whose car had been seen driving away — and who would already have disposed of whatever he might have been wearing and secured himself an unbreakable alibi. Kyle Sykes was far too experienced to leave anything to chance. They could bring Michael Hoban in, if they could find him, but like as not whoever had been involved with setting the fire would be away from home and alibied to the hilt for the night in question. It would be a matter of, "*Anyone could have taken the car, Inspector. Perhaps it was stolen.*"

Another car pulled into the drive and Clarke's boss, DCI Henderson, got out and walked over to them. "Messy. How soon before we can get forensics in here?" He directed the question at the fire chief.

"Should be cool enough by midday, but you know how it is at a scene like this. Just putting the fire out destroys a hell of a lot of evidence. My people will work with yours. Your crime scene manager's already been briefed, and we should have a preliminary report by early evening."

Henderson walked back towards his car. Clarke followed. Henderson paused before getting in. "I've called a full briefing, the whole team, an hour from now. Finish up here and then come in. You heard the news about Charlie Perrin?"

"I heard that he was dead. I don't know the circumstances."

"Apparently, he was drunk and playing with a shotgun. He's in the morgue and the family have fast-tracked the post-mortem. You can do that when you're as rich as Croesus. Funeral's arranged for the end of the week, so they're assuming nothing will turn up at the post-mortem that involves a police investigation."

"Of course they are. What about the inquest? Can't we hold the body until then?"

Henderson shrugged and spread his hands in a *Why ask me?* gesture. "I expect they'll get an interim certificate after the PM."

"Interviews?"

"You can have that honour. Of course, it's all informal, this being an '*accident*.' Unless something turns up at the post-mortem, which of course it won't. That's scheduled for two p.m., by the way."

"And you want me there?"

"And I want you there."

"Can I ask how we first got to know about Charlie Perrin?"

"We had a heads up about four o'clock this morning, but the news broke around six. The parents phoned one of their pet media outlets and announced the sad fact of their youngest son having gone to meet his maker. The shotgun that supposedly did for him is licensed, by the way. Supposedly, he dropped it when he was pissed out of his brain, gun went off, bye-bye, Charlie Perrin. He was alone at the time. The family found the body after hearing the gun go off from the other side of the premises."

"Then how do they know it was an accident?"

"How can we prove it wasn't? Their legal team will be all over this. They let our officers in to view the scene, didn't get in the way when the CSI did their job. In fact, they made sure tea and coffee was on hand for everybody. There was even the offer of breakfast. The post-mortem is going to be carried out by Sir Geoffrey Connor, and who's going to argue with him?"

Clarke was thoughtful. "I thought it was Sykes who had Connor in his pocket, not the Perrins."

"So did we all. Perhaps the rumours about the families coming together aren't so exaggerated after all. Watch this space, as they say."

"I've been watching this particular space for too long. It's been about as interesting as watching paint dry. About as informative, too."

"Then spare a thought for those of us who've been on this a hell of a lot longer," his boss told him. "Right — to recap, this is how your day will go. You come to the briefing, and then you visit the Perrins. Then you swing by and talk to Kyle Sykes, seeing as the owner of this now ex-house was in his employ. See what he *doesn't* have to say. That's not going to take very long, you know that as well as I do, so you should have time for a spot of lunch before the post-mortem."

Thanks, Clarke thought, as he watched his boss drive away.

CHAPTER 6

Charlie Perrin's final journey back to his family had not been the most dignified of affairs. He had been laid out on a blanket in the back of a Volvo estate car, with the seats down, and covered with the pink, floral quilt from Lauren's bed, just because that had been handy.

Kyle Sykes had never been one to delegate the difficult stuff, and he had gone on ahead, roused the Perrins from their beds at three in the morning and explained the situation before Charlie's body arrived. It was now nine a.m. and he was still talking. A funeral director had already been called in and arrangements made. The wake would be closed casket, of course, and the story was that Charlie Perrin had met with a bit of an accident. No one, funeral director included, was going to question that. His business was part owned by the Perrins and his family had provided funerary services for theirs for the past three generations.

Gus Perrin had been in a wheelchair for the last five years, having suffered with his own accident in the shape of a rival and a handgun. What he had lost in physical capacity, he made up for in both business acumen and rage, and it had taken all Sykes's ability to keep the lid on the latter.

"We do this subtle," Kyle Sykes said, not for the first time. "We don't draw attention. No need for the families to go to war over this. You've lost your son — my daughter will pay for that — but there's nothing to be gained by going off half-cocked. By getting the wrong kind of attention from the wrong kind of people."

Charlie Perrin's mother had been distraught and had been packed off upstairs with Charlie's sister. A doctor had been called to give her a sedative. Both Gus and Kyle had agreed about one thing, this was no place for wailing women. Sykes was surprised therefore when, after a quiet knock on the door, the sister came in, leaving another woman standing uncertainly in the doorway. Carole Perrin was a familiar enough figure, tall and slim like her mother and remaining brother, and dark-haired. She, unlike Sykes's daughter, had married when and to whom she was told and, if Karl remembered right, she was also some kind of artist, exhibiting here and there, spending her dad's money to put on shows of weird sculptures.

The other woman was new. He didn't recognize her at all. Not as tall, slightly built and with short, very neatly styled blonde hair. Kyle preferred long hair but she was, nevertheless, a looker. Her eyes were surprisingly dark, a grey that shaded almost to brown, and there was a wariness to them, which was familiar enough. Most of the women Karl knew carried that same expression in their eyes.

"What?" Gus demanded.

"Just wanted you to know, all the arrangements have been made for the funeral. There'll have to be a post-mortem, but Dr Brookes is dealing with all that. Sam here came up with a good story about an accident with a shotgun."

Gus's eyes narrowed. "He weren't shot with a friggin' shotgun."

Carole exchanged an awkward glace with the other woman. "He will have been by the time the post-mortem takes place," she said. "It'll make a mess, but if it's done right, will cover up the original . . . injuries. Dr Brookes will make sure no one asks too many difficult questions, you know that, and it's well-known Charlie was a bit careless when he'd had a few. Dr Brookes explained matters to Sir Geoffrey Connor, and he'll be doing the post-mortem for us, so there'll be no bother." She cast a look at Kyle Sykes, acknowledging that this had been his doing.

Gus narrowed his eyes and looked hard at the small blonde still standing in the doorway. She looked away but didn't move, though Sykes could see she was scared. Eventually, Gus nodded.

Carole took a deep breath and then continued. "I've asked Sam to sort out the wake, but we didn't know where you wanted it to be."

The blonde woman came hesitantly into the room and handed a sheaf of papers, at arm's length, to Gus, as though she was anxious not to get within reach. Kyle smirked. She was probably very wise, though if Gus wanted her within reach, that's where she'd be.

"What's this?" Gus demanded.

"We've drawn up a list, a guest list. Carole wondered if there was anyone you wanted to add. And the last page is arrangements we've made so far, and a rough order of service. " She made this sound like a question, as though he might not know what an order of service was.

Gus looked it over. "Good enough."

"Any additions?" Carole asked.

"If there are, I'll tell you. John will tell you," he said, referring to her surviving brother.

Carole nodded and she and Sam withdrew, closing the door softly behind them.

"Who's the new girl?"

"Works for our Carole, she reckons she's busy enough to need a secretary or a PA, or something or other."

He sounded deeply dismissive and Sykes did not question further.

"I'll keep the peace," Gus Perrin said. "Fourteen days I'll give you. Find that bitch, get rid. You do that and I'll consider honouring our former arrangement. Consider, mind.

Fourteen days, two weeks. Plenty of time in anybody's book to take care of a kid and an old man."

And that was what rankled most, Kyle Sykes understood. Rankled with both of them. Charlie Perrin had been taken out by a kid half his age. Charlie Perrin, who had beaten one man to death with his bare fists. One that Sykes knew about, anyway. He'd disposed of at least half a dozen others but had finally met his match. Shot with his own gun by a teenage girl.

CHAPTER 7

A strange scene unfolded as Clarke drove through the very modest five-bar gate and onto the farm that had been Gus Perrin's home for the last eighteen years. Perrin was a man who believed in keeping everybody close. He'd had three children — two now — and when the eldest two had married, they had moved into their own accommodation, but that accommodation had still been on the Perrin farm. The locals still referred to it that way, despite the fact that little in terms of agriculture had happened since Perrin took over the forty acres. It was perfect for the Perrins, Clarke reflected. The big house, and a whole load of tied cottages and barn conversions. It was almost like a village from which the Perrin business empire was run, the legitimate and not so legitimate. If the rumours were correct and the Perrins and the Sykes were prepared to become one big happy family, then, Clarke thought, it was about time somebody reported them to the monopolies commission.

A man in a sharp suit stood talking to a uniformed officer in front of the main house, a mellow old brick and weathered stone construction that Clarke knew had featured in at least two interiors and one country life magazine. It settled into the landscape, looking sleepy, contented and self-satisfied.

A building that knew its place and was obviously well-loved and well-maintained. The two men, one from his side, one from theirs, were sharing a joke and what looked like a large flask of coffee. *Very cosy*, Clarke thought. But then the Perrins were known for cosying up to all and sundry, even uniformed constables. Local school needs a new roof? Gus Perrin's your man. The vicar is running a garden fete? The Perrins will provide security and organize the car parking. Big on community was Gus Perrin, his actions engendered by the policy that Clarke's boss summed up as "*Don't shit where you live.*"

Clarke was willing to bet that within a ten-mile or so radius of the farm, no one would have a bad word to say about the Perrin family. Get further out and it would be a different story.

He pulled up in front of the house and the tall man in the Perrin uniform of smart, dark suit and white shirt bent down to speak to him through the window. "Follow the drive round the side of the house and you'll see your lot outside Charlie's bungalow. Refreshments have been set up in the storeroom next door. You need anything, you just shout, OK?"

It was, Clarke thought as he followed the drive around the house as per instructions, an almost surreal experience. The man might have directed him to a family picnic or some kind of seasonal celebration. The illusion was ruined only by the fact that Clarke recognized him and knew that he had been imprisoned for three counts of GBH and had *not* been imprisoned for many more.

The bungalow had obviously once been a farm building of some sort but had been converted, as had every other available space on the farm, into quite luxurious accommodation. The crime scene manager, Paul Collins, spotted his car as he pulled up and came over. Clarke got out and stretched. No car ever felt like it had enough leg room. At six foot three, he was a head taller than Collins — though not quite as broad. Collins was built like a rugby prop forward.

"So, what have we got?"

"I've allowed the body to be moved, your DCI sanctioned that earlier this morning. We got everything we could from it, and frankly it was in the way, you'll see what I mean when we get in there. It's not an easy scene to work and is going to take us time. But on the face of it . . ."

"On the face of it, he got pissed, dropped a shotgun and it went off."

"It happens," Paul Collins said. "All I can say is that the angle of shot would *appear* to be consistent with the victim standing and dropping the firearm. The blood and brain matter on the wall would also appear consistent with that story. I suppose what I'm saying is, prove it *didn't* happen that way."

Clarke nodded and followed the crime scene manager into the chalet bungalow. The front door opened into a large living room. Off that, he could see a kitchen and a flight of stairs. Collins led him through the living room and into a second room set out with the dining table and four uncomfortable-looking high-backed chairs, then into a small room at the back. This room was separated from the rest of the property by a heavy door, and the tiny window, high up in the wall, was barred. Clarke whistled. "Most people in the hunting, shooting, fishing set have a gun cupboard, not an entire bloody room."

The room was small and cramped and Clarke, as he examined the crime scene photos, understood what Collins had meant about the body being in the way. Apart from the gun cabinets, the only furniture in the room was a small table on which was set an almost empty decanter, a single glass and a box of shotgun shells. The body had fallen backwards against the cabinets, arms outstretched, the gun to one side. This was still in position on the floor. The CSI working here would have ended up stepping over the body, almost on the body, whenever they moved. Clarke indicated the box of shotgun cartridges.

"What was he planning on doing? Going out shooting in the middle of the night?"

"According to the family, it wouldn't have been the first time. He was unmarried, lived alone most of the time and, they claim, had a tendency to wander out in the middle of the night with a lamp and a shotgun looking for rabbits." Paul Collins shrugged. "What do I know? Maybe he did."

"And was he generally half-cut when he went out for a spot of lamping."

"According to the family, half-cut tended to be his general state from about six o'clock in the evening. He'd start drinking before dinner and wouldn't really stop. They reckon he was never exactly what you'd call incapacitated, just not entirely sober."

Clarke nodded. That fitted with what he already knew about Charlie Perrin. The series of drunk driving offences, a final ban last year when even those magistrates under the Perrin thumb could no longer prevaricate. Clarke doubted there was any shortage of people to drive him around, so it was not likely to be too much of an inconvenience. "And the sister found the body?" he confirmed.

"She lives in the nearest cottage. She heard the gunshot, came over, and found him."

"How did she get in? The front door wasn't forced. Did she have a key?"

"Apparently, no one locks their doors around here. This is the countryside, you know."

Clarke laughed. "And your average burglars are going to know to keep clear of Gus Perrin's farm," he agreed. "So she finds the body — and then?"

"DS Sheldon's taken her statement but apparently she went up to the big house and told them what had happened. The other brother came back and took a look, decided that life was extinct, called their doctor, phoned the funeral directors and then finally phoned the police."

"And how much time had passed by the time we got involved?"

Collins shrugged again.

"Plenty of time to stage the scene to their own liking."

"You don't believe the 'accidental shooting while pissed as a fart' scenario then?"

"You might say that," Clarke returned. "But I couldn't possibly comment."

Clarke went in search of Sheldon. As he had been told, a makeshift incident-come-refreshment room had been set up in the storeroom about fifty yards from the bungalow. An assortment of gardening equipment and machinery had been parked over at one end, including a ride-on lawnmower the size of a small car. A trestle table had been set up, on which were Women's Institute-style tea urns and an assortment of cakes and biscuits. A tray of mostly demolished sandwiches had been set nearby. Folding tables and chairs crowded the remaining area and Sheldon sat at one of these in the corner of the room, sorting a stack of paperwork into some kind of order. Clarke helped himself to coffee and biscuits and went to join him.

Sheldon looked uncomfortable. "It's not normal this, boss. We spend most of our working life trying to trip these buggers up, we come out here expecting trouble, and everyone's playing nice. Like they can't do enough for us. All in the cause of transparency, so Gus Perrin says, doesn't want us thinking there was anything untoward going on." He laughed. "I tell you, I don't like this."

"Ah, don't worry about it. Come next week, it'll be back to normal. We'll be dragging one or other of them in for questioning, they'll be lawyering up, we'll be banging our heads against the same brick wall. Status quo will be back in place. In the meantime, enjoy their coffee and their cakes and their bloody sandwiches. So, statement from Carole Perrin or whatever her married name is. Carole Josephs?"

Sheldon nodded and handed him the statement. Clarke skimmed it. It didn't tell him anything he didn't already know.

"The time of death is down for around five thirty in the morning," Sheldon said. "And Carole Josephs claims that she was woken up by the shot. Apparently, her husband's not there, he's away on business. She gets dressed, goes over to her brother's place, and finds the body in the back room."

"The walls in that room are thick. You reckon she could have heard the shot? How far away is her cottage?"

"Not as far as from here to the bungalow. But across on the other side. I don't know, you'd have to fire a shotgun in that room and sit on her bed to find out, but I'd imagine it's pretty quiet round here at night, so the sound would carry. And she's going to know what a gunshot sounds like, being as how she's part of this family."

"But is she going to automatically think it's coming from her brother's place?" He scanned the statement again. It was clear and simple and to the point. "How was she when you interviewed her? Nervous, upset, hesitant?"

"Exact opposite. Cool, calm. She knows that you want to speak to her. She's at home and expecting you."

Clarke nodded towards the stack of paperwork. "And what else do we have?"

"Statements from the brother, from the two men who went with the brother to look at the body, from the undertaker and from the family doctor." Sheldon looked expectantly at Clarke, waiting to see if there was anyone else he should have spoken to.

"We'll go and have another chat with Carole Josephs. Come along and make the introductions, then."

Outside, the grey had subsided a little and weak sunlight did its best to filter through the clouds, though it did nothing to lift the temperature. Over to the left of this building was a stand of trees, ancient and tall, the last leaves still clinging on. The sunlight caught the red of the big house and the bricks glowed. Clarke could glimpse at least a half-dozen other properties — cottages, the converted barn. He'd long since ceased to believe that crime didn't pay. Sometimes, when looking at places like this, he wondered if he was on the wrong side. The opportunity had certainly been there when Clarke was younger, given his father's involvement in the less than legal.

Sheldon led him across the open yard in front of the storeroom and past Charlie Perrin's bungalow. Walking down the side of the bungalow, Clarke noticed that there was another door leading into the kitchen. The bungalow backed onto a grassy area that sloped towards yet another bank of trees. Carole Josephs's cottage nestled into a dip in the landscape and was, unexpectedly, surrounded by its own hedged and very beautiful garden. At this time of year, much of it was dormant, but tall, clipped yews and even the last few roses spoke of a carefully tended and much-loved little corner of the farm. His attention was caught by a striking sculpture sitting between two yew trees, to the right of the path. He paused to look at it. It looked like a stone seed, carved and then polished to bring out the beauty of the material. *Granite?* he wondered. The colour and texture reminded him of a curling stone. It invited touch. A sinuous groove curved from tip to base and then curled around into a spiral. It was incredibly simple, but oddly satisfying.

"One of hers, apparently."

It took a moment for Clarke to understand what DS Sheldon meant and then he remembered reading that Carole Josephs was an artist. She might live on her father's estate, financed by his money, but she also went out into the world and presented it with things she had made — as opposed to things she had shot, stolen, smuggled or defrauded. *Interesting,* he thought. *But that doesn't mean she's any less her father's daughter.*

Sheldon knocked on the door. It opened immediately and a tall, dark-haired woman he recognized as Carole stood there. She led them through to the kitchen, where a smaller, fair-haired woman was about to plunge a cafetière.

"We saw you walking over," Carole said. "Have a seat, but there's nothing much more I can tell you."

Clarke introduced himself and looked pointedly at the younger woman. She set cups on the table and then put out a hand to shake his. He was surprised by that.

"Sam Barker," she said. "I'm Carole's assistant." She glanced at her employer. "Do you want me to stay, or to go and get on?"

"Thanks, Sam. I'll join you in the studio in a few minutes."

She does not, Clarke thought, *seem particularly upset by her brother's death.*

* * *

DI Clarke left the farm about an hour later, having revisited the scene and spoken again to Collins and his CSIs. He had gone up to the big house and spoken also to Gus Perrin himself. His manner had been as gruff as ever, but he'd basically repeated what his daughter had told both Sheldon and Clarke.

He had asked how long the police and the CSIs were likely to remain.

"I expect we'll be out of here by the end of the day," Clarke told him. This was, after all, still being treated as an accident. From the way he was behaving, Gus Perrin must be very certain that they'd find nothing to contradict that. *Maybe*, Clarke mused, *it was even true.*

"No rush," Perrin said. He sounded almost bored.

"It must have been a shock," Clarke speculated, wanting to stimulate a reaction from the big man whose disinterest seemed odd, to say the least. Clarke couldn't bring himself to be sorry for his loss or to express any of the other trite phrases they were taught to use these days. He wasn't particularly sorry. Death, however it had been visited, meant that Charlie Perrin was now one fewer arsehole to worry about.

"Charlie was always a fucking idiot when it came to the booze," Perrin said. "I always reckoned an accident would take him, but I had assumed it would be in a car."

"Hmm, well, at least this way he didn't take anyone else with him." Clarke could not resist.

A hard look came into Perrin's eyes and he shifted restlessly in his chair. Clarke watched him. He had known Gus Perrin before his shooting. Perrin had been tall, broad, built like a brick outhouse, but quick as a rattlesnake and just as vicious. He might not be as quick these days, but that look reminded Clarke that he was still as vicious.

"Be careful, DI Clarke. He was my son. I don't take kindly to people mocking me."

The implied threat still sat between Clarke's shoulders like a target as he drove out through the main gates and back onto the main road. *Stupid to goad*, he told himself, *but so hard to resist*.

CHAPTER 8

Clarke's next stop was Sykes's home, a drive of about five miles but one which took him into a different world. Sykes had not taken on the role of lord of some rural manor — he'd stuck close to his roots on the edge of town. His house was built at the edge of an industrial estate, which seemed like an odd location until you took into account that Sykes and his family had initially made their money from scrap metal and their original yard had been less than a quarter of a mile away. Sykes apparently liked to keep in touch with his origins. The house was large, new (Clarke could remember it being built about five years before) and, despite the broad, sweeping driveway and portico entrance, the place was remarkably low key compared to the Perrins' pretensions of landed gentry.

Two large four-by-fours were parked in front of the house and Clarke pulled up in front of the second one. He waved at the camera, which had swivelled to look down at him and then made his way up the steps to the front door. Perrin liked to keep his friends and his family — and probably his enemies, for all Clarke knew — physically close. It seemed that Sykes took a different approach.

Clarke did not have to introduce himself when the door opened. Clarke had no doubt that just as he knew, at least by sight, almost every member of Sykes's organization, the leader of this particular organized crime gang kept himself abreast of Clarke's and briefed his people accordingly.

"Detective Inspector Clarke."

"Mr Sykes." Clarke nodded politely. "I imagine you've heard about Charlie Perrin?"

"Of course. News gets around. I have to say, though, anyone who knew Charlie could see it coming. I have always told my men, 'Booze and weaponry do not mix.'"

Clarke raised an eyebrow. "I don't see you or your crew as the hunting, shooting, fishing types," he commented. "Or are we talking about less legal weapons?"

Sykes laughed. "So what can I do for you? I'm sure you didn't call on me just to bring me the news."

"No, my boss suggested I drop by. He said I could ask you questions, you could give me non-answers, and I could report back to my boss, honour satisfied."

"You do amuse me, DI Clarke. What questions do you want me to answer? Or shall I guess?" He ticked them off on his fingers. "No, I have had no dealings with Charlie Perrin. No, we had nothing to do with his death, which I believe was an accident? Yes, I may be going to the funeral — which will no doubt be the thing that interests your boss. And . . . what else?"

"Is there any truth to the rumours that you and Perrin are about to get into bed together — in a business sense, of course? Like you said, news travels and there are rumours about uniting the two families. I've got to say, your girl seems a bit young for Charlie, but what do I know, girls grow up fast these days."

He was watching Sykes carefully and saw a tightening of the mouth, a slight narrowing of the eyes. *Sykes would never make a poker player*, Clarke thought.

"There's always talk," Sykes said. "Now, that must be all, DI Clarke."

"Not quite. I was over at Harry Prentice's place this morning. I left two fire crews still damping down. The fire chief is talking about arson. So, my next question is, where's Harry?"

Sykes shrugged. "Well, if you've not found a body, I would assume he's not there."

"No sign of a body."

"Well then." Kyle Sykes spread his hands wide. "Harry must be away. Nasty shock for him when he comes back."

"Away, where?"

"How would I know? Why should I know, for that matter? Harry's retired. For all I know, he spends his time fishing."

"Fishing."

Sykes laughed and shrugged again. "If there's nothing more, Inspector?"

The front door had been opened again and the man who had let him in was waiting to let him out. Clarke reflected briefly that Sykes seemed to prefer his people in grey suits. *A rich man's livery*, Clarke thought. Unlike Gus Perrin's men, Sykes's thugs were always white. Toby Clarke, with his white father and black mother, could never have applied for a job with Kyle Sykes, not unless he had a particular skill to sell that didn't involve him being front-of-house. Besides, he could never have afforded the tailoring bills.

"See you at the funeral, then," he said.

Clarke got into his car and sat for a moment, fiddling with his radio, tuning it to a fresh station. He was surprised to see that Sykes had followed him out onto the top step and was now standing chatting to his flunky and trying to look casual. *There's something odd here*, Clarke thought. He didn't know what, but something was definitely off.

He fastened his seat belt and prepared to drive off. He'd been to the Sykes house three, four times before and it definitely felt different this time. He was through the gates before it struck him. Where was everybody? Usually the house was buzzing with men lounging around, like they did at the Perrin place, or in the garage at the side of the house, tending to the many vehicles. Today, the garages had been closed, and it had seemed few people were there, other than Kyle Sykes and the man who had let him in. He'd heard footsteps elsewhere, other people coming and going but nothing like the usual bustle, the usual numbers of hangers on paying court to their boss.

"So where the fuck is everybody?" Clarke wondered aloud. On impulse, he keyed his phone and called the office. DS Denise Allwood answered. "Find out if the Sykes girl's been to school today," Clarke told her. "Dig around and see if there's anything unusual going on there."

What was I hoping to find? Clarke wondered. He didn't know for sure, just something had been out of kilter and it wasn't just at the Perrin end of things.

CHAPTER 9

Clarke knew that many of his colleagues disliked post-mortems. Personally, he found them fascinating and often wondered if, had he done better at sciences at school, that was where he would have ended up. His genuine interest often helped him gain insights that his more squeamish colleagues did not.

It was just after two in the afternoon when he arrived, sidling into the room as Si Levrov was making his preliminary observations for the benefit of the recording. The pathologist raised a hand in greeting, as Clarke positioned himself where he could watch without getting in the way. Observing Si and allowing him to deal with the more routine matters before the post-mortem properly began was a man Clarke recognized from his appearances as an expert witness. Sir Geoffrey Connor was an affable man with an abundance of white hair, currently tucked beneath the obligatory net, and half-moon glasses.

He smiled at Clarke. "Toby. Good to see you again. I don't imagine we'll be detaining you for long."

Clarke hadn't realized they were on first name terms, though he decided such familiarity would probably only travel in one direction. "Sir Geoffrey." He nodded his greeting. "You think this will all be straightforward, then?"

"Of course! Why would you think otherwise?" Humorous blue eyes turned their full gaze on Clarke. "I'm afraid to say our Mr Charles Perrin was a very silly man. A very silly man indeed. A careless man. You can't afford to be careless around firearms now, can you?"

He glanced over at Si. "Ready for me? Good, good. Now, let the dog see the rabbit."

Clarke caught Si rolling his eyes but Sir Geoffrey was too busy removing what was left of Charlie Perrin's brain to notice.

There was not a lot left of Charlie Perrin's head. Half of his face was relatively untouched, but the other half reminded Clarke of the kind of meat a butcher might make into burgers. He watched without comment as Sir Geoffrey made his examination, keeping up a stream of commentary for the recording, occasionally asking Si for an opinion. Clarke, excluded from the discussion, was content to watch. Sir Geoffrey seemed to be enjoying himself, his voice confident and loud. He was one of those expert witnesses who spoke directly to the jury, who had the knack of presenting evidence in an erudite manner but in language that could be understood by the layman. He was the author of several influential papers and had advanced knowledge in his field, and Clarke knew he was also as corrupt as any Kyle Sykes or Gus Perrin — it was just that no one had, as yet, been able to prove a damned thing.

Clarke knew Si well enough to notice that he was looking uncertain about something. He pointed to something on what was left of Charlie's skull. Sir Geoffrey looked at it dismissively and moved on. Clarke frowned but didn't like to interrupt. Instead, as they moved away from their examination of the wound and onto the ritual of weighing and measuring internal organs, Clarke took himself off to get a coffee and a bite to eat. By the time he returned, Si was alone and finishing up his notes.

"I hoped you'd come back," he said.

"Oh? I noticed you seemed concerned about something. Anything important?"

"Not according to Sir Geoffrey Connor. He's gone, by the way. Left me to close up and do the washing down. No doubt he's off to collect his fat fee."

"Not like you to be bitter." Clarke grinned at his friend. "So, nothing wrong according to him. And according to you?"

Si hesitated. "He knows his stuff," he said. "He's far more experienced than I am, but . . ."

"But?"

Si took a notebook from his drawer. "But this," he said. "To my mind, this doesn't add up."

* * *

Evening saw the return of Kyle Sykes's missing people, those whose absence Clarke had noted earlier in the day. They returned in twos and threes, a half-dozen cars in all, but none had news.

"What the hell have you been doing all fucking day?" Sykes demanded. "You're looking for a kid and an old man, how hard can that be?"

An awkward silence followed, a shuffling of feet. These were men who didn't think twice about inflicting violence, who were in the business of causing others to be afraid. But, confronted by the raw rage of Kyle Sykes, well, that was enough to cause a bit more than general unease in their ranks.

"So," Sykes said. "We know she's with Harry. We know what car Harry was driving. What about the bloody ANPR?"

"Our people are onto it," someone said. "But it takes time, boss. It ain't like opening an email. No one knows what direction they went in. There's no cameras out by Harry's place."

"'There's no cameras out by Harry's place,'" Sykes mimicked. "He'll have gone through town, he'll have taken the bloody motorway. How hard can it fucking be?"

"We've got people on it, boss. They'll come through."

"Better bloody do," Sykes said. He cast a scathing look at his troops. "Tomorrow morning, you get out there again and you knock on any doors you have to. You talk to every single person that kid of mine ever had contact with. Every frigging man or woman Harry ever had dealings with. Be in no doubt, you will find them or I'll want to know why."

He paused again, this time seeking and holding eye contact. "And not one of you should be in any doubt of what I'll do to those who let me down."

CHAPTER 10

The cottage really was remote. They had left the motorway, stopped in the first small town they had found with a decent-sized shop and had stocked up with food. Harry had spotted a CCTV camera by the door but nothing inside. He had wanted to avoid big supermarkets. They had too many cameras, too much surveillance.

He knew that they'd be remembered, this older man with a limp and this tired, pale, young girl buying what looked like a weekly shop in this little convenience store, but that couldn't be helped.

They had then driven ten miles off their route and stocked up with kindling and firelighters, Harry having remembered that the cottage had a wood-burning stove. He'd added a bag of logs from a garage and a couple of bags of coal and hoped there were further supplies at their destination. Harry planned on holing up for the duration, facing whatever came on ground he had surveyed and understood. He didn't give much for their chances, long-term, but figured they may as well be fed and warm in the meantime.

"Won't somebody see if we light a fire?" Lauren had asked.

"There is no one *to* see," he said. "Nearest cottage is a mile away and that's a holiday let, too. The North Sea's too chilly for most folk this time of year."

They had left the main roads soon after and driven along increasingly narrow lanes until finally Harry turned off, up a long, muddy, grassy track. Soon Lauren could see their destination at the end of the track. Beyond that lay the ocean, grey and cold and fierce, crashing high on the shingle.

She got out of the car, shivering in the sudden blast of cold, fastened her coat and helped Harry get their stuff out of the car.

Lord, she thought, *this place is bleak*. They had passed no houses for a mile or more before reaching this place and in this spot, apart from the tiny, stone cottage, was a not a single item of anything human-made, in whatever direction she looked.

Harry bustled about, finding the key behind a brick in the garden wall, switching the electric on at the mains and checking that the fridge was working. "Get the kettle on," he said. "And then help me get this shopping stowed away while I light the fire. The sheets might need airing before we make up the beds, but if I remember right, there's a dryer in the shed next to the back door."

He seemed relieved to be here, but Lauren was worried. Harry clearly knew this place well. "Harry, who owns this cottage? How come you've been here before? Harry, if you know about this place . . ."

"You think your dad will, too."

Lauren nodded. "He keeps tabs on everything anyone ever does, you know that."

Harry hoisted two carrier bags onto the kitchen table and set them down. He was clearly working out how to respond.

"Harry? Look, I know nowhere's safe, but to come somewhere he knows about, that's just asking for trouble. He'll search everywhere you've ever been. Threaten anyone I've ever even been in the same room with." She sat down on one of the kitchen chairs and placed her elbows on the table, face in her hands, trying hard not to cry.

"He'll find us, no matter how far we run," Harry said. "He'll put out the word to every Tom, Dick and Harry, the length and breadth of the country. I don't suppose he'll value my old head very high, but there'll be a price on yours, pet, so the best thing we can do is get as far away as possible from anyone and anything that might recognize you and — you're right — any place your old man might be able to think of where I might have been. He *doesn't* know about this place. Granted, that don't make it safe, but I came here only once before. Found it by chance. It was just after my Jeanie passed away and I needed to just go off for a while. You remember?"

Lauren nodded. As it happened, her dad had been out of the country and had missed the funeral. Harry had caused something of a flap, going off like he did. She'd heard about it, heard the gossip. Some of her dad's lieutenants had even started a book on whether or not old Harry had topped himself — and how. Her dad had been informed but had been remarkably sanguine, reckoning Harry knew which side his bread was buttered on and that he'd be back.

"Dad said you and Jean had been married a long time. That you were bound to be cut up about her dying." He'd also started to get impatient when Harry had not returned by the time he had come home. Grieving for a dead wife was allowed: Sykes had even taken a few days for himself after his own wife had gone, though he'd gone on a bender, not on a road trip like Harry. But there were limits, according to Sykes. A few days was expected. A few weeks was '*Just fucking self-indulgent*'. She could remember her father saying that the day before Harry returned. She recalled being so scared in case Harry's absence might cause her dad to go off on one, as her mother used to say. Kyle Sykes, generally cool and calculating, could be dangerously unpredictable when the mood took him.

"You came here?"

"Eventually. I just drove. Stopped . . . I don't really remember where. Then this particular day, I pulled into a car park about three, four miles down the road. There's a little cut-through onto the beach, a pub, fish and chip van in the summer and a few caravans, though it was all closed up, bar the pub, when I came here that time too. It was winter, you remember."

"Of course I do." Lauren had been utterly devastated when Jean had died.

"I walked on the beach and after a while, I came on this place. It was empty but I liked the look of it and it didn't take much to get inside."

"You didn't know where the spare key was then."

Harry laughed. "No, not then. Anyway, I walked back along the beach, asked about it at the pub. The landlord said it was rarely rented out this late in the year so, well, let's just say I camped out for a couple of days. Never saw a living soul apart from the birds."

Lauren considered. Harry was evidently spinning this whole story to make this place seem safer and even more cut-off than it was. Trying to convince himself as much as her. He wasn't fooling himself and he wasn't fooling her, but that was OK. For the moment, both of them wanted, *needed*, to believe that things might just somehow be all right.

"Best get this food put away," she said. They could take refuge in ordinary, safe activity.

He nodded. "You do that. I'll light the fire and find the sheets, get them in the dryer. Anyone comes asking questions, we tell them I've come up here on a birdwatching holiday and dragged you along with me."

"Yes, Harry," Lauren said. "Like you'd know a buzzard from a seagull."

* * *

A couple of hours later, as darkness closed in and they sat down to their evening meal, Lauren raised the issue again of what they were going to do next. Harry had brought the four-by-four round to the side of the house and covered it with a tarpaulin he'd found in the storeroom at the back, so that the large green vehicle did not stand out quite so incongruously. He'd made sure that all the curtains were tightly closed, so that light did not show through the windows, particularly those facing out towards the sea. The cottage was not really in view of the little road, but he worried about local fishing boats perhaps noticing the cottage was in use. As he had told Lauren earlier, if anybody did happen upon them and enquired, then the excuse of a late holiday would be the one they would use and they would just hope that whoever they were talking to did not have the owner's phone number on speed dial. That, Harry thought, was really the least of their problems, anyway.

"Did you tell *anybody* about this place? I mean, people must have asked where you'd been. It was the longest you'd been away for, well, like . . . years. I missed you, Harry."

"I know you did, pet. I kept telling myself that I should stay around for you, that Jean would want me to stay and look after you, but I just couldn't. I needed to be on my own for a bit."

She nodded and cut another slice of pizza. He was glad that she was eating. There were a few chips left in the bowl and he shared these between their plates. "Cheesecake for dessert," he said.

"God, how many calories have I eaten today!"

"Who cares?" Harry grinned at her. Kyle Sykes liked his women thin. Harry knew that he kept a tight rein on what his daughter ate. Famously, he kept a tight rein on what she wore, where she went, what friends she had. As a result, she really didn't have any friends, not that Harry would have considered worthy of the name. There were just a few girls who she occasionally did things with, but that was about the size of it.

Had he told anyone else about this cottage? The truth was, he couldn't remember. He'd still been knocked sideways by grief even after he had turned the car around and headed for home, knowing that sooner or later he'd have to get on with life. Not that the house had ever been home after Jean had gone, it had just been the place where they had lived. He was surprised how little regret he felt now that he'd left it for good. People had asked of course, "Harry, where did you get to?" and he had managed to remember odd places on his route, enough to satisfy them, but the fact was, he had, as he told Lauren, just driven. What he hadn't told her was that the day he'd walked along the beach and found this little cottage, he had considered walking straight out into the sea, pockets full of stones. He had considered putting a gun to his temple. After all, he was never without the means, but that day it seemed like he decided that he did actually want to live. Or maybe it was simply that — despite having no hesitation about taking other lives — he didn't have the courage to take his own.

Lauren took their plates over to the sink, filled the kettle yet again, and then faced him with her arms folded across her body and *that look* in her eye that Harry knew so well.

"So, what next?" she said. "What are we going to do? We need to get ready, Harry. We need to decide. Do I go to the police? Like I said, I know things, we both know things. Maybe they could put us in witness protection or something."

"Maybe they could. Maybe your dad has fingers in that pie, too."

Laura nodded. That was a very real possibility. Her dad's organization was like a big spider sitting at the centre of an even bigger web. Looking at it, you might think the spider was the most important thing. But Lauren knew it was the web that really mattered and she had no idea how big that web was.

"I should have brought my passport," she said. "We have money, we could have gone somewhere else." She saw Harry's sceptical look and sighed. "Yeah, OK, I know that we'd have just bought us a bit more time. I don't wanna die, Harry, and I don't believe you do either. So how are we going to get out of this mess?"

Harry looked at her admiringly. Only seventeen, and yet she had the cool and determination of someone much older. She was very much like her mother had been.

"Look under the sink, I think I spotted some old newspapers there earlier. Spread them out on the table, I don't want to get grease on the wood." He left the kitchen to go and get a bag he had brought in earlier, and also to retrieve the gun that Lauren had kept in her pocket all day. He figured she'd all but forgotten about it. When he came back in, she'd spread the newspapers on the table. Next, while she washed the pots and made more tea, Harry stripped the gun that Lauren had taken from her father's desk.

Lauren brought mugs of tea and sat at the table watching him. "You need to teach me to shoot, Harry. I mean aim and that sort of thing. I didn't need to aim with him. He was so close, I could feel his breath on my face."

He was so close that after the breath had come the blood. She'd been covered in it. She closed her eyes for a moment, trying to block out the memory. She took a deep breath and opened them again, looking steadily at Harry. "So you need to teach me to shoot properly."

"I'll teach you," Harry said. "But more important than that, girl, you need to learn how to hide, because when they do come, your job is to get out of here and stay out of sight, no matter what happens. Your job is to stay alive, you got that?"

He saw her eyes widen as she took in the full impact of what he meant. Harry would die to keep her safe.

"No. I'll fight. I won't leave you, Harry. They might get us both, but I won't leave you."

He reached across the table and grabbed her hand, looking intently at her. He was angry now, and he wasn't sure where the anger had come from — only that it was there. "You get killed, and this is all for nothing. You might as well have stayed there, in your room, waiting for your dad to come home. But you didn't, you ran, you came to me and you asked for help. And I've helped you, and it will all be for nothing if you die. Got that?"

She nodded slowly and he could see that he had almost frightened her. Almost. Lauren had only ever known one side of Harry. He'd been careful not to let her see the other, but she needed to know. From this moment, she needed know all of Harry and what he was capable of. And the truth was, he would rather put a bullet in her head himself than let her father get to her. Harry's way at least would be quick. Kyle Sykes liked to get every ounce of satisfaction from his killing, prolonging the moment until the body could take no more — and it was shocking how much a body could take and still keep breathing. Harry and Lauren both had cause to know that.

"Now," he said. "If you have a weapon, you need to clean it, to maintain it. To treat it like a friend. So, lesson one." He took the rest of his armoury from the bag and laid it out on the table. "While you strip one gun, another is kept on hand and loaded. You go nowhere unarmed. Even in the house, you keep something always within reach, you understand?"

She nodded, eyeing the stack of weaponry that Harry laid out on the table. It was enough to start a small war.

"Now, this will fit your hand better. Your dad's gun is really too heavy for you. This is a Walther, a PPK, small enough to put in your pocket and not too much of a kick. This doesn't have the stopping power of your dad's gun, but it's good enough to put a man down. You aim for the centre of mass, not the head, nothing fancy. Keep cash with you at all times and go nowhere without this gun. And go nowhere without this, either."

From his bag he took a mobile phone, still boxed. They'd bought a couple of them and some spare SIM cards at one of the garages they'd stopped at. "It goes without saying you make no calls, you do nothing that can be traced." He paused until she nodded affirmation and then she watched as he unpacked the phone and inserted the SIM.

"Now, wherever you are, inside or out, this is with you. Within reach. The gun too. You leave the cottage, these go with you. Now, I'm going to program the phone with one number and you're going to memorize that number, just in

45

case, just in case you lose this phone. If the worst happens, you call that number and ask for help and tell them Harry gave it to you. You got that?"

"Whose number is it?"

"Hopefully, you'll never need to find out. But if you do, if you do have to call this number, then you do exactly what they tell you. Promise me. Because if you have to call this number, it means I'm gone and you need help from someone else. This is your last resort, girl. You understand that?"

"Harry, I don't want to . . ."

"I said, '*You understand that?*'" He allowed a hard edge to creep into his voice again and was satisfied when she nodded.

"So if this is someone who can help us, why don't we call them now?" Lauren asked.

A fair question, Harry thought. So why didn't they? The truth was, Harry wasn't sure what calling this number might also bring down on their heads. He would trust his contact to help Lauren, if only because they would see some advantage in it.

"It's not as simple as that. Lauren, you've got to trust me on this. You understand? My contact will help, but there'll likely be strings attached. And I don't like strings."

She waited as though to see if he'd say more but seemed to give up when it was clear he was done with the subject.

"If everything else goes wrong, I call that number," Lauren said.

"Good girl. Now, we watch a bit of telly and then we go to bed and get a good night's sleep."

She looked at him, wide-eyed. Then she seemed to relax a little.

"OK, I can do that. I'm not sure I'm going to be able to sleep, Harry, but finding a film or something would be good."

Lauren glanced at her watch and looked surprised. "I thought it was much later, but it's only six thirty."

Harry nodded. It did feel later. The day and the previous night seemed to have stretched out in an eternity of anxiety and running and tension. She had slept in the car, despite what she had been through, but Harry knew that sometimes shock did that to a body.

"And we'll have hot chocolate," Harry said. "I picked up some marshmallows, we can do hot chocolate just like we did when you were a little thing. You used to love Harry's hot chocolate."

He saw Lauren blink back tears. He was trying so hard to focus on the normal and the ordinary and he needed her to try equally hard if they were to keep their spirits up.

"I'd like that," she said. "I'd like that, Harry." And he could see how surprised she was to find that it was really true.

CHAPTER 11

At evening briefing, Clarke took his seat and listened as the rest of the team reported back on their day. It was finally his turn and he filled in the gaps, talking about his odd feeling about the Sykes place and then asking DS Denise Allwood about the Sykes girl.

"Not at school today, and it took me a while to get that out of anyone. They're all, '*We can't give out confidential information to anybody but parents.*' But I hung around the gates at leaving time, and asked one of the girls, who looked about Lauren's age, if Lauren had left yet. Said I had a message for her from her dad. She looked at me a bit funny, but she told me that Lauren hadn't been at school. So I looked worried and she said she'd tried phoning Lauren but got no answer on her phone. Goes by the name of Sophie Richardson, apparently in the same class, so I struck lucky. Then one of the teachers came out and wanted to know what I was doing there, and Sophie's mum came over and hustled her daughter away. I had to explain who I was to the teacher, but by that time everybody had gone. Sorry."

"Find an address for this Sophie Richardson," Clarke instructed her.

"Anything from the post-mortem?" DCI Henderson asked.

"Nothing conclusive, but again, the whole thing stinks."

Someone cracked a joke about dead bodies tending to have a bit of an odour. Someone else laughed. Clarke ignored them. He indicated photographs on the operations board. "As you can see, a good chunk of face is missing, brain, back of head. Blast caught him full on this side of the face so anything that might have happened before, will have been mostly obliterated."

"Mostly?"

"Probably completely," Clarke conceded. "But there is one small thing which is interesting." He indicated another photograph. "This section of skull, you can see the break where the rest is shattered and at first, we thought it was simply that. But you look more closely and there's a distinct curve on this section and a particularly distinctive pattern, star cracking around it. If you looked at a single bullet wound, and the skull was otherwise intact, this is what you'd see." He pointed to the drawing that Si had made for him. "It might be nothing, it might just be a chance artefact, but it is suggestive."

"Suggestive of what? That someone shot him first, then fired a shotgun in his face to cover it up?"

Clarke shrugged. "It's a small anomaly, probably nothing."

"Note it," his boss agreed. "If it's nothing, no harm done. What's the interest in Sykes's daughter?"

"We caught a rumour, a couple of weeks back, that the Perrins were looking at wedding venues. Charlie is the only unmarried Perrin, or was. You put that together with the rumours that the Perrin and the Sykes OCGs are planning combined operations, and it again is suggestive."

"Lauren Sykes is just a kid," someone objected.

"She's seventeen. She's legal. Carole Perrin was only a year older when she became Carole Josephs."

"And Josephs is now Perrin's right-hand man. Though you didn't see him today?"

"No, I spoke direct to the boss. Carole Josephs said her husband was away. To be honest, when I went to the cottage,

I didn't get the impression of a man living there with her. It struck me as being *her* place. The kid's away at school, I believe."

"Thomas Josephs. Yes."

Clarke was thoughtful for a moment. "And do we have anything on this other woman, this Sam Barker?"

Detective Constable Janice Owens stood up. She had a sheaf of papers in her hands. She came to the front and asked Clarke to start passing them along. "There's not much, but her background is interesting. She started working for Carole Josephs about two years ago and is her PA and studio assistant. She's got a PhD in History of Art, studied at the Courtauld Institute which I'm told is pretty high-end and she's arranged four exhibitions for Carole Josephs in the last couple of years. She's only twenty-nine but seems to have some really good industry connections and she seems to know her stuff. She studied art restoration at the Courtauld and she's had a couple of solo exhibitions. She's a painter, not a sculptor."

"And anything interesting in her background?" Clarke could feel the excitement and guessed Owens had something up her sleeve.

"Barker's her mother's name — her mother reverted after she got divorced. But Dad is far more interesting. Timothy Hughes O'Farrell. Originally from round here, but . . ."

"Took himself off to Manchester about fifteen years ago. Made a name for himself up there. Killed in an armed robbery, if I remember right," DCI Henderson commented.

Clarke raised an eyebrow at his boss. "You've got a good memory."

"I arrested him once or twice. Before he graduated to the armed robbery gig. Right little scrote he was. Then he got married and seemed to straighten himself out for a bit, or at least I don't remember him being arrested for anything. Marriage didn't last and he was back to his old ways again. I don't know what happened to the wife, she left town and took the kid with her."

"And now the kid is back and working for the Perrins. Gus Perrin will have checked her out. His background checks would put MI5 to shame."

"She has no record. Not even a parking fine."

"Does she live at the farm?" Clarke asked, skimming down the sheet he had been given. "Ah." The current home address was recorded at the bottom of the other side. "So she's shacked up with someone called Marty Baines. What do we know about him?" The name ran a vague bell, but he could not place the man.

Owens was ahead of him. "No record, he sometimes drives for Perrin, but not in *that* way. He's actually employed as Perrin's physio. Does hydrotherapy sessions with him in the pool and that sort of stuff. Like the rest of his employees, Perrin insists he lives on site and they've got a cottage right on the edge of the estate, just where the boundary meets the village. I've got his bank records, nothing untoward, or with hers. They don't seem to pay rent on the accommodation, but they pay their own utilities and food. Council tax . . ."

She trailed off as though suddenly disappointed that there was nothing more to tell, but it was interesting, Clarke thought, to get even more of an insight into the way Perrin ran his business. Like Sykes, he had moved into more legitimate areas in the last decade but Clarke assumed this had been largely so that he could launder his money from the less legitimate areas. And it seemed in keeping with the way Perrin liked his life to be organized that he should want his own personal physiotherapist living on site. He wondered if this Marty Baines was fully comprehending of Perrin's organization. He'd have to be completely stupid not to know what Perrin was.

"And no sign of Harry Prentice?" he asked. "Sykes reckoned he might have gone fishing." There was laughter in the room at the idea that Harry Prentice might do anything as peaceful as sitting on a riverbank.

"Anything further on the fire?" DCI Henderson asked.

Clarke consulted the notes he had been looking through earlier. "Not much more than we knew this morning. Four points of combustion, petrol as the accelerant. It looks as though cans were emptied out and left in situ. Everything would have gone up pretty fast. The fires had already been started, is the guess, by the time the patrol car came by. The arsonists were *almost* unlucky."

"I've had a word," Henderson said. "Suggested that they should have continued with the pursuit, just radioed in. But they were understandably worried about anyone being inside and potential threat to life overrides other concerns."

"They made the best call they could under the circumstances," Clarke said.

Henderson nodded. "So let's summarise what we have here," he said. "We have the death of Charlie Perrin. We have Harry Prentice AWOL and his house burned to the ground. We have a seeming absence of personnel at the Sykes place and Sykes's daughter also seems to have buggered off. We have rumours of a proposed marriage between the two families. The groom's now dead and the girl nowhere to be found . . . Of course, she might just be staying with friends. She might be playing hooky for the day, but I personally can't see Kyle Sykes allowing his daughter to be anywhere but under his eye."

"Just because she wasn't at school, doesn't mean there's anything up, Allwood commented. "She could simply be off school sick."

"In which case, the school would have been informed. They insist on that. Her class teacher would have known and so her friend would probably have known, too. Besides, what teenager fails to answer their phone?" Clarke knew he was playing devil's advocate and Denise could probably be right. But that feeling remained, nagging at the back of his brain, that things were not right at the Sykes place. That something else was going on here.

"So we presume the girl is missing," Clarke decided, looking to his boss for approval.

Henderson nodded.

"And we assume that Charlie Perrin's cause of death has been fudged or otherwise lied about."

"We assume that's possible." Henderson was a little more chary of agreeing to that. "But, yes, we keep an open mind."

"Do you think the two things are linked?" Allwood sounded almost contemptuous of the idea and, glancing around the room, Clarke could see that others felt the same way.

"She's just a kid."

"Agreed, she's just a kid." DCI Henderson nodded. "But she's Kyle Sykes's kid, not some little innocent who knows nothing about anything. I'm inclined to agree that the two incidents may be linked. I'm more interested in the fact that Harry Prentice seems to have gone off the radar at the same time as Lauren Sykes. Prentice and his wife practically raised the kid after her mum was murdered."

"And we all know what Harry Prentice was, back in the day," Clarke added.

"And that was?" Allwood asked.

She was still relatively new to the team, Clarke remembered, as she cast him a puzzled look.

"Harry did time for GBH and conspiracy to murder," he explained. "Though Sykes's legal team got him off on a technicality that led to a retrial."

"But he was guilty?"

Clarke waited until the knowing sniggers from various members of the team had died down.

"Anything or anyone Kyle Sykes wanted dealt with and Harry was the one to do it. Harry was Kyle Sykes's trigger-man. Sykes wanted someone out of the way — Harry saw it was done."

CHAPTER 12

Sophie Richardson was on the phone to her friend Cora. "You mean she's gone missing?" Sophie was both impressed and a little scared at the idea. "No, no one's found her yet. But there was that woman asking questions outside the school. Did you see her? She had this, like, reddish hair and a scruffy old coat on."

Cora had not seen the woman. Sophie remembered that she'd already left by then. "I thought it was funny when Miss Harris didn't know where she was today. She'd not called in sick, anything. What did her dad say?"

"Only that he was worried about her. He wanted to know if she'd said anything. But I mean, Lauren never says anything."

Sophie laughed. Wasn't that the truth? She'd done tennis club and swimming club and music with Lauren, all after-school activities that had thrown a group of them together. Lauren was friendly and that, but she was always a bit distant. "Do you think she sounded a bit weirder than usual this last week or two? I mean, that day when Miss Bence was talking about all our A-levels and she said something like, 'I probably won't be here for them anyway, so what does it matter?'"

"Do you think she was thinking of running away, then? Do you think she's been kidnapped? I mean, I know her dad's meant to be loaded."

"What, like yours, you mean?" Sophie could hear her mother calling her from downstairs. Something about a phone call. She wondered immediately if Lauren's dad was calling her home as well. After all, she and Cora were probably the closest Lauren had to what you might call friends in the entire school. "Got to go, Mum says there's a phone call down on the house phone. Do you think it's him?"

Moments later, she was telling a very polite-sounding Kyle Sykes she had no idea where his daughter might've gone to. That, yes, she did extra classes with Lauren, and that, yes, they did the swimming club together and the school orchestra. No, they didn't get much chance to talk about anything. It wasn't like Lauren ever came to sleepovers or anything like that. And, no, she didn't know who else Lauren might be close to.

"Close to," she said to her mother after she'd hung up the phone. "No one's close to Lauren Sykes."

"She's come here a time or two," her mother objected. "She came to the barbecue in the summer and I think one time before that, didn't she?"

Sophie rolled her eyes. "Yeah, but that doesn't mean we're close. She isn't like the rest of us. She's dead serious. And anyway, you didn't like it when she came here for the barbecue. Uncle Andrew said something about her dad, and then you got all worried and you were so pleased when she went home early." She looked at her mother, letting the observation hang. She'd listened into the adult conversations, of course, the almost-row that Sophie's mum and dad had had later in the evening. The one that implied that Lauren's father was not just a businessman but was a criminal as well.

"Yes, well. She seemed like a very nice girl, that's all I can say. And hopefully nothing's happened to her. Are the police involved, did Mr Sykes say?"

Sophie shook her head. She was already on her way back upstairs, eager to let Cora know this latest bit of gossip. Eager to speculate and to find out who else Mr Sykes had phoned that evening.

* * *

Lauren curled up next to Harry on the small sofa. She'd brought a blanket from the bed and sat with it round her shoulders, with a mug of Harry's hot chocolate in her hands. They were watching *Die Hard*. She had watched the film many times, as had Harry, but they heckled and cheered and held their breath in the tense moments and just forgot themselves for a while. By ten o'clock, Lauren was drooping with exhaustion and the film was almost ending. She was relieved when everything was done and dusted and she could legitimately take herself off to bed.

Harry hugged her. "Go get some sleep," he said. "I'm just going to have a quick look outside."

She couldn't bring herself to move until he was back. It seemed like forever but in reality was only about five minutes. He seemed unsurprised to see her still on the sofa, staring absently at the television.

He switched it off. "It's a filthy night out there. The wind is coming off the sea and bringing the rain with it. You can't see a hand in front of your face." He seemed quite happy with that, apparently taking solace in the idea that nobody would want to be out on a night like this. "Off to bed with you now." He picked up the mobile phone, the gun, and a package of cash off the table and handed them to her.

It was like being slapped with a dose of reality. Lauren found again that she wanted to cry. But instead, she hugged Harry goodnight and went to her room. She put her coat on the back of the chair next to the bed, her jeans and jumper where she could grab them quickly and her shoes, unlaced, beside the bed. Shove your feet in your shoes, tuck the laces in so you don't slip on them, and get out. That's what Harry had told her. Money in the pocket of your coat, phone in the other one, gun by the bed on the bedside table. She had planned her possible routes out of the cottage, thinking about all eventualities. The doors, the window, where she could hide if they got into the cottage and she was still there. Harry had left the keys to the four-by-four in the ignition, just in case. She'd never driven anything like his big car, but she figured she could manage if she had to.

Still in her underwear, socks and T-shirt, she crawled into bed, convinced she would never get to sleep. But ten minutes later, when Harry looked in on her, she was totally gone. Harry knew that he'd have to sleep too and had set booby traps around the house. Nothing sophisticated, just stuff that would make noise and people would trip over if they tried to come through the doors or windows. He had placed weapons strategically around the cottage and had taken his own particular favourite, an ageing Smith and Wesson J-Frame, and placed it on the bedside cabinet, just as Lauren had done with hers.

Settling into bed, he spoke quietly to his dead wife. "It's a right pickle we've landed ourselves in, Jeanie. I might be seeing you sooner than we thought."

CHAPTER 13

A dozen miles from Kyle Sykes's house lived a man called Joe Messenger. He and Harry had come up through the ranks together and were of a similar age, though not particularly the same disposition, Messenger always being on a shorter fuse. But he and Harry had been close at one time. Sykes knew this. If anybody knew anything, it would be Joe.

Joe was not expecting the knock on the door and had certainly not expected his boss to come visiting.

"Mr Sykes. I mean, come in. What can I do for you?"

Sykes and his two enforcers practically filled the living room of the little terraced house. Joe's wife came in. She'd been getting ready for bed and was in her dressing gown. She halted in the doorway, eyes wide.

"You go on up to bed, love," Joe said, trying to keep his voice steady. Sykes coming here meant trouble. Big trouble.

"Yes, you do that. I just want to ask Joe here a couple of questions." Sykes took a seat and gestured for Joe to do the same. Joe was relieved to see his wife sidle out of the door and to hear her feet on the stairs.

"Where's Harry gone?"

Joe was genuinely surprised. "I didn't know he'd gone anywhere."

"Well, he has, and I want to know where."

Joe shook his head. "I've not seen Harry in weeks. I called him the other day, we arranged to go for a pint next Friday, but that's the most communication I've had with him in a long time. Harry's taking his retirement very seriously."

"Not seriously enough." Sykes leaned forward in his chair. "I'm a reasonable man, Joe, and a good employer. You can't argue with that."

"I would never argue. You know that." Joe felt the blood drain from his cheeks and was trying to control the tremor in his right hand. He'd rarely been this physically close to Sykes. His orders generally came down the line via two or three others. Joe just carried them out when they got to him. Joe was a foot soldier, that was all. Harry had been a lot more.

"So," Sykes said. "We look at this from another angle. I'm prepared to believe you don't know Harry's gone off, but I'm not prepared to believe you couldn't guess where he might have gone to."

For a moment, Joe's mind was a complete and utter blank. He couldn't think of a single place. He couldn't think of a single reason why Harry *might* have gone, except that he'd obviously crossed his boss in some way. Joe would never have reckoned Harry as being that stupid.

"I don't know where he'd go. Harry never went anywhere. Not without your say so."

"And what about when his wife passed on? He went away then."

He did, didn't he? Joe thought. *But buggered if I can remember where.* Harry had gone missing for over three weeks, the longest time he'd ever been out of touch. When he'd come back, he'd been vague, as though he hadn't really noticed where he'd ended up or how he'd got there. Joe racked his memory for any clue.

"North. He went north. I think he went to that island place with the causeway. Lindisfarne. He said something about monks and Vikings. And then he stopped off in York, or near York. I'm sure that's what he said." Joe looked expectantly at Kyle Sykes, looking for some sign of approval, fearing the opposite.

"North. That's the best you can do?" But the Lindisfarne connection rang a bell in Sykes's mind. Harry had mentioned something about it, but he couldn't recall the context.

"He said he found a holiday cottage. Right on the coast. Up there somewhere, I'm sure it was. He reckoned there was nobody staying there on account of it being winter." Joe dredged his brain again and found another tiny fragment of information. Somewhere Joe recalled Harry saying he'd had the best sausage cob he'd ever eaten, something of the sort. Something really random. *What the fuck was it?*

"There was a pub. He said there was a pub somewhere nearby. Reckoned he had lunch there and that's how he found out the cottage was empty. The Red Lion, that was it," Joe had never been more relieved to remember anything in his entire life. "I don't know no more. I'd tell you if I did."

It wasn't much, but it was better than nothing.

Sykes got to his feet. Joe was about to rise, but Kyle pressed him back down into his chair, his fingers claw-like on Joe's shoulder. Sykes tightened his grip, pressing his steely fingers into muscle. Joe gasped.

"You remember anything else, you be sure to tell me. We don't want to be upsetting that wife of yours now, do we?"

Joe shook his head. Moments later, Kyle and his entourage were gone. Joe didn't move until he heard the car drive away and then he went and closed the front door, which in characteristic fashion, Sykes had left wide open. He turned the key and shut the bolts top and bottom, knowing that if Kyle Sykes wanted to get into his house, no bolts in the world would stop him. His wife came to the top of the stairs and called down.

"Joe?"

"It's all right, love, they've gone now." He rubbed his shoulder. His arm was numb. But the mood he sensed Kyle Sykes had been in, he knew this could have been a whole lot worse. Joe wondered what the hell Harry had done and what would happen when Sykes caught up with him.

CHAPTER 14

Nine o'clock in the morning found Toby Clarke back in the mortuary.

"I wanted you to see them fresh," Si told him. "We've got identification on two, but I'm hoping you can help me with the third." He unzipped the first of the body bags and stepped back so that Clarke could get close. "Roughly the same injuries on all three. Approximate time of death, some time between midnight and six this morning, I would say. The first of the bodies was found at eight, a woman walking her dog."

Clarke nodded. "Our lot turned up, found two more close by." The three bodies had been dumped on waste ground, a brownfield site earmarked for redevelopment close to the canal. The dog walker was still being interviewed. She'd been badly shaken up, but Clarke, who had met her very briefly, had been left with the impression that she was more angry than upset. She was elderly, neatly turned out in a tweed skirt, quilted jacket and sensible shoes, and said that she walked the same route nearly every day. She had seemed more annoyed by the person who spoiled her walk than she was scared about finding a dead body.

Clarke studied the wounds on the first body and then went to look at the other two. Two white males, one black, all with livid gashes that had opened flesh and muscle, and in one case, dragged out entrails and sliced into them deeply as well.

"I'm willing to bet you can guess at the weapon," Si commented. "Though it's been a while."

"It has," Clarke agreed. "Five years, six?"

"About that."

The first time Clarke had observed this kind of injury, he hadn't understood what had caused them or how a single weapon could cause these kinds of entry, internal and exit wounds. But he knew now.

"A docker's hook," he said. One that had been sharpened at the point and then sharpened along the inner edge. The last one he'd seen had been attached to a T-bar handle. It was a formidable weapon that could be swung to impale, and, when pulled, it sliced through whatever had been impaled. The injuries were deep, gaping. Shocking.

The two white men seemed to have been attacked mostly on the body, while the black guy had had one side of his face practically torn off. The hook had impaled the sinuses and then been dragged through the face. His shoulders and belly were also deeply cut. They were not wounds that anyone could have survived for long. He was, Clarke reflected, also one of the few exceptions to Kyle Sykes's usual preference for white-only employees — an exception due in no small part to the intervention of Harry Prentice.

"What do you think — punishment or torture?" Si asked.

"Either or both. But it's something of a coincidence that they all work for Kyle Sykes and even more of a coincidence that they were all known to be close to Harry Prentice, at one time or another."

He pointed at the older of the two white men. "Phil Stern, one of the best wheelmen in the business. Could drive any damn thing. The younger one's his son, Davy. The third, he's a bit of a newcomer, but before Harry Prentice retired, Harry was . . . How would you explain it . . . ? I suppose you could describe Harry as his mentor or sponsor, or whatever. Harry certainly got him the job. His name is Kristy Young but the strange thing is, he was strictly white-collar. He was brought in for his computer skills. He was a hacker, IT expert. Harry found him, apparently."

"So, are we saying this has to do with Charlie Perrin's death, or Harry Prentice disappearing, or what?"

"I have no doubt all of those things are linked," Clarke said sourly. "Thanks, Si, anything unexpected turns up, let me know."

He left and went to brief his boss, wondering exactly how all of this fitted together. These were Kyle Sykes's men, but he doubted the Perrins had anything to do with the killing of them. After all, Sykes was the man with the hook.

CHAPTER 15

Harry and Lauren were up early. Surprisingly, they'd both slept well and as they ate breakfast, they discussed what they would do with their day.

"As soon as it's light, we'll go and survey the area," Harry said. "Make sure that we're totally familiar with every part of the beach and the land going back to the road. It looks kind of marshy back there, and I noticed a few cows when we were driving up. That means someone's likely to come and check on them from time to time, so we need to keep our eyes peeled."

Lauren was immediately anxious. "What if they see us?"

"We're on holiday, remember. Birdwatching. And before you tell me I don't know a sparrow from a hawk, there's a book about local birds on the shelf behind the telly. I spotted it this morning."

She laughed. "OK, Harry. Best read it then, before someone tests us."

Usually the first thing Lauren did in the morning was check her emails and social media. She wasn't particularly friendly with anybody, but she liked to know what was going on and she belonged to a couple of WhatsApp groups linked to the extracurricular activities they all did. The other girls all went out together but Lauren rarely joined them — her dad didn't exactly approve. Watching from the sidelines in a virtual sort of way was about as close as she got to a social life, but she found herself missing even that now.

"Harry, do you think it's safe to look at the internet on my phone? I wanted to see what was on the news."

"I suppose if you just go to the main news websites, it would do no harm. But the phones are pay as you go, I don't know how much credit it would use and it might be a while before we can top up."

"We could do that online . . ." Lauren began. Then she stopped. "No, we can't, that would mean using a credit or debit card, and we can't do that."

"We're in a cash economy now, pet. And that only when we have to. OK, go on, take a quick look at the local news, let's see what's going on back home."

Lauren shuffled her chair over beside his so they could both look at the phone. It was a cheap and basic smartphone, but it could still connect to the internet. Harry had swapped out the SIM card that had come with it on a just-in-case basis. Lauren navigated to the local news sites, back from where had been home. It didn't take long to find what they were looking for. Charlie Perrin's death had been reported as a tragic accident and she read the details with a growing sense of unreality. "Do you think the police will believe this? Why are they lying about it?"

"The families are saving face," Harry said. "It wouldn't do much for Charlie Perrin's reputation if it came out he'd been shot to death by a seventeen-year-old girl."

She could feel him observing her as she took that in. She took a deep breath. "But do you think the police will believe it?"

"They'll know something's fishy, but I think they're the least of our worries right now."

She scrolled down, finding a report of the house fire at Harry's place. They read it together and Harry thought she looked more shocked by this than she had by the item on Charlie Perrin.

"*He* did it, didn't he? My dad."

"I expect he did," Harry said. He took the phone from her and logged off the internet and then checked her credit. "Leave it, we've got the here and now to deal with, not the there and then."

She nodded and went off to get herself ready for the morning's trek. She paused just outside the kitchen door and looked back. Harry had picked up his own phone and she guessed he had gone back to the news site that they'd just shut down. She'd only glimpsed the headline but immediately it had set off an alarm bell in her mind. She guessed he had spotted it too and had not wanted to scare her even more. It was brief and fragmentary but made abundantly clear that three bodies had been found on wasteland, close to the canal. In the pit of her stomach, Lauren knew that they were something to do with her and Harry running away.

She fetched her coat and was careful to make a noise as she came back into the kitchen. She pretended not to see as he blacked the screen and put the phone in his pocket. But he couldn't hide the renewed level of anxiety on his face.

Outside was bitterly cold. Lauren was grateful for her coat and for the bobble hat and matching gloves that they'd picked up at one of the garages when they'd stopped for petrol. Her pockets were weighed down: gun, phone, cash. Harry made her recite the phone number he'd given her, just to make sure she knew it by heart. But he would not be drawn on whose number it might be.

They turned right and walked along the beach in the direction that Harry had come the first day he had found this cottage. Back towards what he called civilization. Tramping along on sand and shingle in trainers that, despite two pairs of socks, still let in the cold and damp, the walk seemed interminable to Lauren. Harry seemed to have eyes everywhere, watching the gulls, looking out at the fishing boats, trying to predict the weather. Lauren laughed at him. Harry was a city boy — she doubted if either of them would recognize that a storm was imminent until it actually started to rain on them.

Harry paused, touched her arm and pointed. "You see up there, the low bit of the cliff and a few steps in the rock?"

She nodded.

"Well, up there is a pub and the car park, a few caravans. You know, like I told you. This is the nearest way back into the rest of the world, unless you take the car from the cottage and drive back the way we came. And you only do that if you're sure no one is going to be able to follow you. Quickest way to make sure they can't follow is to shoot the tyres out. You make sure your engine's running first, so you're ready for a getaway, you got me?"

"I get you."

"Now we head back," Harry told her. "And we keep our eyes open every step of the way, just in case."

"Who are we likely to meet? Who'd be stupid enough to be out in this wind?" She felt like her face had been blasted raw by the chill of the wind off the sea and the sand it had blown into her eyes.

"Dog walkers, kite flyers, I suppose."

She laughed. "Try and fly a kite in this and you'd be dragged out to sea. What's past the cottage in the other direction, Harry?"

"Beach for about a mile and then a steep cliff. It juts out into the sea and blocks your exit, so don't go that way. If you need to run, this way is the one." He turned away from the sea and began to head inland, up towards the line of dunes that separated the beach from fields and then road. The sand was looser here and the wind free to pelt it in her face with even more ferocity. She pulled her scarf over her mouth and nose and hauled her hat down to her eyebrows. "God's sake, Harry, it was bad enough near the sea. I can barely walk in this."

Harry said nothing but led her right into the heart of the dunes. "Look," he said finally. "Look around you, what do you see?"

She was puzzled. "Just sand dunes. Oh, look, more sand dunes. And tussocky grass stuff."

"Now look behind you."

"Footprints," she said. "We have to get round that one, Harry. Even in this wind, with all the sand shifting you can still see the footprints."

"Think about it."

She could hear the impatience in his voice, understood that he was trying to tell her something important and she just wasn't getting it. But she was cold and tired and exasperated and the only thing stopping her yelling at him was her trust that if Harry thought this was important, then it probably was.

He was obviously waiting for a response.

"I don't walk on the sand," she said finally. "I walk on the grassy stuff."

"Give it a go."

Lauren glared at him, caught between amusement and total irritation, but then she nodded. "OK, let's go grass hopping."

They made it into a game. It was harder than it looked. Sometimes the tussocks gave way beneath their feet, at others they were really quite slippery or spaced wide apart. But by the time they were halfway back to the cottage, both were getting the hang of it. Lauren looked back. "No footprints," she said.

"And a lot of loose sand," said Harry. "You ever bury someone on the beach?"

"No, I leave that to my dad. I know what you mean, though," she added as Harry drew a breath that told he wasn't joking.

She watched as he bent down and began to scoop loose sand from behind the dune, on the leeward side where it had tipped over, fine and loose. He showed her how she might burrow in, keep out of sight, hide herself. At first, she thought he was joking, but as it became obvious that he wasn't, she gave it a go. She could understand what he meant, Lauren thought, as she drew the loose sand around her and peered out, seeing nothing but a bit of sky, other dunes, more tussocks of grass. It all looked the same. Every dune looked a bit like every other dune, every clump of grass like every other clump of grass. No doubt if you were used to looking at this stuff, you could orientate yourself, but to Lauren it was much of a muchness, and she began to see how that might be useful.

"Harry . . . " she said, as he helped her to her feet and they went on their way once more, "is this the best we're going to come up with? My dad sends men with guns and we hide in the sand dunes?"

Harry nodded. "Best I can come up with at the moment, pet. You have a better plan, tell me about it."

They walked the rest of the way back in absolute silence, each with their own thoughts. *How much would a bullet hurt?* Lauren wondered. She'd seen men suffering gunshot wounds on a couple of occasions. Had seen the doctor come, knowing that she shouldn't have. That, as far as her father was concerned, she *hadn't* seen anything. He had told her on both occasions to go to her room and to stay there until he said she could come out. On one of those occasions, she had heard him ranting at his lieutenants for having brought the injured man to his house. He hadn't seemed as angry the second time around, but then that second time around, the injured man had been Harry. When Harry had stopped a bullet and saved her father's life in the process.

She knew it must hurt a lot, but she found that oddly she was not particularly frightened of that part. It was almost as though if she did get shot, that would be the ending of things and there would be nothing she could do about it after that. Her father's men were all well-trained, all good shots — chances were, she might feel one shot but certainly not the second, because by then she'd be dead.

No, what scared her far more than that was if she *wasn't* shot or at least, not killed outright. If her father had decided that an example needed to be made, Lauren knew full well what he was capable of. She could not forget what Kyle Sykes had done to her own mother when she had crossed him.

They were almost at the cottage now and Harry paused, observing the scene, checking that nothing seemed out of place. Lauren found that she was looking too, following Harry's gaze.

"What are we looking for?"

"Anything that don't feel right."

She wanted to tell him that nothing felt right just now, so how was she going to tell if anything felt even more not right, but she didn't. Instead she took a deep breath and looked around as carefully and cautiously as her mentor was doing. At the side of the house she could see the four-by-four still under its tarpaulin. There was no one on the beach, no one anywhere in view. The seagulls still argued and squalled and the tide had receded a little since they had begun their walk. It didn't appear to go out very far, though obviously at certain times of the year it came up the beach a good deal further. The debris from its furthest reach was clearly visible, just a few yards from where the dunes began. Something in her memory spoke of spring tides but she wasn't quite sure what that even meant.

Harry had started to move forward and Lauren relaxed a little as they crossed the pebbles, then the gravel and then the path, and went into the house. She suddenly realized how tired she was and wondered how far they had walked that morning. "Any maps here, Harry? Local maps, I mean."

"I think there's a couple with the tourist information brochures, over on the bookshelf. Behind the television." His attention was still on the house, on checking anything that was slightly out of place, but eventually he gave up and went into the kitchen, suggesting they have some lunch.

Lauren retrieved the maps and glanced at her watch. It was too late for the lunchtime news. She wondered if Harry would be OK about her checking her phone again. She really wanted to know what was going on. Knowing felt like power, somehow, even while she was scared of finding out, just in case something came up that frightened her even more. Background terror was becoming almost like a heartbeat. It seemed as though she was operating on some level that over-laid it. It never went away but she was still functioning, even though she was not really quite sure how.

Harry had shed his jacket and hung it on the back of a chair. He was washing his hands and preparing to make sandwiches. "There's ham and cheese in the fridge, but we didn't get any mustard. Which is a shame, because I like a bit of mustard on my ham. You found the maps, then?"

She nodded. "There's two OS maps, one of the whole area and one of this bit. I suppose they get a lot of walkers here in the summer."

"I suppose they do. You spread it out on the table, the large-scale one, and we'll take a look while we are eating our sandwiches."

Lauren did so, trying to orientate herself. She found the Red Lion pub, the car park and the small cluster of caravans up on the cliff. Someone had stuck a Post-It note to the map with a scribbled message that '*the pub does good lunches*'. Beyond the pub was a narrow track leading back to the main road — if you could call it a main road — that also passed the cottage. Lauren calculated the route they had walked along the beach. It had been a little over nine miles there and back, so no wonder she was feeling it. Her usual lifestyle didn't include a hell of a lot of walking. For exercise, she played tennis and swam and did a bit of basketball in the winter, when there was no tennis to play. And she had those ridiculous DVDs her dad had given her, some blonde he fancied who had released a set of exercise programmes that mixed some kind of dance moves with boxing. She'd used them a few times just to please him, deliberately leaving them lying around so that he was satisfied his gift had not been ignored.

"Shift it over a bit," Harry said, nudging the map. He set the sandwiches and mugs of tea on the table. "So you've figured out where we are."

She nodded. "Nearest village is Holdsworth," she said. "That's about five miles in the opposite direction to where we went today, so further on along the little road out there. The

Red Lion and the caravan site are about four and half miles in that direction. So we walked a long way today, Harry. There's a church stuck on its own on the cliff a bit further along. I suppose it must have had a village at one time, but it looks like there's only a couple of farms down there now. And on the other side of the cottage, there's the cliff you were talking about, the one that blocks the route along the beach. If we wanted to head towards Holdsworth, we'd have to go by road or . . . no, look, there *is* a cliff path. I'm not sure where we'd pick it up, looks like you'd have to go back to the road and start from there. Did you go to Holdsworth when you were here last?"

Harry thought about it. "I might have done, I really don't remember."

"OK, so the nearest real civilization is about ten miles away." She was consulting the other map now and pointing to a settlement that looked about the size of a market town. "If we have to drive away from here, that's probably the best bet."

"I should give you some lessons. You've not driven anything as big as my Landy."

Lauren regarded him steadily. "And I'm likely to attract a lot of attention driving a thing like that. It will be obvious to anyone I'm just a kid."

He's started to object, so she interrupted. "Harry, if I need to drive it, I will drive it, believe me. I've no intention of letting my dad or his men get to me, if there's any way I can avoid it. I've seen what he does to traitors, I know better than anyone else what he's capable of. I won't freeze, I won't make this a waste of your time or your life, if it comes to that. I promise you, Harry."

He nodded, accepting her word. "Eat your lunch," he said. Then, as an afterthought, "Make sure you memorize that map, make sure you know what the satnav location of this place is. If you have to ring that number I gave you, they'll need to know where to come and get you, and this isn't exactly an easy place to find."

CHAPTER 16

"I had to pay a visit to the mortuary this morning," Toby Clarke said.

Kyle Sykes nodded. "I saw the news reports. Never a pleasant duty, visiting the mortuary."

"Three men who worked for you."

"Three men who have done work for me at one time or another," Sykes corrected him. "It's not quite the same thing, you understand. Anyone who does work for me is responsible for their own tax and National Insurance. They are freelance. You see the subtle difference, Inspector."

They were sitting in Kyle Sykes's large conservatory. A very new detective constable by the name of Hopkins sat close by, her notebook open in her lap and pen poised. Small, with a mass of dark brown hair that was usually tied up on top of her head with a scrunchie, she seemed to be doing her best to be invisible. She didn't have to try too hard, Clarke thought. Sykes had ignored her thus far and would probably continue to do so. The conservatory overlooked the green space at the back of the house. It was, Clarke thought, an underutilized space, being mostly lawn with a few trees down at the end. It looked as though Kyle Sykes wanted the space to have a large garden, wanted the status symbol of it, but had never quite got around to creating the garden itself.

"Not a pleasant task for their relatives, either. Identifying the bodies. They were all badly mutilated."

"Identifying the dead is never a pleasant task," Sykes said. He had a South London accent, all sharp edges and angles. Clarke had noticed that when he was stressed, his accent became more prominent. Today, he sounded relaxed. "I had to go and identify my own wife, if you remember."

Clarke nodded. He remembered. He'd been present and it was not something easily wiped from your brain. He put that aside. "I have to say that these three were a random selection of your not-quite employees."

"Of my freelancers. Definitely *not* my employees. Her Majesty's revenue office makes that distinction very clear."

"Nevertheless, they were an odd collection," Clarke insisted. "Phil Stern — in his day, one of the best wheelmen in the business. Strictly old school. If you were planning a bank job and needed a quick getaway, then Phil was your man. And his son, Davy — David — carved out a nice little niche for himself in your organization."

"Davy was an excellent mechanic. He will be missed."

"And then Kristy Young. Now he was a bit of an odd-ball — IT expert, one-time hacker so I'm told. Never actually arrested for that, but his reputation is solid enough. The word is, Harry Prentice brought him to your attention. So, like I say, an odd mix."

Kyle Sykes shrugged his shoulders and spread his hands as though weighing what Clarke had said. "What can I tell you? Modern business requires a broad skills base. We pride ourselves on our talent pool."

"And how do you advertise these days? Local paper? Online? Word-of-mouth?"

Sykes smiled. "There's never a shortage of young men wanting well-paid work."

"Young men? So not an equal opportunities employer, then?"

"As I told you, not an employer at all."

"They are freelancers responsible for their own tax and National Insurance, yes, I get it." Clarke was silent for a few moments. He glanced around the large conservatory as though considering the use of space, the advantages of UPVC framing.

"A conservatory is a good addition to any home," Sykes told him.

"A little difficult when you live in a third-floor flat," Clarke said.

Sykes laughed. It was an oddly genuine sound, as though he really did enjoy the small joke. Clarke saw DC Hopkins shift in her seat. She was uncomfortable in Kyle Sykes's presence and not experienced enough to hide the fact.

"So, speculate for me, who might want these three men dead? One of them, I could maybe understand. Father and son, perhaps. But that combination, and with that degree of unnecessary violence?"

"I imagine you are a man who argues any level of violence is unnecessary." Sykes looked at him with interest. "So when a man regards any level of violence as unnecessary, you have to agree it's difficult for them to create a meaningful scale. What might be excessive to you is no more than a gentle tap to someone else."

"I think even you might agree that these men received more than a gentle tap."

Sykes shrugged. "And I can't tell you who did it to them. I have enemies, I suppose. Every successful man has enemies."

"Gus Perrin?"

"Mr Perrin and I have an agreement. We don't tread on one another's toes where business is concerned, that merely complicates matters. We're both successful men, and there is room for more than one of those in any community."

His tone was cold now, Clarke noted. The accent a little more pronounced. So the mention of Perrin had touched a raw nerve. He was unsurprised when Sykes got to his feet, signalling that their interview was at an end. Clarke didn't argue. He'd expected nothing from Sykes. They were both just going through the motions and Sykes, he suspected, would probably have been a little disappointed if Clarke had not turned up on his doorstep that morning asking questions to which he knew he would receive no proper response.

There were still very few people around, Clarke thought, as he led Hopkins back to his car. When they pulled out of the drive, he glanced towards Hopkins's notepad. "I saw you scribbling frantically. Did you actually record anything of any use?" he asked.

Hopkins looked mortified. "We needed a record, boss."

"And so we did. Even if it is a record of empty comments and random information about the desires and requirements of the HMRC." He glanced at her again and decided that he was being unfair. "Not a criticism," he assured her. "Kyle Sykes has been playing this game since before I was born. His father and grandfather played it before that. He's had a lot of practice."

"So who do you think killed them? Gus Perrin's lot? Do you think he believed they had something to do with the death of his son? Should we expect revenge killings?"

"That's a lot of questions in one. OK, so who killed them? I wouldn't put it past Sykes himself. Perrin, no, I don't think so. I have no reason to think that, mind. Just that it doesn't sit right. And, no, I don't think it had anything directly to do with the death of Charlie Perrin. I don't believe that was an accident — that strains the limits of credibility — though I don't think any of those three were involved in it anyway. Phil Stern never committed a violent act in his entire life. He drove a lot of very violent people in his car, but his job was to drive them and it was something he was very, very good at. There wasn't a local route he didn't know, not a speed limit he wasn't aware of and not a tactic he couldn't have taught to the experts on the defensive driving course."

He saw her cast a look in his direction that suggested he was naive. In her book, a villain was a villain. "And what about the son? Was he *just* a mechanic?"

"Like the man said, you need a broad set of skills when you're in business and it doesn't make any difference whether or not that business is legitimate. You still need skilled men. Some are skilled mechanics, some are brilliant drivers, some are very adept killers."

She stared at him for a moment as not though not fully comprehending how he could be so flippant. The truth was Toby Clarke, now approaching forty, had been dealing with men like Kyle Sykes and Gus Perrin since he'd been a kid. He had almost become one of them, the option being there to follow in his father's footsteps rather than follow his mother's teaching. They'd been an odd match, his parents. It was no surprise it hadn't lasted. What was surprising was that he had no complaints about either parent. In their own way, they both cared about him and he suspected his father had been glad that he had not stepped through the doors that were always half open for him. He had come to realize that it was out of something like respect for his father that he had delayed joining the police force until after his father had been dead and gone for a good eighteen months, though he'd been thinking about it for quite a while before. He had, however, put a good distance between himself and home before signing on the dotted line. It was his mother who had been oddly disapproving of the decision.

"What happened with Sykes's wife?" Hopkins asked.

"Murdered."

Hopkins glanced at him. "How? What, in a revenge killing or something?"

"Anyone ever tell you, you have an obsession with revenge killings?"

She looked slightly huffy. "Well, they do happen."

"Of course they do. But you'd be surprised how many times some kind of agreement is made between the families, some other way of resolving things. Believe me, Hopkins, most of the time the OCGs keep off each other's turf. It's too much of a hassle, too expensive to do otherwise. It's often when they join forces that the trouble really starts, because overnight an organization can double or triple in size, resources, knowledge. You have to stop thinking of them as stupid criminals and start thinking of them as business-men — and a few women for that matter, who strategize and plan and don't just respond by lashing out with random violence. The stupid and the randomly violent ones, we deal with very quickly. They end up inside. Having said that, when an organization like this decides that violence is required, everything goes tits up very fast and very badly. Most of the time, though, we're not dealing with the likes of the Krays these days. We are dealing with people who have a finger in so many pies . . . and a hell of a lot of those pies are legitimate businesses, run by people who have no idea who they're in bed with."

He paused, thinking just how mixed up that metaphor was and also whether this was one of those times when what-ever was going on would be resolved by negotiation or by violence. From the look of things, it was not going to be one of the former occasions. Hopkins might well be proved correct in her assumptions.

"Did you catch who did it? Who killed the wife?"

"We had a suspect and we had someone go to jail for the offence, not necessarily the same thing."

"What do you mean?"

"Our main suspect was Kyle Sykes. Our main scapegoat was a man called Ronald Hardwick. He was known to be violent but had the intelligence of, I don't know, maybe a five-year-old on a good day. He was found covered in blood, with the murder weapon in his hands, his footprints and fingerprints all over the scene. Circumstantial evidence was overwhelming and what's more, he confessed to it. Though whether he was mentally capable of making a confession is another story. He's now banged up in a secure psychiatric unit, doubtful if he'll ever make it out into the world again, but there you go. A result."

"But if the circumstantial evidence was overwhelming, what makes you doubt it?"

"When you have half a day to spare, you can read through the case notes for yourself. But the fact is, the man was well known to Kyle Sykes, he was an impressionable soul, and by the time we got to him he was so jacked up on drink and drugs he would have confessed to the assassination of Franz Ferdinand."

"France who?"

Clarke shook his head in mock despair. "What do they teach you at school these days? Anyway, Kyle Sykes was behind it. Jennifer Sykes had been having an affair. She thought she'd been careful and discreet but nobody is careful or discreet enough around our Kyle. The man she was having the affair with also turned up dead two days later. It's likely he'd been killed at the same time, but his body had been dumped in the canal and he was lucky. Just a bullet to the head."

"How had she been killed?"

"Same way as those three men in the morgue."

"Jesus!"

Clarke wanted to tell her that Jesus had never been a suspect but he wasn't sure that she had that sense of humour. "Quite," he agreed. "It was the daughter who found her, in the garage of their old house. Found her and found Ronald Hardwick bending over her. Not unreasonably, she started to scream the place down, turned and ran, and of course in moments, Hardwick was surrounded by Sykes's men, we were called, and so it goes."

"How old was the kid?"

"She was eleven," Clarke told her. *And now there's no sign of her*, he thought. *We still have no idea where's she's gone. If she's gone.* "But after her mum was killed, she went to stay with Harry Prentice and his wife, Jean. Her dad made a big fuss about not being able to live in their old house anymore and had this current one built. She didn't go back home until he'd moved in. He spent the eighteen months in a luxury hotel. She spent it with Harry and his wife."

"And now she seems to be missing, and Harry Prentice's house was burned to the ground."

"And four men are dead, including Charlie Perrin. Word is, Lauren Sykes and Charlie Perrin were going to be man and wife. Two families joined in hellish matrimony."

"But she's just a kid. He was old."

"Older, not old," Clarke objected. "He was younger than me."

"Sorry, did I touch a nerve?" She grinned at him, then looked worried as though she might have offended him.

"Older," he conceded, smiling back at her. "A lot older than Lauren."

"So maybe she's run off to avoid getting hitched."

"Hell of a coincidence that he's wound up dead."

He glanced at Hopkins, seeing her taking this in. "You think she killed him?" Hopkins laughed.

"I think we have to consider anything and everything," he told her. *And*, he thought, *there's a hell of a lot to consider.*

CHAPTER 17

They had not discussed it, but by some sort of tacit agreement they had both settled in front of the television for the evening news. Harry had checked the internet several times that day and knew that the story was growing. The burning of his house was not likely to have made national level, but the murders of three men already had. Lauren had sensed Harry's mood darkening throughout the day. Now she curled up beside him on the settee and held his hand.

The report he was expecting was the third item, coming after political visits and bombing raids and the number of civilian dead overseas. "*The bodies of the three men found close to the Grand Union Canal where it passes through Wandsborough have now been named.*"

Cue footage of an all-too-familiar place. On one bank of the canal where redevelopment had taken place, old warehouses were now luxury apartments. On the other was still waste ground, surrounded by loose chain-link fence but easily accessible from the towpath. The buddleia and the birches had moved in, evidence that it had been derelict for about a decade. Kids from the local high-rise played there, avoiding the syringes and condoms. Harry had known it before the rows of terraced houses had been demolished. Lauren would have passed it on her way to school most days, but he doubted she'd ever actually been there.

Photographs of three men replaced the landscape. Two looked like mug shots and the third looked more like a passport photo. All three had been depersonalized, the immediate message being these men might have deserved to die. Who knows what they might have been getting up to?

Beside him, Lauren shifted uneasily. "It's not fair to the families to use pictures like that. They should use family pictures, you know, Harry. They were still human beings. They still had people who loved them."

"I know," Harry said. "I know." He knew that she was remembering the news reports from when her mother had died. Her mother had no criminal record, being from a respectable background, so initially most of the newspapers had carried images either of her wedding day, or of her at some social gathering or other. It was only much later when newspapers began to speculate about her husband and report that Kyle Sykes was involved in darker dealings that the images changed. The media seemed to pick those pictures in which her mother was no longer beautiful, no longer innocent.

"I know them, don't I, Harry?" Lauren said suddenly. "The younger white guy often worked on Dad's cars, I think sometimes his dad helped too. The other man visited our house a couple of times to sort out the computers — Kristy. He was nice. Netflix kept crashing out on my laptop. He got it working. And he said my computer had got a virus so he cleaned that up and installed some software to stop it happening again."

She sat forward, scrutinizing the television — it was important to her that she recall every tiny detail. These were not just pictures on a TV screen, pictures calculated so that the general public would dismiss them.

"If we get killed, no one's going to care, are they, Harry? Because of who my dad happens to be. It'll be just *'That old lag, Harry Prentice'* and *'That slut of a kid.'*"

"No one will think anything bad about you, pet."

"Oh, no? Harry, if you're gone, there's no one to tell them anything else, is there? I've got no real friends. My dad doesn't give a shit, he just wants me dead. Who's going to tell them any different?"

Harry gripped her hand but didn't really know what to say. Would they get the same treatment? Would their deaths be seen as unimportant just because of who her father happened to be?

Probably, Harry thought. And on his own behalf, he couldn't argue with that, but Lauren deserved better, she really did.

He realized the report had gone in a new direction, and that he was looking at the burned-out ruins of his own house. Lauren gasped. "Your house, Harry."

"We knew it had happened, love."

"Yeah, but . . ." Until she saw the footage, it hadn't seemed real.

No details were released about how the men were killed, only that the police were treating this as a triple murder enquiry. The report went on to outline the petty criminal careers of the two Sterns, father and son, and to hint at the criminal activities of Kristy Young — small-time hacking when he was a teenager, petty theft and a troubled childhood.

Charlie Perrin's death did not seem to have made the national headlines, at least not in the evening news. Either no connection had been made or this had been restricted to local interest only. After all, from what they'd read on the internet, Charlie's death was being treated as an accident.

Harry stood up and switched off the television. "Come on, let's get ourselves something to eat." He was forcing himself to sound casual, but one look at Lauren's face told him that he wasn't fooling anyone. He didn't have to tell her that this was definitely something to do with what they had done, she in killing Charlie Perrin and he in helping her to run away.

"They were friends of yours."

"I knew them all, yes. Kristy was a good lad. He made mistakes but he was never violent. It was me who brought him in, to give the lad some work. Stupid. Stupid thing for me to do."

He was relieved that she didn't waste her breath telling him that it wasn't his fault. But she did ask one more thing, and he realized that, perceptive as she was, she had been conscious of a sense of relief from Harry. "You expected it to be someone else, didn't you?"

Harry cast a fierce glance in her direction, then nodded. "I was afraid your dad might have gone after old Joe. We've been friends since we were kids. We were close at one time."

Lauren looked back at the television, as though the empty screen might tell her something more. She followed Harry back to the kitchen and helped to prepare a meal. Neither of them spoke — there wasn't a lot that they could say.

Four deaths now, Harry thought, *and there will be more.*

"Should we go back, Harry?"

Harry almost laughed. Go back? Face her father, give themselves up to his anger? He'd kill her, and Harry knew that Kyle would kill him, too. There would be two more deaths if they went back, that was for certain. But would there be more?

"Your dad wouldn't stop, not until he was properly satisfied. And your blood won't satisfy him, mine neither. He'll use this as an excuse for all the times he didn't act, didn't get payback. He'll use it as a diversion and an excuse. Anyone who's ever slighted him, they'd better watch out. I've seen it before, pet."

"After Mum died."

Harry nodded. He remembered it all too well and he knew that Lauren did, too. Her father had started drinking the day of the funeral and not stopped for . . . well, Lauren wouldn't really know that because she was at Harry's just after that. But Harry knew she'd heard the rumours, the gossip, the fearful whisperings in corners. His wife had betrayed him. She was dead. The man she'd had the affair with, he was dead. The sister-in-law who had tried to protect them, she and her husband disappeared, their bodies never found, but Lauren must have realized that they were gone. Others had run, some were *rumoured* to have run, but Harry doubted they'd got far. But of course, Kyle Sykes was alibied for every single incident. Drunk for most of them, though Lauren and Harry both knew that didn't stop him. All the drink ever did was break down what few boundaries he observed on a day-to-day basis.

Lauren was watching Harry frying eggs.

"You want fried bread?" he asked.

She shook her head. "Don't think I can eat anything, Harry. The smell of bacon's making me feel sick."

He took the pan off the stove and came over to her. "You'll sit down, and you'll eat. You'll keep up your strength. You keep up your *normal*, OK? The way we survive is to keep up our normal, you got that?"

She looked a little scared. He'd been louder than he'd intended. "I've got that, Harry," she told him. *But what the hell is normal anymore?*

CHAPTER 18

Clarke called at the local supermarket on his way home, realizing rather late in the day that he had no food in his flat. As he pushed his trolley down the aisle, collecting bread, milk and ready meals, and a bit of fruit, just to balance the whole thing out, he was surprised to see a familiar face. Sam Barker turned down the aisle he was in, inspecting apples and pears. Beside her stalked a tall, well-built, mixed-heritage man. Chinese, white British, maybe. Clarke caught himself classifying. Occupational hazard.

The man touched Sam's arm and pointed something out and she laughed. Clarke watched as they shared what was obviously a private joke. *They're a good-looking couple*, he thought. *This must be her physiotherapist boyfriend, Marty Baines.*

"Good evening, Miss Barker," Clarke said.

She looked up, startled and he could see that it took a moment before she recognized him. "Oh," she said. "You're that inspector."

"Guilty," he laughed. Marty Baines was observing him with interest, but there was no caution from either of them, and that in itself was unusual, Clarke thought.

Baines put out a hand. "Marty," he said. "Sam was telling me about everything. It's a bit of a bugger, isn't it? I knew

Charlie got a bit careless, but I never expected anything like this to happen."

"You knew Charlie Perrin well?"

Marty Baines laughed. "No, I did not. To Charlie Perrin, I was just one of the hired help. I give his father physio three times a week, more if he has a lot of pain."

"What you do the rest of the time?"

Marty raised an eyebrow. "Do the police always carry out their interrogations in Sainsbury's? The rest of the time I work in my specialty, which is sports medicine. I'm attached to the Colbert Academy, it's part of the university complex now. I work with athletes, and I also work with some ex-military personnel. The Colbert has a rehab unit attached. Mr Perrin paid for the building." He grinned at Clarke. "And, yes, I know it's probably dirty money, but it's for a good cause, so frankly, I don't give a damn."

"So you have no illusions about your boss, then."

"He's not my boss. He's my patient or client, or whatever you want to call it, three times a week."

"But you live in a house on his estate."

"I live in a house he happens to own. We've come to an arrangement, a business arrangement if you like. Effectively we pay no rent, and I give him physio three times a week. It might be unconventional, but it goes through the books via my accountant. She found some way to make it simple — I bill him, he bills me, and the amounts cancel each other out."

"Convenient."

Marty laughed again. "Actually it is. Mr Perrin owns a lot of property. Most of it legitimate, though you probably know that. He owns two gymnasiums, a hotel and I believe he part owns the golf course at Amerby. I am fully aware that he's dodgy, but I'm just his physio."

Cocky, Clarke thought. *He enjoys his little brush with criminality. Probably even boasts about it to his friends — "Oh, you know, Gus Perrin's not so bad once you get to know him . . ."*

He'd seen it all before. It was the same attitude, the same naivety that got young kids involved in selling drugs or teenagers believing someone actually loved them when they were being groomed for sex. But a man like Marty Baines should really not be that stupid.

He bit back on a direct challenge. "And you, Miss Barker, are you as sanguine about Mr Perrin and his contacts and connections?"

She frowned, as though the question was offensive. "I work for Mrs Josephs. I've worked for Carole for two years now, and I'm very happy. She's an extremely talented artist and she allows me to use the studio for my own practice. I've only ever met Mr Perrin a few times. And, no, I didn't know Charlie well, either, though of course with him living just across from Carole, I did see him quite often."

Marty Baines, Clarke thought, had been almost amused by his questions. Sam Barker was definitely getting more irritated. "It must have been a terrible shock for Mrs Josephs, finding her brother's body like that."

Sam regarded him coldly. "I don't think they were close," she said. "Not everybody is close to their siblings."

"Nevertheless, finding a dead body is not a pleasant experience. Though I suppose growing up in the Perrin household, that will have been inevitable at some point."

Marty Baines laughed at that. He was looking critically at Clarke, but seemed genuinely amused by him. Sam, on the other hand, was bristling.

"Carole is a respected artist and a good woman," she said. "She's not her father. And now, we have shopping to do, so if you'll excuse us, Inspector Clarke."

"I'll no doubt see you both sometime soon," Clarke told them. *Interesting*, he thought, as they both walked away. At first, she had seemed mildly surprised to see him there, had seemed almost to not realize who he was. And then, when Marty had started to chat to him, she had grown more discomfited. So at what point had Marty said something that had caused her to become concerned? Clarke reran the conversation in his mind as he finished shopping and went to the checkout. He decided that Sam had become a little colder when he'd asked about the arrangement with the house and Marty had been open in explaining it. He made a mental note to look into this, to see how legal it actually was. He guessed that he would find it was above board, if a little unusual. He found he was still irritated that Marty actually found it entertaining, on some level, that he should be working for a crime boss, and perhaps that he enjoyed the imagined kudos of acknowledging that dirty money had gone into the building of the rehabilitation unit, that it had come to some good in the end. *Not a healthy attitude*, Clarke thought. *It will come back to bite him in the end.*

The rehab unit, Clarke remembered, was a charity. How would they square this? He had heard of a great many charities turning down money that came from questionable sources and no doubt the investment in these good works was a convenient way of laundering this dirty money. Had the charity hesitated? But then, it occurred to him, who would want to say a direct no to Gus Perrin? Who would take that kind of risk?

CHAPTER 19

The funeral of Charlie Perrin took place on the Thursday afternoon. Local press were in attendance, and the crematorium was full, with people standing outside. Clarke and his spotters logged those they knew and added those they did not to a growing database. Lauren Sykes was still conspicuous by her absence.

Clarke's orders were to stay back, to keep a respectful distance from the funeral party, which was attended by representatives from every OCG he could name from up and down the country, and probably a few he could not, alongside local civic dignitaries who had benefited from Gus Perrin's largesse.

Clarke wondered how many of them were fully in Perrin's pocket and how many just didn't want to risk causing offence.

Kyle Sykes was there, of course. Pausing on the crematorium steps to survey the onlookers, he caught Clarke's eye and nodded before going on inside with three of his sharp-suited thugs. He had refused point blank to say where Lauren might be, telling Clarke it was none of his business. None of her school friends or teachers had any clue as to where she might have gone either, but Clarke was building up a picture of a rather lonely young woman. He hoped she'd done a runner for no better reason than that she was sick of her father, but common sense told him that was hardly likely. The fact that Harry Prentice was also nowhere to be seen was also interesting. Day after day, Clarke had been expecting the body to turn up but so far Harry Prentice was not definitively dead and no one was saying anything about his whereabouts.

The service over, everyone disappeared off to the wake, which was being held at one of the hotel and golf course complexes in which Gus Perrin was a major investor. Clarke's task of the day was over.

Out of idle curiosity as much as anything, he followed the main funeral party to the golf course, parked up on a grass verge and watched as the rest of the cars went by. This, he thought, was a major social event. He had spotted Sam Barker at the funeral, but noticed that she and a few others had left and headed in a different direction. Their status was perhaps not high enough for them to be invited to the wake. He noted also that some of the local dignitaries had departed after the funeral service. Was that significant? Did it speak of a connection or a lack thereof, or was it simply that they had meetings to go to? Or were they heading home to family, having put in a strictly formal and expected appearance?

The final car drove through the gate, the gates closed and Clarke was left outside looking in.

CHAPTER 20

Joe Messenger had not expected visitors that night. He'd watched the funeral on the local news and seen his boss standing on the crematorium steps. Now his boss was standing on his own doorstep. Joe went cold inside.

There were two identical cars outside the house, at least one running on false plates. Joe had been around the organization long enough to recognize that.

"Get your coat," Kyle Sykes said. "It's cold where we're going."

Joe's wife came out into the hall. She looked from Joe to Sykes and the colour faded from her lips and cheeks. "Just nipping out for a bit," Joe told her with as much cheerful conviction as he could muster.

She opened her mouth to speak but he shook his head. There was nothing she could do and he didn't want her involved in whatever this was. Inwardly he cursed Harry — this had something to do with him going off with the girl. No one had told him that's what Harry had done, but he'd asked around and it didn't take a genius to work it out.

Sykes directed Joe to the lead car and Joe sat alone in the back seat. Kyle Sykes liked to travel up front with the driver. The four-by-four following contained five men. They pulled out of the end of the road and then headed straight towards the motorway.

It was dark. All the street lights were on and it began to rain, that fine mizzly rain that's almost fog and soaks you to the skin in no time.

"Have you any idea how many Red Lion pubs there are in the country?" Kyle Sykes asked Joe. "Even when you're only looking up north, and on the coast. Dozens of the fuckers."

Joe knew he didn't need to answer that one. *Harry*, he thought. *You've gone and got us both dead.*

* * *

In the last couple of days, things had fallen into a sort of routine for Lauren and Harry. They'd watched the news religiously, had eaten regularly, at Harry's insistence, and Lauren had studied the map, familiarized herself with the lay of the land and practised stripping, cleaning and firing the weapons that Harry had brought. He'd dared only let her use silenced pistols and even they, to Lauren's ears, seemed absurdly loud.

"Who the hell called them 'silencers?'" she had asked. "They're more like just-a-bit-quieters."

Mostly it was just aiming and dry firing, something Harry really didn't like to do, but he didn't think they'd got much option.

Lauren had ventured out on her own on a number of occasions, generally staying within sight of the cottage. She needed thinking time and knew that Harry did too. She sensed that Harry needed this time to make peace with whatever he believed in, and she also caught him on occasions talking to his dead wife. She wasn't surprised he still talked to Jeanie — she did it herself. She'd loved Harry's wife almost more than she loved Harry and certainly more than she loved either of her parents. She wasn't sure that she'd actually ever felt anything much for her father, but much as she had wanted to be close to her mother, she had often been cool, distant and, Lauren now recognized, often profoundly depressed.

Lauren had gone beachcombing and had found some sea glass on her first foray away from the cottage. Now she went looking for more, loving the subtle colours, greens and blues of the glass washed smooth by the ocean. She found the occasional fossil and picked up shells just as she had when she was a tiny child. Twice she had seen dog walkers in the distance and had beaten a hasty retreat, concealing herself in the dunes and watching them go by. Beyond that, there had just been the sound of the gulls and waves and sometimes the pounding rain to break the monotony of waiting.

They had talked twice about moving on. But where to? Harry had mentioned Scotland. He had contacts there who might shelter them for a while. Lauren had agreed, but had asked, "And where after that? What if my dad threatens them, too?"

It had struck her that the more people who were involved the more likely her dad would find out where she was, even if they were in Scotland. *He* had contacts everywhere.

Harry had agreed that might be an issue. But, more of an issue, she'd come to realize, was that Harry simply didn't have the energy to keep on running. Harry had come here to hole up, decided this was where they would make their stand, and that was that. It disturbed her that she'd found this weakness in him, but at the same time she understood it. Once or twice, she'd thought about taking his Land Rover and leaving him. She'd analysed her motives for doing this and found they were twofold and neither of them made a hell of a lot of sense. On the one hand was the speculation that if she left him, she could perhaps draw her father away. But she knew her father would never forgive Harry and that his life would be forfeited, whether she was with him or not. The second motivation was anger. She was occasionally furious with Harry that he had decided that they would stay in this one place when what she wanted to do was keep on running. This anger bubbled beneath the surface and threatened to burst out when things got too much. When this happened, she would come down to the ocean and throw stones and rocks and anything she could find into the sea. The sea didn't care, but she knew Harry would if she said even half the things that were going through her head, and one thing she had decided on was that she was not going to hurt Harry. She couldn't prevent Harry from *being* hurt, but she wasn't going to add to it. After all, he was all she had. The one person left in the world who loved her.

When she got in from beachcombing, they checked the internet briefly on their phones, and found footage of Charlie Perrin's funeral on the local news from back home. Lauren saw a fleeting image of her father and the sight of him chilled her to the core. He was looking around as though expecting to see someone, surveying the scene much as Harry did when they went outside the cottage.

That night, it took her a long time to get to sleep and it felt as though she'd only been asleep a very short while when she started awake, aware of a presence in her room. Harry stood over her, his finger on his lips. "Get dressed," he whispered.

Lauren's eyes widened and she felt panic rising in her chest. *But it's the middle of the night*, she wanted to say. Surely her father would not arrive in the middle of the night? And yet when she thought about it, it made perfect sense.

She got out of bed. Pulled on her clothes, her shoes, her coat. Checked the pockets for the gun, the phone, the money . . . the little fragments of sea glass. Harry was in the kitchen. He was listening intently.

He pointed back towards her room and Lauren knew that he wanted her to go out of the window. "Oh, Harry," Lauren breathed. "Come with me."

"Go." His expression told her that he would brook no argument. "You're wasting time, girl."

He was right. If her father really was here, with however many men he had brought with him, there would be no time for hesitation. In the distance, she heard a car engine approaching. She wondered what sound it was that had woken Harry. Obviously, something much more subtle — she, too, would have been roused by the sound of an approaching car. It never occurred to her that Harry might be mistaken and that this might be a false alarm. Harry was too good for that.

In the darkness of her bedroom, she felt for the window catch and slid the window open very, very slowly, then she slid herself through and crouched down. For a moment, she did not move. Harry had told her that she must observe the scene first, that she was to keep in the deep shadows and use her senses. If she couldn't see, then she must listen. Her heart was thumping so loudly and so fast, it made her tremble. It took a few seconds for her to make out the sounds that were not just the pounding of blood in her ears.

Harry had been right. They were here. An advanced guard must have come up the track on foot. They were moving slowly and quietly, but she was still aware of them. Her father specialized in deploying big men and big men had big feet. Big men with big feet found it hard to move as silently as a small and frightened teenager. And now she could hear the vehicles clearly too, coming up the track towards the cottage.

Harry had bought her time — she had to use that.

She made to go round the side of the house, towards the beach and the dunes but almost immediately realized that way was blocked. She saw a shadow move and turned back the way she had come, keeping as close to the side of the house as a rat running against a wall. The Land Rover had been parked under the tarpaulin only a step away from the wall, and she slipped softly into that new shadow. Another tiny movement startled her and she slipped beneath the tarpaulin and held her breath, mouth open so that she could hear better, straining to interpret the sounds. A scuff of shoes on gravel — Lauren was so grateful for that gravel. She suspected now that this was what had alerted Harry. The sound of shoes on shingle.

She crept out from beneath the tarpaulin. There would be a few steps in the open before she was in the dunes and she gathered up her courage to make that brief run. She paused, listening intently, and it was then that she heard the first shot. It had come from inside the cottage. Harry had fired out. He was giving her a chance. She couldn't waste it. She heard shouts and she leaped for the cover of the dunes, hoping that in the dark, no one would see the few footsteps she might have made before she got onto the grassy bank. Crouching low, she slithered away.

Gunfire was returned now. Muzzle flashes that lit the night and sounds that burst the silence. Lauren was only about a hundred metres from the house but she dared not move further for fear of being seen by the two men who had stormed round the side of the cottage. There were louder shouts in the night, more gunfire and the sound of someone breaking down the door. There was only one of Harry, he couldn't cover everywhere. She tried to count the voices, the moving shadows, to work out how many men her father might have brought with him and where they might be, and guessed there were perhaps half a dozen. That seemed a large number to send after an old man and a young girl, but then her father never went anywhere unprepared.

Lauren knew she had to try and put a bit more distance between herself and the cottage but something else had occurred to her that momentarily froze her in place. She was on the *wrong* side of the house. She had been forced to turn left instead of right and now she was on the beach on the side that led only to the cliff. The cliff that blocked her way. Lauren knew that her only chance lay in hiding and keeping still and in calling for help from whoever the hell it was that Harry had instructed her to phone.

She took advantage of the noise and the darkness beyond the cottage in a place where the lights couldn't reach. A strong wind was blowing now and she knew from experience over the past week that any footstep she did make would be obliterated quickly. The rain had also started to fall, which, though unpleasant, would actually work in her favour. So she took a chance and she put about another hundred metres between her and the cottage, then another, before suddenly bright lights flooded the little house and the surrounding beach. The headlights of a car, and then a second car behind it. Lauren flattened herself against the ground and burrowed into the sand as deep she could go.

* * *

Inside the cottage, Harry slumped in the corner of what had been Lauren's bedroom. He was bleeding from a head wound where a bullet had grazed his scalp and from another bullet wound in his side. It was through-and-through and he didn't think it had done too much damage. It was eminently survivable — in other circumstances. Sykes stood in the doorway. Joe just inside the room. Joe was shaking as though he would fall apart and looking down at Harry. "I never told him," Joe stammered.

"Oh yes, you did," Sykes said. "You told me enough."

"We're a bit beyond playing the blame game," Harry said quietly.

"You think? I blame you for filling my kid's head with ideas she shouldn't be having. I blame you for bringing her here. Now, where is she?"

Harry shrugged. Shrugging hurt. "I don't know. I hope she's over the hills and far away by now." He laughed. That hurt too.

Sykes stepped aside. Two men came in, lifted Harry to his feet and hustled him through to the living room. His hands were zip-tied behind his back, a rope was put around his neck and thrown over the top of the living-room door. On the other side, someone took the strain, pulling Harry's head up and back and exposing his throat. His feet were now just touching the ground. Harry tried to prepare himself for what was going to come next. He could see Joe, his arms pinioned by another of Sykes's men. Joe could hardly stand, he was so scared. Harry hoped that he'd given Lauren enough time to get away. With a bit of luck, she should be part way along the beach heading towards the Red Lion by now. She would call the number he'd given her, and rescue would come. She just had to hold her nerve and do what he had told her. Believing that Lauren was safe was all he had to hang on to now, even now he knew Sykes had sent out men looking for her. But she knew the territory, this was her ground and not theirs. She would be all right, Harry convinced himself of that, and then when a little bit of doubt crept in, he convinced himself again. Then he stopped convincing himself about anything because the pain began.

Sykes drove the hook deep into Harry's flesh and pulled. Harry screamed.

"Where is she?" Sykes asked him.

"I told you — I don't know." With his head pulled back, chin forced high by the rope, Harry was struggling to breathe. He had managed to scream, but he couldn't figure out how. Surely there wasn't enough breath in his body for so much sound to come out. The hook swung again, into Harry's side this time and again he managed to make that wailing, keening sound, the sound an animal makes when despair is absolute and it knows it is about to die.

He knew that Sykes would ask him again and again and again until the screaming stopped, and it was a relief in Harry's mind, the only little tiny bit of relief, that he really didn't know were Lauren was and so couldn't tell.

* * *

Shadows passed in front of the headlights and then out of view. The firing of guns had ceased but, carried on the still night air, Lauren could hear as Harry cried out over and over again. She put her hands over her ears, pulled her hat down tight, but it couldn't shut out the noise. "Harry, Harry, Harry," she whispered over and over again, as though by saying his name she could somehow relieve him of the agony. What could she do? She had a gun, and for a moment she had a wild idea about storming into the house just firing randomly and hoping she hit something. Hoping she hit her father. Harry had taught her how to aim, had taught her well — surely there was something she could do — but she had figured out by now that there were at least half a dozen men. She had seen at least three of them out looking for her. Big men, armed men, men who might be merciful and shoot her in the head or, more likely, would shoot her in the belly and take her back for her father to finish off. But what really hit home, what really stopped her in her tracks, was the idea that Harry might still be alive when they did that. That Harry would die knowing she had failed him.

So she had to make that phone call. She was terrified of someone hearing but she dared not move further into the dunes because the lights from the vehicles might pick her up if she did.

Curling as tight as she could in her hiding place, Lauren found the number Harry had programmed into the phone and held her breath. Would anyone answer at this time of the night? What would she do if they didn't?

"Hello?" The voice sounded cautious and Lauren realized with a shock that it was a woman. "How did you get this number?"

"Harry gave it to me," Lauren whispered. "Said I should only use it in an emergency. In an *emergency* emergency. But they've got Harry and if Harry isn't dead already, he soon will be. They've come for me. You've got to help."

There was silence on the other end of the phone and for a moment Lauren thought the woman had hung up.

Then, "Where are you?"

The voice was guarded, thoughtful and noncommittal, but Lauren could have yelled with relief. The question seemed to open the possibility that this woman would help.

Lauren told her where Harry's cottage was, gave her the grid reference and satnav reference, which Harry had made her memorize, and told her about the Red Lion pub and that she was hiding out in the sand dunes. Again, the silence. Then the woman said, "It will take me a while to get to you, two or three hours, perhaps."

Lauren's heart sank. It seemed such a long time. They would find her. And then the worry came back that she was on the wrong side of the cottage. She had to somehow sneak around the back and head towards the Red Lion. But the woman told her to stay put. For a moment, Lauren was desperately confused about what to do next.

"I'm scared." It was all she could manage.

It sounded to Lauren as though the woman took a deep breath and made a decision.

"I'm coming for you. Now, listen. Stay hidden. I'll come along the beach, when you see me, you need to follow — don't approach, don't come anywhere near me. Follow me and I'll lead you back to where I parked my car and we'll work it out from there."

"How will I know it's you?"

"I don't imagine many people walk on that beach at this time of year. You'll recognize my voice. I'll have two dogs with me. Their names are Tod and Abe, you've got that?"

"Yes, but . . ."

"No buts. Stay put, stay hidden."

"What if I can't?"

"You're still alive," the woman told her. "That's how I know you can."

CHAPTER 21

Lauren dared not move. She had wriggled herself into a position where she could see the side of the cottage and one of the cars with its headlights on, but that was about it. She would like to have seen more, to try to monitor what was going on, but there was no way she could risk shifting position. The headlights illuminated two big patches around the cottage. They did not reach where she was lying, even though they had been put on full beam. Beyond the range of the headlights lay shadow made deeper by the lights themselves. She knew that it would be hard for anyone to spot her in the greater darkness, so long as she didn't move, so long as she didn't try and run. So long as she didn't lose her nerve. But that still left her with the problem of having to get past all of this and either back onto the beach or — the option that she had begun to see as more likely — through the marshy field onto the main road. From there, she knew that she could walk back to the Red Lion. If she could make it that far, then perhaps she could phone this woman again, let her know what was going on. It was a plan of sorts. But the idea of finding her way through the field that she knew to be full of holes and hollows and sucking mud filled her with dread. It was also open, with no cover anywhere.

She glimpsed shadows crossing in front of the car, the shape of two men heading back along the track. Obviously, somebody had thought of that option already. She stayed still and listened. There were shouts from inside the cottage and she recognized her father's voice. Harry had ceased to cry out. If he was making a sound now, it was too low for her to hear and she found herself hoping that it was over.

Another shout, this time from behind her. The two men seemed to have spotted something in the field. Lauren froze. What if they had seen her? She curled even smaller, closed her eyes, as though that would make them go away. She heard a shot fired, running feet and then fervent cursing and coarse laughter. "It's a frigging cow," someone said. "You shot someone's frigging cow."

She heard them coming back, grumbling and complaining about being covered in mud. Complaining about wet feet. Complaining about normal stuff. A door opened and closed as they went inside the cottage. The slight creak told her that it was the door into the kitchen and not the front door facing onto the beach.

She realized she was holding her breath and released it in a deep sigh. She was crying. Her cheeks were wet with tears, the rest of her with rain. Already she was chilled to the bone and this woman on the phone was still hours away. Lauren wondered how she was going to cope, how she was going to get through the wait, how she was going to get past the cottage. She wondered if those men had tried looking in the field for her, and realized what a lost cause it was, that this might now be the best route for a getaway. She raised her head a little, then ducked down as the door opened again. It crashed closed and someone came out. He stood in the shadow of the Land Rover and lit a cigarette. If she raised her head just slightly, she could see the ash glowing in the dark. He was, she guessed, about two hundred metres away. She was estimating this by recalling the distance of the running track at school. He was smoking in the rain, standing in the lea of the vehicle. The tarpaulin had been dragged off almost as soon as the men arrived, and she realized that she had got away just in time.

"Thank you, Harry," Lauren whispered and somehow that strengthened her. She was pretty sure now that Harry was dead. When she thought about him, there was a kind of absence where Harry should have been. A kind of negative space that she couldn't quite explain. She knew that Harry had always talked to Jean, that his dead wife still figured solidly in his thoughts. She wondered if Harry believed that he would be with Jean now. She wondered if he was. Then she suddenly realized how much her thoughts were wandering and she wasn't staying focused.

Just got to wait, she told herself. *She'll come, and I'll find a way of getting past the cottage. I'm going to have to do it soon, because once it gets to daylight, I've got no chance.*

She set herself to visualizing the lie of the land. She had a pretty good idea of where she was in the dunes, and knew that there was a breakwater that came up the beach approximately lining up with her current position. If she could get through the dunes, and get behind the breakwater, then she'd have some chance of getting down onto the strand line on the beach, climbing over and running along the damp sand. She should be far enough from the house then that she could avoid being seen. Deciding she had no other option, she waited for the smoking man to go back inside and then slowly began wriggling out of her hiding place, shuffling backwards through the sand and across the tussocky grass.

She had moved barely two body lengths when a new sound came. Vehicles on the main road — and not just any vehicles, but vehicles with sirens. *The police*, Lauren realized. *Who the hell had called the police? Had the gunfire been heard further along the coast, or was it the woman on the phone?* Offhand, Lauren couldn't think of a single reason why this should be the case. *Unless, unless . . .*

There were shouts from the house, men piling into cars and taking off back down the drive, the lights that had been pointed in her direction suddenly swung at right angles, sweeping across the dunes and then across the field. She flattened herself as much as she possibly could, wriggling flat to the earth, just in case she might get caught in the beams. In the distance, she heard screeching brakes and gunfire, some of it automatic, a staccato *rat-a-tat-a-tat* puncturing the night air.

Lauren knew she had to take this chance.

She rose from her hiding place, shook off the wet sand, and ran towards the front of the cottage. The police could be here any moment, but she had to know. She had to know. She pushed the door and went inside and then just stood, looking at the blood, looking at Harry. He was laying on the living-room floor, his body gouged and his throat laid open. Harry was dead.

She could hear the cars getting closer now, vehicles coming up the track. She had to get out of there. She turned and ran down to the beach, and along near the tideline, where the sand was firmer. Only when she'd put distance between herself and the house did she look back. Lights, bright blue lights this time, shone out over the sand. Men were shouting and someone was picking their way down to the shingle. She froze and again crouched down, making herself small. The man just waved his torch around and headed back to the house. Grateful, trembling, she ran at a crouch back to the dunes that had offered her safety before. This time, she was on the right side of the cottage. She was heading in the correct direction. She silently blessed whoever had called the cavalry, burrowed back into the sand and waited for the daylight and rescue to come.

CHAPTER 22

It didn't take long for a mobile incident room to be set up next to the field. Three police cars sat at the back of the house with a scientific support van and a mortuary ambulance.

Another, proper ambulance, as Lauren thought of it, had already come to the house, which told her something astonishing. Someone was alive in there. It sure as hell wasn't Harry, but someone was. Had Harry wounded one of her father's men? Had they left him behind? That seemed unlikely, but they'd left in such a rush it was possible.

As the sky had lightened, Lauren had hit upon a way of finding out what was going on. She had taken the chance on three occasions of raising her phone above the level of the dunes, setting the camera on the phone to full zoom, snapping a quick photograph and then examining whatever it was she had captured. She'd been aware, from shouted instructions, that the senior officer was keeping his people close to the house until someone had arrived with big lights. These were now set around the crime scene. Even then, he'd kept them within the lighted perimeter. It seemed his colleagues had been injured and perhaps killed and he wasn't about to risk anyone else. He was obviously anxious about a gunman hiding out in the dunes and for a brief while, Lauren had been worried too.

When the ambulance had come along the main road towards the cottage, it had been accompanied by two others. They, however, had halted back on the main road so she assumed there were at least two injured.

One of her snatched photographs showed armed police standing at the perimeter of the scene. For what felt like a crazy moment, she thought about simply getting up and walking over to them. What would they do? Would they shoot at her? Probably not, as long as she kept her hands raised. But she was terribly aware of Harry's warning, that he had no idea how far the spider's web of her father's business extended. Besides this, Lauren had learned never to trust the police. Her father, of course, cultivated this mistrust, but so had Harry. She realized now just how ingrained it was and wondered if it was actually something she should be letting go of. Were they really the enemy? The trouble was, Lauren decided, she didn't really have a clue *who* she could trust.

She didn't even know who this woman was who was supposed to be coming to rescue her. But Harry had trusted her and Lauren still trusted Harry, even though she felt that she had been right and he had been wrong. They should have kept moving.

Later that morning, police officers left the cottage with spiked poles and tape and set up a wider perimeter. She saw them looking for footprints and evidence and pointing out where men had trampled tussocks and left deep imprints in the sand. She moved further away from their activity, which meant she could no longer use her camera, but she did feel a little more relaxed about taking the occasional look. They were so focused on the area around the cottage that only occasionally did they look further out and she could sense their reluctance to go tramping around on a difficult beach or through sand dunes when there was no evidence that anything had taken place there. She supposed that later on others would arrive and the search perimeter would be widened but she hoped she would be long gone by then.

The clock on her phone told her that the three hours had long passed — it was now closer to five. She was tempted to ring this woman again. She held off. She had no idea what the situation was at the other end. Had the woman been delayed because she couldn't get away from somebody or something? Lauren had no wish to put anybody else risk. She would give her another hour, then she would make her way along the beach to the Red Lion, search for the numbers of a local taxi firm on her phone and get a lift to the nearest small town. She'd figure things out from there. Thanks to Harry, she had money and, if the worst came to the worst, she told herself, she was also armed.

Lauren's new deadline was almost up when she heard another sound on the beach. A whistle and then someone calling the names of two dogs. One looked like some kind of terrier and it was having a wonderful time dodging in and out of the waves. The other was larger and more sedate and occasionally cast a look of tolerant exasperation at its smaller companion.

The woman walked past where Lauren was holed up, on towards the cottage. Lauren wasn't sure what she'd been expecting. Perhaps someone older . . . and bigger. This woman was maybe in her thirties, she wore a thickly padded coat and a bright red hat, which concealed her hair. She looked small, Lauren thought, slender, and the spotted wellington boots were not the kind of footwear Lauren had ever associated with this kind of life-and-death rescue mission.

The woman paused as though suddenly noticing the police cars and wondering what was going on. She called the dogs to heel. *Yes*, Lauren thought. That was definitely the voice on the phone and the dogs were called Abe — the larger one — and Tod. Abe obeyed and sat down beside her. The smaller one joined them after a moment or two but it was evidently having too much fun to want to be still for long. Lauren found herself wanting to laugh. It was a strange feeling, a nice feeling. A desperately sad feeling.

The woman began to head back the way she had come. She was halted by a shout and one of the police officers came running down to her. Lauren held her breath. The strong wind off the sea carried snatches of conversation and she heard the police officer ask the woman if she often walked along here. She told him no, not often. But that the dogs liked it, whatever the weather.

She must've asked what was going on, gesturing towards the police cars and the cordon. Lauren could almost imagine the official response from the way the officer suddenly stood more upright and looked more formal.

Then he said something that made the woman laugh and she was on her way again, calling the dogs and strolling back along the beach.

Lauren watched carefully until the officer had returned to his post by the cottage, then began to follow the woman and the dogs, placing every step carefully. The woman never looked in her direction. The larger of the two dogs seemed conscious that she was there and would occasionally lift his head and sniff. Each time he did this, the woman directed his attention away. She had a tennis ball that she threw at regular intervals. The smaller dog would chase after it, but once he caught up with it, would leave it lying on the sand. The bigger one would amble along and pick it up and hand it back to the woman, then watch as she threw it again. Lauren had the sense this was a well-established routine.

It seemed to take a very long time to get back to the gap between the dunes, the car park, and what Harry had always referred to as "civilization." The women still did not look around. She opened the boot of an estate car, shut the dogs in, dropped her coat onto the back seat and got into the driver's seat. She leaned over to open the passenger door. Lauren hesitated for the briefest moment. *Here goes, Harry*, she thought. She ran to the car and got in.

"Fasten your seatbelt," she was told. "There's water and chocolate in the glove compartment and the heater will soon warm up. If you look behind you, there's a blanket and a flask of coffee in the footwell. Can you reach it?"

She was pulling away, not waiting for an answer. There was no one about, but she seemed eager to be gone anyway. Lauren tugged on the blanket and wrapped it gratefully around herself. She began to shiver as though her body had suddenly realized just how cold it was. She fished the chocolate out of the glove compartment and managed to pour some coffee, thankful that she had something warm to drink.

"Are you a friend of Harry's? Harry's dead, did you know that?"

"I supposed he must be, otherwise he'd be with you. I'm Petra, by the way." They had halted at the junction with the main road and she took the opportunity to turn and look at Lauren. The look was cool and appraising but not unkind. "You seem very young for someone to want to kill you," she said.

"I'm seventeen. I didn't realize there was an optimum age."

The woman laughed. She had a phone in a cradle on the dashboard and at that moment, it began to ring. She put a finger to her lips and signed to Lauren that she must be quiet. A man's voice. "I've been calling you, where have you got to?"

"Had one too many last night, slept over at Gail's house."

"Wondered if you might like to meet me for lunch."

"Sorry, no can do. Got a hair appointment booked."

"You could cancel it."

"No, I can't. Need to look my best for Saturday."

Lauren heard the man laugh. They exchanged a little more conversation and then the man rang off. But he had called her Pat, not Petra, Lauren noted.

"Your boyfriend?" Lauren said.

"For my sins." Her tone had changed and now it was Lauren's turn to scrutinize her.

"He might be a boyfriend, but you don't like him very much, do you?" she asked.

Petra glanced over at her. "What makes you think that?"

"I've grown up around a lot of women who don't like their husbands or their boyfriends," Lauren told her. "He called you Pat. So what is your name, is it Pat or Petra?"

"Depends who's saying it," she said. "Harry called me Petra."

Lauren considered. Petra it was, then. "So how did you know Harry?"

"Now that is a long and complicated story and I think we'll save that for later. First things first, are you hurt or just cold?"

"I'm not hurt. Harry woke me and I got out before they arrived."

"And you know who they were, the men who came? Were they your father's people, or were they from the Perrins?"

Lauren looked at her in astonishment.

"Let's just say I'm aware of what's going on and leave it at that. Or at least, I'm aware of part of it. You'll have to accept that I can't tell you any more."

Lauren looked at her more closely but nodded. "My father was with them. He's Kyle Sykes, but I take it you know that already."

"I know who you are, yes. So what have you done that put a price on your head? Has it got something to do with Charlie Perrin's death?"

Lauren took a deep breath. "He tried to rape me, so I shot him."

"I'd say 'Well done' but that's probably not the accepted reaction. But well done, anyway. No wonder your father's annoyed."

"Incandescent, more like."

Petra was shaking her head. "I don't think so. On the Kyle Sykes tantrum scale, we are currently still in mild annoyance mode. Believe me, I've seen the results when he's been fully, as you put it, incandescent. But then I suppose you have, too."

When my mother died, Lauren thought. She nodded. "It's ramping up though, you didn't see what he did to Harry."

Petra took that in. "OK, so I want you to tell me absolutely everything. Start with the night Charlie Perrin died and go from there. Every single detail, you got that? In about an hour, we'll be changing cars, and then we'll stop and have some breakfast."

"This is not your car?"

"Not my car, not my dogs, though I wish they were. Don't worry, the car and the dogs belong to a good friend and there is absolutely nothing to connect me, Harry, them or you."

Lauren wasn't sure about that. "Harry didn't think there was anything to connect him to the cottage, but my father found him anyway."

"Harry had been there before?"

"He found it by accident when Jean died. He went away, just drove, ended up there."

"Well, he must have told somebody about it. Or maybe just a few details that gave your father the clues he needed. He's got a hell of a network has Kyle Sykes."

"And how do you know so much about it? What are you?"

"*What*, not *who*. An interesting choice of words," Petra said. "No — your story first. Don't leave anything out, it doesn't matter how random. Just don't leave anything out."

* * *

Over the next hour, Lauren talked. She ate chocolate and drank coffee and she began to warm up and feel a little more human. Somehow, explaining everything to this stranger was helpful. It allowed Lauren to clarify her own thoughts. She found it hard to believe that only three full days had passed since she'd left Charlie Perrin's body lying dead on her bedroom floor. The man was a brute, he had deserved what had happened to him.

Petra asked the odd question, clarified the details, but otherwise let her talk. After they had travelled about an hour and a quarter, Petra pulled into a layby behind another car. "This is us," Petra said. Lauren got out, bringing the rest of the chocolate, the coffee and the blanket with her. A young man with dark hair took Petra's place in the driving seat. He didn't speak to either of them but from the cheerful yapping of the dogs, it was obvious that they knew him well.

They got into the second car, a smaller hatchback and Petra adjusted the driver's seat. "He's got such long legs," she complained. The estate car had already gone, turning back the way they had come.

"His dogs and his car?"

"No, borrowed dogs, borrowed car."

"Borrowed from yet another friend? How big is *your* network, Petra?"

"Not as big or extensive as your father's. Certainly not as big or extensive as the Perrins'"

"So what now?"

"In about another hour, we'll change cars again. Then I put you in a hotel for the night, and I go back to being Pat for a bit. You can order room service, you can watch as much TV as you like, and you can sleep. Just don't leave the hotel. And then we'll figure out what to do with you next."

"And who is Pat?" Lauren asked. She was beginning to formulate some ideas about this woman but wasn't certain yet. "You're someone who's pretending to be someone else and you know a great deal my father and the Perrins. I can only think of a few reasons why that should be."

"What did Harry tell you about me?"

"He said you were someone I was to call in case of an emergency. He didn't call you a friend. He just said you were someone who would help me, if the worst came to the worst. I asked him why we didn't call you straight away if he thought you could help, but he said there were strings attached to the kind of help you could give, so we should wait."

Petra nodded, accepting that.

"You'd have liked it more if Harry had called you a friend," Lauren suggested. "You liked Harry."

"I liked Harry," Petra confirmed. "Look, there's not a lot I can tell you. I'm really not supposed to get involved like this. I'm really not supposed to break cover — I figure you've worked that one out."

Lauren nodded. "So, you're an undercover cop? Believe me, I'm not about to dob you in. Who am I going to tell?"

"Your dad, if he catches up with you. You won't want to, but he won't give you any option. You'd be telling him anything just to stop the pain, you and I both know that."

"Better make sure he doesn't catch up with me then," Lauren said.

CHAPTER 23

In the hotel, Lauren took a long bath and finally got warm. They had stopped off on the way to the hotel and in a shopping centre bought her a small wheeled suitcase, an overnight bag and some clothes. She got dressed in new jeans, a T-shirt and a hoody, relishing the soft fleeciness of the inside. They had also picked up a loose-leaf pad and some envelopes and pens. When Lauren came out of the bathroom, Petra was sitting at the desk scribbling notes.

Someone knocked on the door and called out, "Room service." Lauren was immediately alarmed.

"It's OK," Petra told her. "I ordered us food. You need something a bit more nourishing than chocolate."

Even so, Lauren ducked out of sight, angry with herself that her coat was hanging over a chair close to the radiator, by the window and out of her reach. The gun, the cash, the phone, they were all still in the pockets. How could she have been so careless?

The door closed and Petra set an overladen tray down on the bed. "Eat," she said. "I'll join you in a minute."

The food immediately reminded Lauren of Harry's offerings. Harry had not been much of a cook, so eating with him had mostly been pizzas and burgers and chips. Petra had obviously resorted to that now, presumably going with the reasoning that all teenagers liked pizzas and burgers and chips. Right now, Lauren was just happy to have something to eat, but she noted that there were also little plastic cartons of fresh fruit and she quietly put both of those on her bedside cabinet. She didn't think that Petra would mind.

The woman came over and perched on the other bed, helping herself to a slice of pizza and some napkins. "I didn't know what you'd like, so I played it safe. But there's a room service menu over there, you can order anything. If you don't want to open the door, then just shout through the door that you're getting out of the shower and to leave it outside. I'll put the 'do not disturb' notice on the door when I leave and that will keep the cleaning staff at bay."

"What were you doing?" Lauren gestured to the notes Petra had been making. "You writing a report?"

"I've got to let somebody know what's going on. Don't worry, I'm not telling them where you are. But this is bigger than I can deal with and definitely bigger than you can deal with." She reached for a second slice of pizza and Lauren grabbed a burger. For a few minutes, they just munched in silence. Lauren finally acknowledged how exhausted she was feeling, the carbohydrate-heavy meal adding to the feeling of lethargy.

"I'm knackered," she said. "I think I could sleep for a week."

"Sleep is probably the best thing you can do." Petra leaned across and took Lauren's hand. "I promise I'll look after you."

Lauren pulled her hand away. "Don't make promises you can't keep. You can promise to try, if you like, but that's all you can do."

Petra nodded. "OK, we'll settle for that. I promise I'll do my best."

Lauren giggled. "You sound like a Girl Scout."

"I'll have you know I was a Brownie." Petra laughed too. "Admittedly, I don't think I was a very good one."

"So what do we do now? I have some money, and I don't do stupid things just because I'm scared, so you can tell me what you think my chances are. I don't want to put anybody else at risk, you understand that? I'm grateful for what you've done, but I'd rather just leave here and go off on my own rather than risk someone else."

Petra nodded, seeing the truth of that. "Look, like I said, this is bigger than you are, bigger than me and we need some outside help. Some protection."

"You mean the police. Harry said . . ."

"No offence, love, but Harry is dead. I understand his reasoning, I know that your dad's got fingers in every pie going, but the only organization big enough to go up against him is the police. They're not all corrupt, you know."

"I get that, but how do you know who to trust?"

"Do you trust me?"

If Petra had been hoping for an instant positive response, she was disappointed. She watched as Lauren gave this question her full attention, her deepest thought.

"I think you see me as a commodity," Lauren said. "I do think you want to protect me but — and don't take offence at this because I do understand, I do get it — you're also looking at this to see what advantage it brings you. Look, I know you're police. I figured out you're undercover. But I don't know exactly what you're trying to do, I don't want to know, because I don't want to be able to tell, you understand?"

Petra nodded. Lauren already knew too much for her to be comfortable with.

"So, rescuing me gives you some leverage, yeah?"

"It might," Petra agreed.

"Because you must realize that I know a fair bit about my dad's organization. I can name names. I can tell you stuff he doesn't know I'm aware of. So that's what you must be thinking. And of course, that's what he must be thinking too. He wants me shut up for good and so do the Perrins. And it's not just about Charlie. Though I get that it's a matter of pride. I shot Charlie when, well, more experienced people than me have taken pot-shots at him and missed. So a lot of people are going to be very offended by that."

Petra was looking at her with fresh eyes. Young she might be, but this kid was not stupid and she was also more in control than Petra expected. Petra had served in the military before joining the police and she'd seen well-trained men and women go to pieces under this kind of pressure. She was fully aware that the kid must be raging inside, fearful and desperate, but she was maintaining her control. "OK," Petra agreed. "Yes, I'm looking for an angle, *you* could be the answer to a lot of questions or you could be such a big complication it blows the whole operation apart."

"Either way," Lauren said. "Chances are you're already compromised, and you should get out now."

"What makes you say that? Look, you drew your conclusions because of the circumstances. Admittedly, you were quick, but—"

Lauren was shaking her head. "My dad's organization has been infiltrated twice before. That's right, isn't it?"

Petra nodded. On both occasions, the UCs had disappeared. No trace of either of her colleagues having been found.

"I'm guessing you've not tried anything with my dad's organization this time. I think I'd have recognized you. So it's got to be the Perrins. And you must have been part of the scene for a while, because Gus Perrin likes to keep his people close and he trains his lieutenants to do the same. I don't think you're a lesbian — Gus isn't exactly known for his openness and tolerance — so you've been getting involved with one of the men. That was who was on the phone to you. So he'll be wanting to see you later, because not seeing his girlfriend for more than twenty-four hours would be unnatural. So you're already compromised by having broken your habits."

"I'll be seeing him this evening," Petra agreed.

"So, you must have gone into really deep cover. Getting out of this mess isn't going to be easy. You don't really have cavalry to call."

"I have an emergency 'out', should I need it. But I don't want to use it because, yes, it would blow the whole thing wide open."

Petra watched Lauren consider that. "So what's the aim? Get rid of Gus Perrin, get rid of Kyle Sykes? And what then? You know as well as I do that nature abhors a vacuum and so does the world of organized crime. You cut the heads off the organization, the organization's still there — someone will just step into the void. You won't smash it, it's too big."

She has a point, Petra thought. Right now, the salient question that sprang to her mind was, *What to do with Lauren Sykes?*

* * *

When Petra had gone, Lauren finished eating, put the tray out in the hall as she'd been told to and made herself a cup of tea. Then she sat down on the end of the bed to think. She knew that Harry had made mistakes, and that Petra didn't think much of him as a strategist, but that was missing the point. Harry had done everything out of love and loyalty.

What would Harry do now, and how could Lauren improve on that?

She glanced at the clock. It was three thirty, more than twelve hours since Harry had roused her from sleep. No wonder she was tired. Despite the room being warm, she felt chilled, but it was not the kind of chill that central heating could easily cure.

She went over to the window and looked out. The room was on the thirteenth floor and as they had come up, Petra had made sure she knew where the exits were and where the fire escapes came out. This high up, she had a good view across the city. She'd noticed that there were tourist maps and information in one of the drawers and she pulled them out now, trying to figure out where the hotel was in relation to everything else. It turned out there was a railway station close by. If she needed to, she could get out of here. A five-minute walk to the station would get her on a train. She had plenty of cash.

And then what? Her father would not give up. Nor, she guessed, would Perrin, if Sykes failed to deal with her. She would have to keep moving, pick up casual work where she could, stay where she could. Although she had cash at the moment, that money would not last for ever.

Sheer exhaustion was winning and Lauren could no longer think straight. Oddly, she felt safer in the anonymity of this standardized chain hotel, in a city she'd never been to and which, she calculated, was at least a ninety-minute drive from where she had grown up, than she had in that tiny, remote, exposed little cottage by the sea. It was easier, she thought, to disappear in a crowd, because no one took any notice of anyone else. Your presence was diluted by the presence of all the other people going about their business and getting on with their day. With that thought in her head, Lauren pulled the duvet tight and fell into a deep and heavy sleep.

CHAPTER 24

A couple of hours after Lauren had been deposited in her room, Petra was in search of a hairdresser. Having used that as an excuse not to meet Billy for lunch, she knew she'd better not see him until she'd had her hair sorted out some way or other — the colour changed, or the cut, something dramatic.

Dealing with Lauren Sykes had not been on her agenda and she knew she had to report it. In the hotel room, she'd written a brief account of what she'd been doing and the mess she found herself drawn into. Then she found a post office, a first-class stamp and posted her report to her handler. Old-fashioned it might be, but it was still the simplest and safest way. She had refrained from telling them where she had stashed the girl. The fewer people who knew that the better. It wasn't particularly that she didn't trust her handler; more that she didn't know who he'd be reporting to or whether she could trust them.

She was surprised that the incident from which Lauren had fled and in which Harry Prentice had died had not made it onto the national news. She eventually found a local news report while flicking through her phone in a decent-looking hairdressers that accepted walk-ins. It went against the grain

— she had a favourite stylist who did her colour and she was very reluctant to let somebody else have a go.

The hairdresser ran practised fingers through her already pristine shoulder-length bob, clearly puzzled as to why she thought it required attention. Petra found herself making up a half-truth about going to a special event at the weekend, and wanting her cut sharpened up so that it looked absolutely pristine. Maybe even a complete change of style? And that she thought she could do with a few more lowlights. Later, she managed to discover a couple of news items that talked of a suspicious death and reports of a major police incident. It had been reported as an RTA. Obviously, someone was trying to keep this under wraps. She figured she was going to have to get her news through other routes.

Sitting in the hairdresser's chair, Petra turned her thoughts to Lauren. She couldn't believe how stupid Harry had been, taking the girl somewhere that might be connected to him. While it was probably true that he hadn't told anyone exactly where he'd gone after his wife had died, he would almost certainly have given bits and pieces of information away without realizing it. After all, he'd had no reason to suspect he should be keeping it secret at the time.

She wondered who was leading the team looking into Charlie Perrin's death. No way her colleagues would take it at face value and accept that it was accidental. But even had she personally known any officer in the local force, which she did not, she had no direct line to anyone. It had been decided she would have no contact with anyone apart from her handler and that was distant enough. She'd been in deep cover for too long, she thought — not for the first time. She'd been involved with Billy Hunter for three years and she was aware that she was riding her luck. This thing with Lauren Sykes just highlighted that.

The hairdresser came back to check the wraps on her hair and declared that she was done, sending her off to be washed and conditioned, ready for the cut and blow dry. Petra slipped her phone back in her bag. When she got out of here, she'd give Billy a call, arrange to meet for dinner or something. She needed to be visible and present, she knew if anybody asked Gail, she would tell them she had stayed with her, but she could not push it too far.

Suddenly Petra felt anxious, shaky. The feeling only lasted seconds but she had learned to take notice of these little warnings, of what her intuition and experience were telling her. Things were moving too fast, the worlds of the Sykes and the Perrins were about to collide, and not in the controlled fashion that Kyle Sykes had envisioned with the marriage of his child to theirs. Billy had told her that Perrin had been biding his time, that he was seeing this as an opportunity to take Sykes out of the picture, to move into his territory. *Old Gus won't settle for a merger. Only a takeover will do.* Billy had been amused at the thought.

He had also told her that Perrin had given Sykes fourteen days to track down his daughter and bring her to heel. And that, Petra knew, meant that Perrin wanted her wiped off the face of the earth. An eye for an eye, a death for a death.

She came out of the hairdresser's salon pleased with the results. She was not really a natural blonde, at least not the glossy "just walked out of a fashion magazine" kind of blonde that Billy Hunter admired, and it was always an effort to maintain. Now her colour had been refreshed and the cut shaped to more of a pixie than simple bob, she would look good for Saturday. She already had a dress and shoes lined up but she could do with a bag. Maybe she should take Billy shopping, get him to buy a nice little something for her. After all, it was a big night for his boss's daughter. Carole Josephs's private viewing at a fancy gallery. Billy would want her to look the part. He'd want his Pat on show and dressed up to the nines.

CHAPTER 25

The body of Harry Prentice had been identified, connections had been made and Clarke found himself heading north. Photographs of the crime scene had been emailed to him and he had recognized the injuries at once. He also recognized the name of the man who had been taken to hospital. Joe Messenger was not expected to survive, but he wasn't dead yet, and so the hospital was his first port of call.

At the main entrance, he was met by a uniformed constable who took him up to the ward, signed him in and introduced him to the deputy SIO, a pale, freckled redheaded young man by the name of Mark Reynolds.

"We'll go straight in and talk after, if that's all right with you. The victim is awake, not totally lucid, but you might be able to get something out of him."

Clarke nodded. "I know Joe. If he recognizes me, it's possible he might talk. On the other hand, he might recognize me and clam up."

Reynolds grinned at him. "Never can tell. This way." He led Clarke past the main ward and through a side room that looked as if it was used for storage. It presently contained a lot of high-tech-looking equipment and an armed police officer. A second armed officer stood inside a small room at the back, which had the look of a space cleared in a hurry and improvised as a secure area.

Joe lay on the bed surrounded by equipment that bleeped and flashed and to which he was connected by a rat's nest of wires and tubes. Clarke sat down beside the bed and touched the old man's hand. "Joe? Joe, can you open your eyes for me? Joe, it's DI Clarke, we've met a time or two. Can you hear me?"

Watery eyes opened and the head turned just a fraction. Joe blinked twice and tried to focus his eyes on Clarke's face. "I know you," the voice was little more than a whisper. Then, more hopefully, "Harry?"

"I'm sorry, Joe. Harry didn't make it."

"What about the girl? This lot won't tell me nothing."

"The girl?"

He glanced at Reynolds, who was about to speak. Clarke held up a hand to stop him. He wanted to keep Joe's attention — the old man did not have much focus or energy to spare. "Was Lauren Sykes with him, Joe? Was she with Harry?"

"Must have been. Her dad reckoned she was. That's why they went up there. That's why they dragged me with them. I gave Harry away. I never meant to. Never thought I'd told them anything what mattered."

He closed his eyes again and seemed to fall asleep. Clarke noted that the rhythm of the monitors had changed and he glanced over at the nurse observing.

"I think that's all you'll get," she said. "He's in a lot of pain and is heavily sedated. We ease off on the sedation every so often, just so we can monitor his obs properly, but we have to increase it again before the pain kicks in. You've caught him at the right moment but it can't last."

Clarke touched Joe's hand again and called his name. "Joe? Joe, can you stay with me just a little bit longer? Joe, did you see the girl? Did Harry say where she'd gone?"

Joe didn't open his eyes but a smile twitched his lips. "Ran off into the dunes, I should think. Harry didn't know.

Sykes sent men out after her, but then you lot arrived. Girl must've called the cavalry."

Joe's face grew slack and it was obvious that they wouldn't get anything more from him.

Reynolds led the way back out. "So this Lauren Sykes was definitely there. We're hoping you will fill in the rest of the story. We've got one man dead and two badly injured, plus the old guy in there. We're keeping a lid on it at the moment. The cottage is so remote that as far as the media is concerned, it was a suspicious death and a bit of a road traffic accident. But that story won't hold for ever. The last thing we want is the idea that gang warfare's come up from the Midlands. This is a low-crime area, or was until last night. Frankly, we don't have the resources for something like this."

Clarke nodded sympathetically. He glanced out the window and noted that it was getting dark already. "I'd like to take a look as soon as. Any point in going out there now?"

"Boss wants you to come to the briefing, tell the troops what the hell is going on. I'll take you out there first thing in the morning, that way you can see the scene in daylight. It's pitch-black out there at night and that's probably what saved the girl. If she got out of the cottage and hid in the dunes, she'd have been hard to find just because of the dark."

"And you found no sign of her?"

"A pair of socks, sweatshirt, and a few bits of sea glass on the windowsill. We're guessing she picked them up. Not likely something the old man would have done."

"Briefing it is, then," said Clarke. "Do you have the emergency call? I'd like to listen to it." He wondered if he'd recognize the voice.

"Sure, but I can't think it would be your girl who made the call. It came in from a burner phone, which is what you'd expect, but if Lauren Sykes was up here, then she couldn't have made it. The provider reckons it came in from your neck of the woods."

"Really?" That put a different slant on things. *Who had Lauren called?*

126

"And your girl is what, seventeen?"

Clarke nodded.

"I've listened to the call and I'd reckon it for an older woman. Muffled, like she was trying to disguise her voice."

"But the handler took it seriously, despite that?"

Reynolds nodded. "The handler was reluctant. You know we've got to check these things out if firearms might be involved, but—"

"But you didn't just check it out, you sent a full team." Clarke looked curiously at Reynolds. "So?"

"So the woman gave a code word and a contact. The code checked out, the contact said we should throw in everything we'd got. So we did. One man is now dead and another critical. What have your girl and that old man brought up to my patch, DI Clarke?"

"Right now, your guess is as good as mine," Clarke told him.

CHAPTER 26

News of Joseph Messenger's death came through to Clarke as he was driving back to the hotel after the briefing. He immediately diverted to the hospital. He arrived to find Joe's wife sitting at his bedside. The machinery around him no longer beeped and flashed and the tubes and wires had been extracted from Joe's body. Now there was only the old man, his arms tucked somewhat unnaturally under the bed clothes and the sheets pulled up to his chin.

Ruby Messenger had arrived only a few minutes before he died. When Clarke had left home for the journey up here, no one had been able to track her down, though Hopkins had still been trying. The neighbours had said they thought she'd gone to her sisters and this turned out to be the case, but the sister lived twenty-five miles away, and the address had not been immediately to hand. When Hopkins had finally tracked her down, she had gone to fetch her. The young DC stood behind Mrs Messenger, a hand resting gently on her shoulder and a look of shock on her face.

"I drove her up here," Hopkins told Clarke. "Sir, it seemed like the quickest way. It took me ages to find her."

"You did a good job," Clarke told her.

Ruby's hand reached up and took that of the young officer. They held on to each other as though they were both family. *Death can do that*, Clarke thought. "I'm sorry," he said.

"Did you see what they did to him?"

"I did, yes."

"And Harry?"

"The same." Clarke didn't feel the need to go into detail. He pulled up a chair on the opposite side of the bed, and then asked, "What happened? Can you tell me?"

For a moment, she seemed not to understand the question. Then she said, "Kyle Sykes came for him, he and some of his men. They had come from Charlie Perrin's wake. He'd come before, to see Joe, wanting to know where Harry was and the girl. Sykes's daughter. Joe sent me upstairs out of the way the first time, and the second time told me to go back into the living room, but I've got ears and I can draw my own conclusions. I knew he wouldn't be coming back this time. And I was scared, so I went to my sister's, but I didn't plan to stop there for long. I just knew Joe would not be coming back this time."

"So Kyle Sykes asked about Harry and his daughter."

Ruby shook her head. "He wanted to know where *Harry* was, he figured Joe might know because the two of them had been friends for such a long time. Joe didn't know, but he told Kyle Sykes about the time when Harry went away after his wife died. He was devastated when Jean went and he just took off. Joe wanted to know where he'd got to, but I don't think Harry really remembered. But he must have told Joe enough though. Sykes guessed the rest."

"What time did they turn up to take Joe away?"

"Gone eleven. It must have been. We'd normally have been in bed, but we stayed up watching some daft film. Besides, Joe couldn't seem to settle. He'd not been sleeping. He said it was Harry's fault, Harry running off like that, and he guessed that he'd taken Lauren with him — otherwise, why would Sykes be bothered?"

"So Kyle Sykes came and asked where Harry and Lauren might have got to?" Clarke confirmed.

"No, that wasn't it. He didn't mention Lauren. That's what Joe said after: that Lauren had gone missing and that she must have gone to Harry for help."

"Did Joe know why Lauren had gone missing? Did he know why she needed Harry's help?"

Ruby pursed her lips as though she'd already said too much and was regretting it. "You know he'll be able to prove he was nowhere near where Joe died, don't you?"

"Sykes? I suppose he'll do his best to prove that. But you can testify that he came for Joe, took Joe away with some of his men, that—"

She was shaking her head. "I'd stand up in court and say that, but what would it prove? It would prove that Sykes came with some of his men, and Joe went off with them. And there would be a dozen witnesses to say that Joe simply went back to his place for a drink, or to discuss business, or any other thing that Sykes might decide he would make up. He'd have double and triple alibis. Alibis enough to drown in."

"There might be forensics."

She laughed. "Have you ever known him to be that careless? If he had been, he'd be banged up by now, and you know it. There's enough of you working on that, isn't there? A fat lot of good it's done any of you."

"This time, they had to leave in a hurry," Clarke told her. "This time, they didn't have the opportunity to clean up the scene. That's probably why Joe was still alive when the ambulance got there."

Ruby was considering again, her lips pursed tight and her eyes narrowed as she looked at Clarke. There was something hopeful in that look.

"He only needs to get careless once, Ruby."

The hopeful look faded. "And how many years have you been waiting for him to get careless just that once?"

"This time *is* different."

"This time will be different," she told him. "Lauren defied him, and she went and killed Charlie Perrin, so, yes, this time will be different. I don't think he's been this bad, not this blazing, since Lauren's mum died, and we all know how well your lot did in stopping Kyle Sykes that time."

Clarke let the criticism slide. "What makes you think Lauren killed Charlie Perrin?"

Ruby's laugh was bitter and derisive. "If you can't put that together, what the hell hope do you have of tripping up Kyle Sykes?"

Clarke organized a hotel for Hopkins and for Ruby Messenger. He booked it with his own credit card and told Hopkins to make sure the pair of them had something to eat and checked that the young DC had cash for petrol for the way home. Hopkins looked exhausted, Clarke noticed, but she'd gone up considerably in his estimation. As they prepared to leave the hospital, he drew her aside. "Don't be surprised if she is not there in the morning," he said.

Hopkins looked shocked. "What do you mean?"

"Her husband is dead, his ex-boss is on the rampage looking for revenge, and he won't care what innocents get caught up in that. Ruby knows the score, she got here in time to say goodbye to her man, and that's thanks to you. But she won't hang around. And if she is gone in the morning, it won't be your fault."

"But should I . . . I mean she's a witness. We should statement her at least."

"We should, so get that done, just so we've ticked the boxes. As Ruby said, all the statement will prove is that Kyle Sykes and some of his colleagues collected Joe on the night of Charlie Perrin's wake. *If* this gets to court, *if* we managed to put it together enough that Kyle Sykes comes up before a judge charged with Joe's and Harry's deaths, then we'll track her down and bring her back to give evidence. She's got family up in Edinburgh — Ruby was a Maguire before she married Joe and now he's dead, that's where she'll go."

"Won't Sykes know that?"

"He will, but he won't risk going up against the Maguires, he's not quite that stupid. Sykes won't piss off the Maguires just to get to someone's widow. Even Kyle Sykes doesn't want that kind of turf war." *And we certainly don't*, Clarke thought.

"Could Lauren have gone up there? She must have known Joe Messenger and his wife, maybe she reached out?"

Clarke shook his head. "The Maguires would hand her back in a heartbeat. Ruby's one of their own and therefore still has the right to claim protection. Lauren Sykes is nothing to them. They'd not risk upsetting the status quo over a teenage girl."

He made his way to his own hotel, noting that it was after ten and therefore the restaurant would be closed, so he ordered room service. He put the television on and laid out his case notes, folders, photographs and laptop, then sat down on the bed in the middle of it all. When his food arrived, he dumped that on the bed too and ate a sausage baguette while re-examining the crime scene photographs.

Harry must have known the risk he was taking, Clarke thought, in trying to protect the girl. This all left one big question — where the hell was Lauren Sykes now?

CHAPTER 27

Lauren woke in the almost dark. She'd fallen into a deep sleep and the only light in the room was a polluted yellow glow from the city seeping in through the window. When she had fallen asleep it had been daylight and the curtains were still open. It took her a moment to remember where she was, and then another to work out what had woken her. It was someone passing her room to get to theirs, drunk and laughing and falling against the walls and doors. She got off the bed and checked that her door was securely locked, then switched on the lights and drew the curtains. She suddenly realized that tears were pouring down her cheeks and her body was soon wracked with sobs, relief, grief, and a whole shipload of other emotions that she had not allowed herself to feel until now. She didn't want to feel them now, but it was as though her brain and body had finally given in and the tears would not stop. She lay down on the bed again and wrapped herself in the quilt and wept until she was absolutely exhausted. "Harry, I'm so sorry, I'm so sorry."

But it was no good being sorry, was it? What was done was done, and there was no way she could change that. All the sorry in the world would not help.

She took a deep breath and went into the bathroom and washed her face. Looking in the mirror, she could see that her cheeks were blotchy, her eyes red and sore. When she'd been younger, she'd always envied women who could cry pretty tears. She splashed her face again and dried it. What was it Harry had said? "*You've got to keep up with your normal.*" Right, so what was normal? She left the bathroom, switched on the television, and made herself a cup of tea. On the way to the hotel, Petra had bought supplies — teabags and coffee, a small carton of milk and a lot of biscuits.

"Just in case you're there for a day or two," she'd told Lauren. "That way, it doesn't matter if you don't get your tea and coffee topped up in your room."

Lauren was grateful for this. She had no idea how long Petra planned to leave her up here, or how long she could bear to be holed up in this hotel, but she was glad of the foresight anyway.

Having closed the curtains and shut out the night, she flicked through the channels on the television. By weird coincidence, there was a repeat of the same *Die Hard* film she'd watched with Harry only a few days before. She clicked away from it, then went back.

"OK, Harry. Here's me working on my normal. I hope you're proud of me."

CHAPTER 28

"And don't you look good?" Billy said, running his fingers through her newly cut hair. He had drawn her close, put one of his big hands on her bum and the other on her waist and kissed her possessively.

"What have you been up to?" she asked him. "Did you miss me?"

"Nah, of course I didn't."

She laughed. This had become their routine whenever they'd been apart. "And so," she said, her tone wheedling, "how do you fancy going shopping with me? I need a bag for Saturday night. I thought we might take in a film and have something to eat, and then, well, who knows?" She smiled up at him. She was tall, but he was taller and very broad. He made her feel tiny and fragile, which was not something she was used to feeling. Sometimes she liked it. Often she did not.

Billy's eyes gleamed, predatory and eager. "Why don't we just cut to the 'who knows'?" he asked.

She giggled. "Because I'm hungry, because I need a bag for Saturday night."

"Don't you have enough bags?"

"You can never—"

"Have enough bags or enough shoes, I know." He lifted the hand from her waist and touched her hair again. "I like it," he said. "It's different."

"That's because I went to a different hairdresser, I felt like a change. So let's be going, the Colbert Centre stays open till eight, so we've got about an hour. That should be enough time. Then we'll get a takeaway if you like, be home all the sooner."

He roared with laughter at that. "Sounds like a plan."

Later, much later, she woke up to find that he was not in bed beside her and that there were voices downstairs. One of them she recognized, but the other she did not.

Slipping on her dressing gown, Petra padded to the top of the stairs. The visitors and Billy were in the kitchen, talking, not loudly but with an intensity that prickled at the back of her neck. She was considering whether she should go down and join them. If this was a *business* meeting, Billy would not be pleased if she did. When the kitchen door opened and the men came out, she took the risk of leaning over the banister, just enough that she could see Billy and the other two. She caught her breath. *What the fuck is he doing here?*

She retreated back to the bedroom.

Later, she stirred as Billy got back into bed beside her. "You OK?" She murmured sleepily. He responded by pulling her close to his side.

Petra calmed her breathing and relaxed, as though drifting back into sleep. There was a tension in Billy's body that took a long time to go. Whatever the meeting had been about, she figured it had not been positive. He was clearly upset, annoyed, even angry at something. When he finally went back to sleep, she opened her eyes and stared into the semi-darkness. She could have been mistaken, of course, but she didn't think so. Although she had never been a serving officer in this region, she had taken the trouble to familiarize herself with everybody who held any kind of rank and she had definitely recognized the men. The first was an associate of Billy's, Freddie Benson, who managed a casino for Gus Perrin. The other man, unless she was very much mistaken, was a police DCI.

CHAPTER 29

At first light, Clarke collected Hopkins and they followed DI Mark Reynolds out to the cottage that had become their crime scene.

Clarke was not surprised when Hopkins told him that Ruby Messenger had indeed left during the night. She'd apparently gone down to the front desk and asked about train times, the night receptionist helping to go through the listings. She checked out just after five and went off to the station. Clarke was somewhat amused to find that she had looked at trains to Edinburgh, to Truro, and to Cardiff, so she was trying very hard to put him off the scent. He would put money on her going north.

"It's a bit bleak out here," Hopkins commented, as they got out of the car. The wind was whipping off the ocean and sandblasting any patch of bare skin. A wide cordon stretched around the cottage and into the dunes and there were police officers and CSI still wandering around looking purposeful. Clarke was surprised there was no media presence, but then the local police were playing it down. The brief reports he had seen had suggested a suicide, tragic but explicable, rather than a major incident. He wondered how long they could keep the story going, then looked around at the emptiness surrounding this small outpost of human habitation and decided that it probably wouldn't be too difficult to do, at least for a little while longer.

Mark Reynolds was waiting for them by the side door and he pointed out the forensic pathway to Clarke and Hopkins. The crime scene manager took over from there and took the tour.

"My God, so much blood," Hopkins murmured. He knew she'd seen death before but nothing like this. Clarke sort of envied her that.

He was comparing locations within the house to the crime scene photographs he had seen. Harry Prentice, slumped in the corner of the living room. Joe Messenger in the hallway between the living room and kitchen. The first officer attending had assumed he was dead until he had seen a tiny twitch of Joe's fingers. The FOA had then quickly designated a pathway and made sure the paramedics came in via that route. He had picked the cleanest bit of kitchen floor in the hope that this would be less forensically important. In the hall, Clarke could see where the paramedics had knelt in Joe's blood.

"They never went into the living room," Mark Reynolds told him. "It was pretty obvious that Prentice was dead. What is astonishing is that Messenger survived long enough to get to hospital and into intensive care."

"Whose idea was it to put him in that little back room?" Clarke wanted to know. Although nobody could fault the care Joe had received, he had not actually been in the main ICU.

"Actually, that was one of the doctors. That side room has been used as an isolation unit before. The doctor knew it could be set up quickly and with the right equipment. We were worried in case somebody got wind of the fact that he wasn't dead yet and came to have another go. The nurse you saw, she was one of the senior ICU nurses. They gave him every chance they could."

Clarke nodded. "I think Joe Messenger was collateral damage. But, no, I don't expect they thought he'd survived the attack here. Kyle Sykes will not be pleased about that, not that he had much chance to speak to me. You saw the statement that Ruby Messenger made?"

Reynolds nodded. "So that gives you confirmation of Sykes's involvement. But is it enough? It proves he was there, that he went to collect Joe Messenger from his home, but does it prove he was here?"

"That is the million-dollar question. We've got the word of a dying man that Sykes was at the cottage. What will that count for?"

They left, knowing that they were in the way and that CSI needed to get on with processing the scene, but Clarke was glad to have observed it first-hand. Photographs only got you so far. He followed the forensic markers out to the perimeter and into the dunes. Lauren might have had hidden out here, then. But then what? Hopkins joined him. She'd got a map from somewhere.

"That way, going left out the cottage, you come to a big fuck-off cliff."

Clarke looked at her. Small but tough and wiry, she was formidable in her own way, but she didn't usually swear. It seemed out of character. "And in the other direction?"

"Down that way is a pub and a caravan park, and a few other bits and pieces by the looks of it. And a track that leads back to the main road. They reckon that's the way the girl would have gone."

"Makes sense. It looks like a long walk, though. And then what?" With Harry gone, who on earth would Lauren Sykes have turned to?

Reynolds was waiting for them by the cars. They headed back to police headquarters. There would be a briefing when they returned. Last night's had been to bring Clarke up to speed on what had happened at this end. This morning, he would be taking centre stage, explaining the Perrins and the Sykes and how they figured this whole mess began.

"Come to the briefing," he told Hopkins. "And then I want you to head back home, the team will need all the data from this end. I'll clear it with Henderson that you act as liaison on this. That might mean coming back up here at some point, but more likely ensuring that information from the two teams is collated."

Hopkins nodded. It was only a few days ago, Clarke reflected, that she'd been sitting in Kyle Sykes's conservatory looking distinctly uncomfortable. In that time, she seemed to have grown, settled. To have found her feet and her confidence.

"If you were a seventeen-year-old girl, where would you have run to?"

"Probably to my nan's, but that doesn't help much, does it?"

Well, Clarke thought, *that is more or less what Lauren Sykes had done.* Harry and Jean were known, even to the police, to be the closest thing to proper family Lauren had ever had. And everybody knew that Jean had been a lovely woman.

* * *

Lauren was having breakfast when her phone rang. She stared at it for a moment. It was Petra.

"I've got to be quick — you OK?"

"I guess so. When can I leave here?"

"Not yet, we need to find a safe place. Look, if I can't make it back this weekend, I'm going to book you in somewhere else. You'll need to take a taxi and I'll tell you where to go. So be ready, OK?"

"How are you paying for this?" Lauren asked. It was something that had bothered her since yesterday when she'd seen Petra pay for the room with a credit card.

"Same card as yesterday, and don't worry it's a legitimate card, registered to a legitimate address, just not my legitimate address."

"Something else borrowed from a friend, like the dogs and the cars?"

"Exactly that. Look, I've got to go. I don't know when I'll be able to call again, so keep your head down, and rest up."

Lauren heard another sound, as though someone was moving in the background. Petra hung up. Lauren stared at the phone, willing it to ring again, even though she knew it wouldn't. She felt in limbo, helpless and was overwhelmed by a sudden surge of anger. Why should she do anything this woman told her to? And how long could she bear to be incarcerated in this small and confining hotel room?

It was Saturday. Most likely, the town would be packed. Perhaps she could go for a walk and get lost in the crowds . . .

Lauren bit her lip, knowing that this was probably unwise, but then the bit of her brain that still asked *What would Harry do?* suggested that this would also be reconnaissance. When they had arrived, Petra had made sure she knew where the fire escapes and the exits were. So, Lauren figured she could go down the back stairs, and at least have a wander round the shopping centre that they'd been in the day before to familiarize herself with the area.

Was that only yesterday? she wondered. It felt like so much longer.

* * *

When Billy came in, Petra was fiddling with her bag. "Have you seen my lipstick?"

He pointed out two that were already sitting on the dressing table.

"Not those, the one I wore last night." She looked slyly at him through the mirror. "The one you said you liked. Ah — there it is."

He came over to her and stood behind her so she could see both of them reflected in the glass. She smiled at him and then leaned forward to apply the lipstick. He put his hands on her hips and pulled her back towards himself. But she could see his mind was occupied on something else.

"You OK? You seem a bit out of it this morning. One drink too many last night, was it?" She leaned back against him for a moment and then freed herself and went over to the camera bag lying on the bed. He watched as she checked the lenses, unpacking and then packing everything again. He'd

141

seen her do this dozens of times. It was her little ritual, taking things out, checking and putting them back, ticking them off her mental list.

"All set for this evening?"

"Yep, looks that way. The gallery is doing the live-stream video, so I don't have to worry about that. I'm just doing stills, and any infill stuff that Carole wants me to do. She'll tell me when I get there. It should be a good evening."

He grimaced. "If you like that sort of thing."

She sashayed over to him once more and put her hands on his shoulders. "Art with a capital 'A' not your bag?" she teased.

"Art with any 'a' is not my bag." He glanced over to her camera equipment once more.

She knew that he was impressed by her talent, and that talent had really opened doors for her. She knew he was also impressed by her intelligence, and the fact that she looked after her body, and that she looked good with her hair done and lipstick on. She looked the part. She knew also that she wasn't Billy's normal type. He normally went for purely decorative — he wasn't usually that bothered about his women being *intelligent* and decorative. Petra knew that Gus Perrin had been highly amused by Billy's sudden interest in 'Pat'. When things had got more serious between them, she knew that Gus had had her checked out. But that was OK, her legend had been well prepared. And it was close enough to the reality that she didn't have any trouble remembering. In fact, it sometimes worried her that what she did have trouble remembering was who Petra really had been. Three years as Pat had been a long time.

Was it all right that she really was looking forward to Saturday night and the private view of Carole Josephs's new sculptures? Looking forward to getting all poshed up in a new dress, new shoes and new bag and showing off her skills as a photographer? Her photos were destined for at least two top-flight magazines, the editors of which were buying her work on merit and not because Gus Perrin was involved. She seemed to have accidentally carved out a whole new career for herself and she was loath to have that ruined.

CHAPTER 30

Frankland reread the letter he had just opened and then ran a search on his computer. The database yielded reports from two police forces, one in the Midlands and one somewhere up north, and he skimmed the information, the action plans, the crime scene photographs and identified the SIO on each team. He had been aware of the Harry Prentice situation, and of the suspicions that Lauren Sykes might have something to do with the death of Charlie Perrin, but this was a major development.

At the end of her letter, Petra had said something that concerned him deeply. "*I have the feeling things are moving very fast, and I may have to ask for an emergency evac, at least for the girl but possibly for me as well.*"

Petra was one of the best undercover operatives he'd ever handled and it was not like her to get jittery. If she felt the tide was turning, then he really ought to take notice.

* * *

Feeling a long way from home, Clarke followed Hopkins and Mark Reynolds into the briefing room. Last night it had seemed larger, but that was probably down to the fact that there were twice as many people in here now. People with questions. Reynolds introduced him and Clarke took the floor. There was an empty board behind him, and a stack of paperwork and photographs on the desk at the side. Clarke scooped them up and began.

"Victim number one: Harry Prentice; and victim number two: Joe Messenger. They've been part of Kyle Sykes's organization for at least thirty years. Our understanding is that this current trouble begins with Lauren Sykes and the death of Charlie Perrin. You have to understand that at the moment his death is down as 'accidental', a consequence of playing with a firearm when drunk. But there are forensic indicators that this *might* not be the case. The rumour mill is definitely suggesting that Lauren Sykes is implicated.

"It seems she went to Harry Prentice for help. Lauren's mother and Jean Prentice, Harry's late wife, were known to be close and the Prentices continued to be close with Lauren after her mother died. Kyle Sykes is also implicated in the death of Lauren's mother, though we were never able to prove that he killed her or even that he arranged for her to be killed. The fall guy for that is still in a secure psychiatric unit, as you'll see from the briefing notes we prepared for you."

"What was Harry Prentice doing here? Your understanding is that the girl was definitely with him?"

Clarke laid out what he knew about how Harry had come to know this place and the evidence that showed Lauren had been with him.

Other questions followed about the Sykes organization and about Gus Perrin.

"Imagine an iceberg," Clarke said. "What's above the water, for both organizations, is a portfolio of legitimate businesses built over three generations." There was general laughter at that, but Clarke knew it was an apt analogy. "A business portfolio that includes everything from corner shops to casinos. If you look at appendix C, you will find a list of legitimate concerns that are either owned or partially owned by the Sykes or Perrin clans. You'll notice that several of them are limited companies, and therefore their books are open to public access via Companies House. You'll notice also that they both use the same firm of respected accountants. Benson Bryce have been in business as long as the Perrin and Sykes OCGs, the only difference is that we have no reason to believe Benson Bryce are engaged in illegal activity. And believe me, forensic accountants have looked at them every which way. They speculate that it behoves both OCGs to have a squeaky-clean surface image and that employing Benson Bryce helps give legitimacy to their respective organizations."

"You're talking about three generations, that sounds extremely unusual," Mark Reynolds speculated.

"Not so unusual for crime families, but what is unusual is that the grandfathers in both cases decided that they needed to run a legitimate business alongside their illegal dealings. It makes perfect sense. Money can be laundered through the legitimate business and those chosen by the present family members all have a high and quick turnover, such as casinos, gymnasiums, golf clubs. It's the spread that makes it so effective. There is no single route for dirty money to be cleaned. A large number of their investments go into the charity and social sectors and undoubtedly a lot of good comes out of that investment, which means that fewer questions are asked by members of the public, local governments, regulators and so on."

"And the murder weapon?" someone asked. "I've never seen injuries like that before, I don't think any of us have."

Clarke opened his briefcase and took out a linen bag. From that, he took a docker's hook. It had been welded to a T-bar handle. The tip, currently plunged into a block of polystyrene, had been sharpened, as had the inner curve of the hook.

He heard a ripple of laughter as someone asked if he'd got Peter Pan in there as well, but once he'd started passing the weapon round, the laughter faded and a mood of distaste and outright horror permeated instead.

He pointed to the pictures of Harry Prentice on the board, the photographs of his injuries. "It's a variation on a standard docker's hook," he said. "It's a legitimate tool of the trade. The old-time stevedores used them for unloading bales of whatever, used the hook to grab the bale or the rope binding it and then pulled it down so it could be unloaded. It took a lot of skill. Trouble was, they also used them when they got into fights and it was not uncommon in the East End of London for someone to be found with part of his arm ripped off — or his face — or even the hook driven into a skull. But Kyle Sykes, and we suspect it is him, he's taken this to a whole new level. Of course, Mr Sykes has been alibied in every single instance, by at least a dozen worthy witnesses, and of course he'd always wear gloves."

"You'd have to be committed to use something like this," a young constable commented. "It's even more up close and personal than a knife. A knife goes in and comes out relatively clean, but with this you've got to jab it in and then pull. The only way it's going to come out is if it slices through whatever you've hooked it into." He mimed the action he was describing.

"It's a nasty thing," Clarke said. "Once you see those injuries, you never forget them."

"Was this evidence in a crime?" Reynolds asked. The weapon had now come back to him and he was holding it somewhat gingerly.

"The first time we came across this was six years ago. Lauren was eleven. She found her mother dead and this is an exact copy of the weapon that had been used to kill her. The man who was arrested and subsequently locked up, he was holding it. His fingerprints were all over it, and we can't prove that he wasn't the culprit. We can't *prove* it."

"You think Sykes used it on his own wife?" This from the constable who had been so curious before. He looked a little green around the gills now.

"That's where the smart money is," Clarke told him. "If Lauren Sykes did have something to do with the death of Charlie Perrin — well, that would have upset her father's plans very badly, and I've no doubt that if her father had caught up with her at that cottage, she'd have been subject to the same treatment as Harry Prentice and Joe Messenger. I have absolutely no doubt that he is still looking for her and that he won't stop until he finds her. Lauren Sykes is seventeen years old, and we have absolutely no idea where she might have gone."

CHAPTER 31

Kyle Sykes was not a happy man. He had one man dead and two wounded. The dead man now had a certificate saying that he had succumbed to heart failure, which, Kyle Sykes thought morosely, was what killed most people in the end anyway. The two wounded men had been patched up and they and their families sent away for the foreseeable future. Sykes had places dotted around the country where they could hole up and recover with local agents to keep an eye on them to make sure they weren't speaking to anybody improper.

Sykes could not believe how badly this had all gone. He blamed Harry of course, and obliquely he blamed Joe — how had that little fucker survived? The news that Joe had in fact died in hospital infuriated him. What infuriated him more was not knowing if Joe Messenger had recovered consciousness or not and the only person he could conceivably ask, the wife, had gone north out of the way. Her sister had followed her. No doubt he could bring pressure to bear if it became necessary, find out what the old woman knew, but even in his current rage, he knew he could do without trouble on two fronts.

Gus Perrin had invited him to a meeting that evening. Sykes had been inclined to tell him to spin on it. He still might.

No, the only person he could blame now was Lauren, and Lauren had gone to ground. It riled Sykes more than anything else that this kid had scuppered his plans twice. Once by killing Charlie Perrin and the second time by simply not being where she should have been when he'd come for her.

So where the fuck was she and who was helping her? There was nobody in his own organization unaccounted for, nobody who could have nipped up there and got the kid away. And it seemed beyond belief that anyone working for Gus Perrin's organization would aid someone who had killed their boss's son.

So had *she* called the police? Did they now have her in custody somewhere? Sykes had put out feelers but so far, no one was saying anything. Even under more focused pressure, his informants either genuinely didn't know, or were a damn sight braver than Sykes had previously given them credit for. Or just more stupid.

* * *

Lauren was at that particular moment standing at the entrance to the railway station and getting her bearings. The station was being renovated, and great swathes of it were blocked off by scaffolding and by advertising boards, from behind which came the sound of hammering and sawing and voices. There were peepholes at intervals through which members of the public could see the progress and when she got past these and into the station proper, she discovered that there were three routes down to different platforms and two temporary ticket offices set up at the top of the stairs.

Someone asked if she needed help. She glanced round to see a guy in uniform. He was smiling and friendly and held a tablet in his hand, stylus poised for any enquiries she might make.

Lauren smiled back and told him she was fine, she was just checking what platform she needed. He looked as though he'd like to ask more, to be more helpful, but she distracted him by pointing out a lady who genuinely looked lost and who had come up to ask him a question. She now stood at his elbow looking anxious and as he turned towards her, Lauren beat a swift retreat.

"Idiot," she muttered to herself. She really needed to be more careful not to draw attention.

Satisfied that she could at least find her way around the station, she left and crossed the triangular pedestrian area, heading back towards the hotel. Three major roads converged at this point, all heavy with traffic and with knots of shoppers getting ready to cross. She had noticed on the night they'd arrived that the Christmas lights had already been switched on. In daylight they were off, of course, but they still looked festive. She would usually spend Christmas with Harry and Jean and of course more lately, just with Harry. Her father gave her presents on Christmas Eve and then, duty done, kissed her goodbye until the festivities were over. It was a relief on both parts. Her dad had no idea how to do Christmas. Lauren knew he'd spend most of it drunk with various women in various nightclubs or in various casinos. It always amazed her that however much he drank, he still had this incredibly acute awareness of what was going on around him. It was something that was quite scary about him. That even when he lost control, he seemed to be kind of in control about losing it.

She crossed the road alongside groups of families, chattering teens and excited kids who were going to see Father Christmas. *A bit early for that*, Lauren thought. When her mum had been alive and Lauren had been a little thing, they'd gone to see Santa Claus in one of the big department stores in town. That had been a tradition every year, but they'd always left it until the last week. Her mother said it made it special that way, like the way their visit to the pantomime was put off until close to New Year. Her mother always argued that there was too much going on in the days over Christmas, and it was better to have something to look forward to afterwards as well. Lauren didn't remember her dad becoming involved in any of this. His biggest contribution was giving her mother some spending money and giving Lauren extra pocket money as well.

Gifts for her father were always very safe — scarf, tie, cigars, a bottle of booze. In her early years, she'd bought these while she'd been out with her mother, but later, Harry or Jean had done it for her. She realized that she didn't know her father well enough to buy anything but safe stuff. Besides, he didn't seem to like very much. He didn't like music, he didn't read, he didn't even watch the telly much and wasn't into films. The only jewellery he ever wore were a watch and a ring and they were expensive.

She passed the hotel. It too was half covered in scaffolding. She turned down the next little road that she knew led to the back of the shopping centre, the way she had gone with Petra. For a while, she wandered around clothes shops, then looked at shoes, stationery and toiletries and shelves packed with "ideal" Christmas gifts. Who were they ideal for? she wondered. She spent some of her dad's money on a notebook and pen, a couple of paperbacks and a bright blue woollen scarf that she just took a fancy to. She also bought a shoulder bag and a small purse, the inconvenience of having to dip into her coat pocket and peel money off the stack making her aware of how odd that seemed. Girls always carried bags, that was a given.

She was aware that sometimes people were looking at her curiously, that she wasn't really blending into the shopping crowd, a teenage girl on her own and clearly a little ill at ease. She suddenly realized that she'd never really wandered round a shopping centre alone before. Her mother had taken her shopping, Jean had taken her shopping, but there had always been somebody keeping a discreet distance behind. She was driven to school. She was picked up after. If she went to anybody's house, she was driven there and was always conscious that there would be somebody sitting in a car down the road, just in case she should break the arrangement and try to go somewhere else.

Not surprisingly, this freaked people out, so the invitations to go to somebody else's house were few and far between. Not that she was particularly close to any of the girls at school anyway. Mostly she shopped online and had it delivered, it was just so much simpler that way.

Bored now, she headed back to the hotel, slipping through the lobby and into the lift. At least no one here seemed to take any notice of her. She fumbled in her bag as an excuse to keep her head down, turning her face away from the many CCTV cameras.

Back at her room, Lauren got a shock. Housekeeping had been in and made her bed and tidied up. She realized with rising horror that she had forgotten to put the "do not disturb" sign on the door when she left. Though thinking about it, she couldn't even remember having taken it off the door in the first place. Looking around her room, she could not find it inside either. She opened the door to her room and peered down the corridor. The door opposite had a "do not disturb" sign hanging on it. Lauren looked more closely. She was sure it was hers. There was a wine stain on it that looked familiar. Perhaps it had been knocked off and put back on the wrong door? She recalled the drunken guest bouncing off the walls the night before. Could they have done it?

Lauren tiptoed across the corridor, unhooked the sign and reattached it to her own door. She locked the door from the inside and leaned heavily against it, breathing hard. Her heart was beating very fast.

She took a deep breath and tried to control herself. There was nothing suspicious about this, nothing at all. It was just one of those random things. But even so, she checked her room carefully and was relieved that she still had the gun, the money and her phone in her coat pockets and that she'd stowed all her new clothes and the bags in the wardrobe. Who turned up at a hotel with that much new stuff?

Lauren decided that she'd done enough for the day. She made herself a cup of tea, called room service for sandwiches and transferred some of the money into the purse that she'd bought.

Now what? Lauren wondered. She could try and read, or she could watch more television. She put the television on low volume and then took out the notebook and pen she'd bought. She remembered how Petra had written what amounted to a statement about what had happened at the cottage. Lauren wondered again who she had sent it to. Petra had promised faithfully that she would not tell where Lauren was and Lauren did find herself believing that. After all, Petra had a lot to lose, too. Lauren guessed Petra had been undercover for quite some time. She didn't imagine that the Perrin organization would treat undercover cops any better than she surmised her father's organization had. Petra had left the rest of the lined notepad behind, but Lauren had wanted something she could keep on her, hence the smaller notebook. She finished her sandwiches before she even attempted to begin writing, mentally recounting to herself what had led to all this mess. She decided she would write an account of everything that had gone on from the moment Charlie Perrin had locked the door to her room. She would then write down everything she knew about her father's organization, about the Perrins. Anything she could remember that she'd picked up, overheard, that might be knowledge she wasn't supposed to have. Exactly what she was going to do with this, she wasn't sure yet, but she wanted to make a record, just in case.

Just in case of what? Lauren thought. *Just in case I end up as dead as Harry? And who the hell am I going to give this to when I'm done? Maybe leave it in the hotel room for someone to find? Maybe post it to the local police?* Right now, she didn't know.

Because she had nothing better to do, she made some more tea and forced herself to begin. At first it was hard, reliving that time with Charlie Perrin. She'd told Harry all about it, of course, but that had been in halting, faltering, roundabout terms. She had told Petra. But now she was trying to put things in proper order. Once she'd begun, it was easier than she had thought it was going to be. It poured out of her — the anger, the fear, the frustration. Having told it all to Petra, it was now clearer in her mind than it had been when she'd told Harry. She'd already gone through a sorting process and that had really helped.

Her hand was cramped and it was dark outside when she finally stopped. She stowed the pen and notebook in the bag she had bought that morning and went to look out of the window. Christmas lights were on now. Below her, between the hotel and the station, lay a pathway of red and gold and white. A sudden wave of loneliness crashed over her. She had always been alone in real terms, apart from Harry and Jean and her mum. She had always been alone and now they were all gone. Was this what it was going to be like from now on? Lauren didn't know if she could cope with that.

CHAPTER 32

The Sydonia Gallery was on the ground floor of the Palace Hotel, occupying space alongside designer boutiques and high-end jewellery stores. It was not large, and it was not quite the kind of white cube space that had become fashionable. It maintained some of the wood panelling and marble tiles that were a hangover from when this had been the atrium of the Palace in more affluent days. The Palace Hotel itself was Art Deco and always reminded Petra of the wonderful cinemas from that era, one of which had been her regular filmgoing spot when she was a kid. That had since been pulled down and replaced by a supermarket, but for a long time she had harboured the plan that if she ever won the lottery, she would buy it outright and turn it into an arts centre.

Carole Josephs and Sam were already there when Petra arrived. Carole turned with a big smile. "Pat, I'm so glad you're here early. I'm in a bit of a panic, I think."

Petra hugged her. She liked Carole Josephs and she got on with Sam really well, too. "You look great," she said. Carole was dressed in deep red, it set off her dark hair and pale skin. The lipstick was a richer colour than she usually wore but it suited her, Petra thought. Though she did look nervous and Petra reminded herself that this really was a big night for Carole.

Sam took Carole's arm. "I keep telling her, it looks fabulous. And everything's set, everything is ready. Buffet's laid out, drinks are chilling — it's going to be a brilliant evening."

"I thought I'd start with some contextual shots, before everybody gets here," Petra said. "And then I can repeat the same shots during the evening and create a layout with them placed side by side. I want to catch the emotional response when people come in. I want to compare that with the way these objects just sit in space, the way they occupy the room."

Carole began to look a little more relaxed and Sam mouthed *thank you* at Petra. Then, patting Carole on the arm, she went to check that everything was in fact absolutely perfect.

The glass doors at the rear of the gallery opened on to the atrium of the hotel and the grand piano had been set up there. Petra could see the pianist and string quartet setting up. She told Carole she was going to nip out and get a few shots of them, too.

"I'll come with you, just to say hello. I heard them in the summer, doing their concerts in the park thing, absolutely fab they are."

It was odd, Petra thought, all this happening just a few days after her brother had died. No one seemed to be mourning Charlie Perrin particularly. She'd heard Carole say that her brother was an idiot anyway and that if it hadn't been this, it would have been something else. At least this way, he'd not taken anyone else with him and Petra knew that Charlie Perrin, despite his ban, still had a habit of driving while under the influence. She wondered if Carole really did think there'd been an accident, if she really had no clue that her brother had actually been shot to death by his reluctant fiancée. Petra sympathized with her. She was trying so hard to be her own person and to crawl out from under the shadow cast by her father and brothers. But to Petra's mind, the only way she was really ever going to do that was to leave the compound, leave the farm and get right away from Gus Perrin's influence. She couldn't see that happening.

She captured some beautiful candid shots of the musicians and Carole and Sam chatting and laughing together, as they got themselves organized. Then she returned to the gallery, examining the way the light and shadows fell and wondering if she could manipulate the lighting later on so that it cast shadows in a different direction. The work had an organic feel to it. There were some bronzes this time as well, which was a new departure for Carole. She hadn't got the facilities for casting in her own studio but she'd worked very closely with the little manufactory who had taken over that part of the job and she'd made the decision that the maquettes should also be put on show and the process explained in photographs Petra had taken during the casting. Petra knew that those who had actually done the casting for her would be guests tonight and that Carole intended to introduce them to everybody. Petra liked that Carole recognized she could not have produced these pieces of art without their input.

Carole came back in, looking much more at ease now.

"What time is your dad arriving?" Petra asked. She knew from experience Gus Perrin would be among the first to get there, and she wanted to be in position to photograph him as he came in. Gus Perrin and his entourage always created an impact.

Carole grimaced. "He said he'd text five minutes before they got here. '*So we can be suitably prepared.*'" She laughed. "After all, he is paying for most of this."

He also owns the hotel, Petra thought.

"Where can I stow my stuff? I don't want people falling over my camera bag. Can I slide it under the buffet table? Under the end there? That way, I can get to things easily but I won't be in anyone's way."

"You just put your stuff anywhere you like," Carole told her. "I'm just grateful to have a friend like you doing this."

Petra gave her a quick hug. She felt a pang of guilt whenever Carole said things like that. She genuinely did like this

157

woman and she liked Sam Barker as well, and Sam's partner. Somehow, she didn't count them as part of the Perrin clan, though she knew that her handler would not agree about that. He saw the whole damn lot as corrupt. She was aware that Carole often chose not to see things, chose not to know what was going on. But quite honestly, she couldn't blame her for that.

Carole's phone chimed. "That was my dad. He says the first three cars are about to arrive. He's early as always but wants to have a look around first."

And to get his pictures taken before everyone else arrived, Petra thought. Pictures that would advertise what an art lover he was, what a champion of culture. Gus Perrin was very conscious of his public image.

A few minutes later, she was involved in her task. She'd exchanged a smile with Billy as he'd come in, wheeling his boss up to the first of Carole's artworks. Petra framed her first shot, Gus Perrin looking thoughtful while his daughter explained what this was about. Billy had backed off and stood in the background, smirking. She tried not to look at him and focused on her task. Others had begun to arrive now, and Sam was helping check the list at the door, taking coats, making sure people had drinks. Petra exchanged a quick glance with Carole's assistant, before turning the camera on the crowd that was now flocking in, booted, suited, bejewelled and perfumed. She was suddenly profoundly glad that Billy had insisted on buying her dress, shoes and bag for the evening. Nothing she could have afforded would have fitted in here.

Billy had wheeled Gus Perrin over to her side and she turned with a smile. "Mr Perrin, this is going to be a wonderful event."

She noted that he was wearing a black armband on his jacket, as was Billy and the rest of the entourage. Charlie Perrin was being discreetly acknowledged, the ghost at the feast.

"And you, Pat, are looking very beautiful this evening," he told her. "Billy is a very lucky man. I'm going to be slipping out of here in about half an hour, just quiet like. I don't want to spoil Carole's evening, but I've got a business meeting lined up. So you'll not mind if I steal your man away?"

Billy leaned in to kiss her cheek and then her lips. "Will I see you later?" she asked.

It was Gus Perrin who answered. "He'll be popping in to collect a few bits, love. But he's got a job to do for me."

Petra allowed her eyes to widen slightly. She lifted her camera. "Better get on," she said. She could feel the nervousness engulfing her, that sense of anticipation that something big was happening. *How is Lauren coping?* she wondered. *What should I do next?* In some ways, Billy being away would make things easier, but where was he going, what was he doing? What was the so-called business meeting about?

She made her way to the buffet table to get a second camera out from her equipment bag and noticed a slip of paper tucked inside that hadn't been there before. She shoved it down beneath a lens that she knew she would not be using tonight, straightened up and went back into the fray.

CHAPTER 33

Lauren sat on the bed waiting for the phone to ring, willing the phone to ring. Petra had not been in touch at all that day and she was now feeling restless and even more alone. All she seemed to be doing at the moment was eating and sleeping, though she'd added quite a bit to her account of her father's doings and contacts. She had no idea if any of this would be useful, or if any of it constituted information the police did not already have. Truthfully, she wasn't even sure she intended it for the police — after all, what had they ever done for her? They'd locked up some poor sod for killing her mother, when she had known, even though she'd only been a kid at the time, that it had been her father's doing. She had pretty much decided that if Petra didn't get in touch the following day, then she would take things into her own hands. She could catch a train and disappear. She felt instinctively that once she'd got used to city life, learned to blend in better, the urban environment would be a better place to hide. Remote did not necessarily mean safe. Remote could mean exposed.

It was very, very late when her phone eventually rang. She snatched it up and answered immediately.

"I thought you'd forgotten about me." She tried to keep her voice light but she wasn't really fooling anyone.

Petra ignored the comment. "Listen, I'm just checking in very quickly. I'll call you later and let you know what's happening, when I know more. Meantime, just sit tight, OK?"

"OK," Lauren agreed. Petra was speaking very quietly, then she rang off abruptly. Lauren didn't need to be told that she must be taking a risk. She was grateful for the contact, however brief. But what was happening? Petra sounded tense and that was not good.

* * *

It was almost two a.m. when Billy finally made it home. Petra was in bed reading.

"I waited up for you. Well, I waited in bed for you, that's kind of the same thing. It was a good evening, Carole sold several pieces so she's really chuffed."

He sat down on the bed and kissed her. "That's good. I'm pleased. She deserves it, she works hard. Look, I've just got to put things in a bag, there's a car waiting downstairs. I'll probably be gone a few days."

"Gone where?" she said in her best wheedling tone. "Or aren't I supposed to know?"

"No, you are not supposed to know. And I can't tell you, because I don't know either."

She pouted, but inside she felt anxious. "So is it because of this so-called business meeting?"

"A business meeting, yes. Our Kyle Sykes was there and boy, did the boss give him a dressing down. He was squirming."

She leaned forward. "Has his daughter turned up yet?"

Billy laughed. "Not likely to if she's got any sense, is she?"

"Oh? Why is that, then?"

Billy tapped the side of his nose. "Best keep out of this, eh? But it seems he can't find her, so the boss says we'll give him a hand. See if we can't sort it out for him."

She opened her eyes wide. She knew he liked it when she looked admiring or even a little shocked. "You want me to help you pack?"

"Nah, just need to slip a couple of other things in my go-bag and then we're done." He went over to the wardrobe and pulled out a soft leather holdall and dropped it onto the bed. She moved her feet out of the way. He took another pair of shoes from the bottom of the wardrobe, put those into a shoe bag and then inside the holdall. She knew it was already packed with shirts and trousers and a spare jacket. It didn't matter where they went, Gus liked his men to be smart. He lifted a panel in the bottom of the wardrobe, removed something wrapped in a red cloth and added that to the bag too. She didn't need to ask what it was — he had shown her once. Billy favoured the Glock 17. A box of ammunition went into the side pocket.

"Billy?" She didn't need to pretend to look concerned. "Billy, I don't like this. What's going on?"

"Not something you need to worry about. You get those photos processed and sorted tomorrow, the boss will want to see them before they go off anywhere else."

She nodded. Of course he would. Everything had to be run by Gus Perrin before it was used anywhere. Though to give him his due, she found herself thinking, he had a good eye. She frowned, annoyed at that stupid random thought intruding, but Billy had not noticed. He had closed the wardrobe doors and was now shrugging on his coat.

"Best get off, they're waiting for me. Laying bets on how long I'm going to be," he added. "They'll reckon I won't be going anywhere without giving you one for the road."

She got out of bed and gave him a hug that she realized was partly meant. She wasn't in love with him, but she didn't particularly want him getting hurt. Nor did she want him hurting anyone else. Especially not Lauren. Not that it was much of a surprise to hear the girl now had Gus Perrin and his organization chasing her tail as well as Kyle Sykes and his men. Petra had been out of her depth before, but now she and Lauren really were in danger of drowning.

There was one question she wanted to ask him before he went. She decided to ask it now, while he had his arm around her, while she could feel he was giving serious thought as to whether another five minutes or so would make any difference to his schedule.

"Did someone come here the other night?" she asked. "I woke up, and you weren't in bed, then I thought I heard voices." She smiled up at him. "Couldn't be bothered to come and find out who it was, so I went back to sleep and when I woke up, you were there again."

She felt his body stiffen, and then he squeezed her bum and said, "Freddie called round. Told him it was bloody late, but you know Fred. Finishes at the casino, and for him it's breakfast time, he thinks everyone else is wide awake too."

She laughed. "Yeah, that's Freddie." Then, as though something had suddenly struck her, she moved in closer and wrapped her arms around his neck. "You will be OK, won't you? Only there seems to be so much going on at the minute. It's got me worried."

He took hold of her, held her away so he could see her face. "What's that supposed to mean?"

"Well, you know . . . on the news, those three dead. Those three who were killed by the canal. Sykes's men. On the way to the gallery, I drove that way, I was just being kind of nosy. It's still absolutely crawling with police. I mean, I know Gus and Kyle Sykes don't get on . . . Do you think . . . I mean . . . Billy, I do worry about you."

To her surprise, he was laughing. "You think Gus ordered that done? Where do you get these ideas from, girl? It was nothing to do with any of us. Sykes did for his own."

"What? Why would he do that? I don't understand, Billy."

He was hugging her again now, stroking her back and groping her bum. She sensed that she liked this display of

163

naivety, liked to think she wasn't always quite as confident or as knowledgeable as she wanted the world to believe. "I thought you had a brain in that head of yours?" he said.

"I have a very good brain," she objected.

"Yeah," he conceded. "You have. But it's a straight brain."

"What's that mean? I can't think round corners?"

He looked at her. "It was something to do with that kid of his, the one we're off looking for."

"Sykes? What about his kid?"

He leaned in and kissed her. "You ask too many questions, you know that? It's a dangerous trait, asking too many questions."

Her heart skipped a beat at that comment, but she pouted and pulled away. Billy just laughed at her. "Sykes did for old Harry Prentice, too. The boss reckons it was him who helped the girl run, after Charlie."

"After Charlie?" She looked puzzled. "You mean after Charlie shot himself? That was just an accident, wasn't it?"

"So the rest of the world thinks." Billy was clearly enjoying himself. "The boss is not a happy man. He told Sykes to sort it. So far, he's not done. The girl's still in the wind, and killing old Harry is not going to have satisfied Gus. Gus is out for blood, but it has to be the *right* blood, if you get my meaning."

"Oh my God." Petra sounded suitably shocked. "You mean the girl had something to do with Charlie's death?"

"Not a word." Suddenly Billy was deathly serious. His gaze hardened as he realized he had told her too much. "You don't talk about this, you got that?"

She nodded. She didn't have to fake the scared look on her face. When Billy's mood spun like this, he was genuinely frightening.

He left, and Petra was very relieved when she heard the front door slam. She had asked too many questions and he had given too many answers. She knew from experience that once he'd put distance between them, he would automatically forget what she'd asked, automatically reassure himself that he had said nothing that could not have been shouted in the street. This, she had learned, was Billy's way of accommodating his own need to boast and hers to listen. He liked to impress her, she knew that.

She reran the conversation in her head. He had said nothing about the other man who had arrived with Freddie and she had known not to push it. Perhaps one of the reasons he'd been expansive about other things was that he had not liked her question about the late-night visitors and had wanted to distract her. She felt that he had not even liked the fact that she'd known they'd called around to see him. And, she sensed, though he seemed fine about Freddie, he was not happy at all about this other man coming into his house.

CHAPTER 34

Petra had not yet looked at the slip of paper she'd noticed in her camera bag. She waited until she was absolutely certain that Billy had gone before she searched it out. It turned out to be a sliver of paper torn from the top of the menu for a local coffee shop and she knew that this was a message meaning that a meeting had been arranged. Somebody would be there at prearranged times in the hope that she could turn up to one of them.

It was rare for a meeting to be arranged. Petra herself discouraged them. It spoke of urgency. Though on this occasion, she was quite glad of it. She wanted to confide in somebody about the DCI she had seen a couple of nights before. What the hell had he been doing here? She also needed help regarding Lauren. She had to get back to the girl with some information. She had to let Lauren know that there was a way out of this, though for the life of her, Petra couldn't fathom what that might be. But she at least had to call Lauren and reassure her that she'd not been abandoned.

She went downstairs and locked all the doors, bolting them from the inside so that even if Billy happened to come back with his keys, he'd have to ring the bell. He knew she did this when she was in the house on her own, encouraged

166

it even, so it would not seem strange. Then she went back upstairs and called Lauren's number. She had her listed under the name of a firm she used when she wanted physical giclée prints of her photographs. Petra had no password protection, or any kind of lock on her phone, nothing that would make Billy suspicious. He would occasionally pick it up and go through her texts.

Lauren again picked up on the first ring.

"Sorry it had to be short earlier," Petra told her. "You understand I have to be careful."

"I understand you're no safer than I am," Lauren told her. "In fact, right now, I'm probably in a better place than you are."

Isn't that the truth? Petra thought.

"Look," Lauren continued. "If you can't get me out of here in the next day or two, then I'm going to catch a train somewhere, I'm going to take it into my own hands. I can't stay here forever eating room service meals and watching TV, and I can't put you in any more danger than you are in already. I won't be responsible for another death."

"It won't come to that. Listen, tomorrow I'll know what to do, but you've got to be ready and, Lauren, you won't like this — but I think we've got to go to the police with this one. No — hear me out — there are people I know I can trust." *I hope.*

"I think my way might be better."

She might be right, Petra thought. "I've got a meeting with someone tomorrow. After that, I'll get back to you and we'll sort it all out. In the meantime, promise me you'll stay put. And, Lauren, there's something you've got to know. Gus Perrin is not best pleased that your dad hasn't dealt with . . . with you."

"So Perrin's after me too, is he?"

She sounds so calm, so controlled for someone at breaking point, Petra thought. "Stay put. If I can't get to you myself, I will send somebody. Tomorrow, I promise."

"I told you." Lauren's voice was steady, but Petra could feel the tension. "Don't ever make promises you can't keep. Promise you'll try, that's enough."

"I promise I'll do my best," Petra told her. *Who is the adult here?* she wondered. "Try and get some sleep and try not to worry." She realized as she said it how stupid that sounded. Lauren evidently thought so too because she hung up.

Petra sat down on the bed and stared at her phone. It was three a.m. and the first meeting that was possible in the morning would be at nine thirty, just after the little café opened. She would have to make it there then, set things in motion. Billy being away simplified matters, though she knew that Gus would be keeping an eye. Gus kept an eye on everyone. Fortunately, the café was on the way to the gallery, so she had the perfect excuse. She could say she wanted to go and have a quick check on everything and stop off en route at what everyone knew was one of her favourite coffee shops. That would raise no eyebrows. Having settled that, Petra sought to take her own advice and get some much-needed sleep.

CHAPTER 35

Petra went out straight after breakfast. She didn't see anybody watching the house, or spot anyone on her walk into town, but that didn't mean anything. She chose to walk because it was easier to observe anyone following her, Gus's men tending to prefer cars to feet.

She popped into the café just after it opened and stood in the short queue chatting to an elderly couple who were also regulars. She sat at a table by the window to drink coffee and eat her croissant and then wandered on towards the gallery. She spent about half an hour there, talking to the manager, checking that everything was in order and gave Carole a ring just to ask if she wanted to be there when she went through the photos later that morning. They arranged to meet up for lunch first, then to go back to the gallery and check through the images there so that the gallery could have first pick for any publicity stuff.

Anybody who happened to be watching Petra would have seen Pat do all of this, but what they would not have noted was the brush contact with the old couple, the exchange of information. The request for a face-to-face with her handler and a memory stick popped in Pat's bag.

After the gallery, she headed to go and see Gail. Gail was a friend and had also been her de facto agent when Pat had been focusing on photographing weddings, christenings and bar mitzvahs. She had contrived to meet Billy at one of these events, a wedding for a distant cousin of the Perrin family. And then again at another social event and after that, well, things had taken their course.

Although it was Sunday, Gail — being self-employed and living above the shop — was working and welcomed her happily. While Gail was making coffee for them both, Pat asked if she could use her computer to send a quick email. She made her way into the back office, borrowing the spare laptop that was used by the girl who came in to do office admin for a few hours a week. She inserted the memory stick and checked the files very, very quickly. She'd expected just a quick message but instead found that she was looking at case files. That she was looking at several gigs of information spread over a dozen or more folders.

"Fuck," Petra breathed. *What the hell is all this about?* There was evidently more here than she could possibly look at now. She pulled the stick, dropped it back in her handbag and then inserted a second, this being a backup copy of the photographs she taken at the gallery. She turned the laptop so that Gail could see as she came in.

"Ooh, will you look at those?" Gail pulled up a chair and put both mugs of coffee on the desk. "These are beautiful. Has she seen them yet?"

"No, I need to forward them over to Mr Perrin and then Carolyn and I are going over them this afternoon. It went really well, Gail. It was a fab evening."

For a little while they sat gossiping, examining the photographs and speculating as to which would be selected to go where. But Petra's mind was racing. *Why the hell had Frankland sent her all that stuff? What did he expect her to do with it? Didn't he know how dangerous it was for her to have this information? Stupid question, of course he did. So what's going on?* She couldn't help but feel it was a warning of some kind. There had been a message on the stick, a tiny Word file that she'd opened extremely quickly and glanced at. What she had seen disturbed her immensely.

No meeting, it had said. *Compromised. Clarke will help.* A phone number followed.

Compromised? she thought. *Who's compromised? What's compromised? Her? Frankland? And what about this Clarke?*

She tried to concentrate on what Gail was saying, knowing that after this she had to go and have lunch with Carole and focus on selecting images, on business. There would be nothing she could do until late afternoon. She had hoped to have something sorted out that she could tell Lauren by then. She was pretty sure that the Clarke in question must be DI Clarke. She'd taken the trouble to keep abreast of who was who in the local force and knew that he had transferred about six or seven years ago. She'd heard nothing negative about him. *Could he be trusted with this though?* Particularly after Petra had spotted the man she was certain was a police officer at Billy's place the other night.

She had to think. She had to figure this out, and she had to know what the hell was going on with Frankland. After leaving Gail, she took a chance and called his direct line. The phone was answered by his secretary, who said he had not come in that morning. He hadn't phoned either to say he was sick. Could she take a message?

Petra told her no, she'd no doubt catch up with him later. But alarm bells were ringing — this wasn't right. She walked back to the hotel and was unsurprised to find Carole and Sam in the gallery. Both looked happy. They wandered together back through the glass doors into the atrium and then into the hotel restaurant. Petra was unsurprised to notice a couple of Gus's men hanging around in the lobby.

"You've got your bodyguards with you today," she joked.

Carole rolled her eyes. "Dad's got a bee in his bonnet about something or other," she said.

Petra, or Pat, never questioned Carole about what her dad was up to. She had long since learned that Carole chose not to know and certainly chose not to talk about it. If her father requested she do something, then she did it. Her personal survival strategy was wilful ignorance.

She was therefore quite surprised when Carole said, "I hear your Billy's off somewhere. I also hear he is planning to pop the question soon . . ."

Petra was genuinely shocked by that. "What question?" she asked stupidly.

Carole laughed. "What question do you think?"

"I never . . . I mean . . ." For once, she was lost for words. Billy wasn't the marrying kind, surely? She was saved from further embarrassment by the arrival of the waiter.

"Now," Carole said, "Dad's paying, so what are we ordering?"

* * *

The phone rang. Lauren leaped at it. All day, she'd waited. Now at six o'clock in the evening, she'd almost given up. She'd packed her bag, promising herself that if Petra didn't phone within the next hour, then she would simply catch a train somewhere and that would be that. She remembered she'd promised herself the same thing when she had been waiting for Petra on the beach and that Petra had appeared just as the hour was up. It was almost as though the other woman felt or sensed her deadlines.

"I thought you'd never phone."

"I said I would. It's difficult, you know that. Right, listen. I'm sending somebody to get you. He'll let you know when he's on his way and how long it's going to take. But his name is Toby Clarke and he is a DI. You can trust him."

"How do you know that?"

"I just do. Lauren, you've got to trust somebody. You trusted me. Keep on trusting me. Clarke is one of the good guys."

Lauren hesitated. "OK, so when is he going to be coming?"

"Like I said, I don't know. I *will* get back to you, I *will* tell you when he's on his way. You just need to be ready and you need to go with him."

Lauren could hear the anxiety in the other woman's voice. "Something's happened, hasn't it?"

"I don't know yet. But yes, I think so. Lauren, there are things going on that I haven't got a handle on yet. Clarke will help us. You just need to be ready to leave."

Lauren promised she would be and hung up. She didn't like the way Petra sounded. What was happening?

She didn't want to use the credit on her phone, so she scoured the news channels on the television to try and find what might have spooked the undercover officer. She managed to find snatches of news about the three men found on the waste ground, and that the case was proceeding but there were no new leads. The news report said that Inspector Clarke had been due to give the press conference but had not been available. The journalist speculated that this might indicate a break in the case. Someone called DCI Henderson had made a statement earlier. It was as Lauren expected, full of platitudes that they were following various lines of enquiry. So that's who Clarke was, she thought. He was local police. Therefore he must know a lot about her father, about Perrin.

Does he know what I've done? For the first time, she really began to think about the consequences of her action. Was she likely to be charged with murder? Surely it had been self-defence? She watched the television for a little longer, hoping that there would be more information, but there wasn't. It occurred to her that she'd spent most of her life being told what to do and she was still being told. But she was no longer certain that she was prepared to put up with that.

She got up and went to the window. Outside it was dark, just street lights and the sparkle of Christmas lanterns. If she left now, it would mean travelling through the dark. Travelling to where? She had a few ideas in mind and no solid conclusions as yet.

CHAPTER 36

Toby Clarke listened as the woman with the soft, almost accentless voice told him that she knew where Lauren Sykes was holed up and that she needed help to get her out of harm's way. She wanted to know that he was alone, that no one could overhear, so he drifted out into the corridor and stood beside the window that looked down into the police car park. He listened for about ten minutes, asking the occasional question, growing more and more concerned.

By the time he'd hung up, he knew how Lauren Sykes had made it off the beach and where she had gone to after that. He still had no idea who this woman was — but he now understood that she must be an undercover officer. She was, he thought, taking the most terrible risks.

He was as concerned as she sounded that she could not reach Frankland and he gave him a try as soon as he got off the phone to her. No response. He tried mobile, home phone and office, but by this time of day even the secretary had gone and the phone rang out into emptiness.

He had been given Lauren's phone number but had been told not to ring it yet. This woman would do that and prepare the girl to be picked up. Lauren would be scared, he thought. For a moment, he regretted his decision to send

Hopkins back home, feeling that a reassuring female presence would have been a good thing. But there was nothing to be done about that. He had promised this woman that he would arrange a safe house and that he would not go through his own force to do so. So he contacted his old boss and explained the situation briefly. Crenshaw took a little convincing but agreed to help.

"And did your contact say why she didn't want you to go through your own division?"

"She claims to have seen a DCI at the house of Billy Hunter. Billy Hunter is a known associate of the Perrin family. Been working for them since he was a teenager, climbed up through the ranks. He's now very close to Gus Perrin and he is among the group that Gus sent to find the Sykes girl."

Crenshaw told him to head down to collect the witness and that he would send an address to Clarke while he was en route. The woman had managed to transmit her fear to Clarke, and Clarke had evidently now done the same for Crenshaw. The sense of urgency was palpable.

He returned to the office aware that he been gone for quite a while. Mark Reynolds looked up from his desk. "Trouble?" he asked.

"Possibly. I've got to head back down, probably be back up here in a day or two if you need me. Apparently, there have been developments, but I'm not sure what they are yet. Everyone's being a bit cagey."

Reynolds raised an eyebrow but made no comment. They both knew that it was often wise not to speculate too much about unfolding events. That could block your thinking, just at the point when you needed to look at it with fresh eyes.

The office was quiet at this time of the evening and Clarke asked Reynolds to say his goodbyes for him. And then he was off, stopping briefly to collect his things from the hotel.

He did not notice the car that pulled out of a sideroad as he left his hotel. It kept its distance as he reached the main road but overtook him as soon as he joined the motorway. Finally it settled two cars behind, matching Clarke's speed as he headed south once more.

* * *

Lauren did not have to wait too long for her phone call. Petra called her back at eight and explained what was happening. That a safe house was being arranged and DI Clarke would come and get her later that night. That he would text to let her know when he was about half an hour away and that he would come to her room. To not worry about checking out because Petra would deal with that over the phone.

"Are you sure you can trust him?" Lauren asked.

"I'm sure. Text me when he arrives, OK?"

Lauren agreed. "Thank you," she said. "I don't how this is all going to turn out, but I hope I can meet you properly one day. One day when we're not both scared shitless."

CHAPTER 37

It was dark outside, and Petra had made up her mind. She had to know what had happened to Frankland. It was out of character for him not to let work know that he wasn't coming in and her sense of dread had risen through the afternoon and into the evening. Something was not right. She had taken a chance to look at the USB drive that the old couple had delivered to her that morning. She hadn't worked her way through everything but what she'd already read had frightened her considerably. It seemed that her handler had already had suspicions about the DCI she had spotted coming out of Billy's kitchen that night. His suspicions had been reported higher up the chain of command, but he seemed to be getting nowhere. Much in the reports stemmed from intelligence that she had obtained, and this had clearly been followed up. She had known that Kyle Sykes had contacts inside the force, had guessed that Perrin did, too, but what she had read was positive proof of this.

She took a backpack from the cupboard. It was designed for camera equipment but it was black and had multiple pockets. She added a camera with an infrared lens and some other equipment, just in case Gus Perrin had people out 'watching over' her. She pulled on dark jeans and a dark sweatshirt and topped that off with a thick, padded jacket. She stuffed the stick drive into an inner pocket, then tugged a knitted hat down over her hair. She left the house via the patio doors and went out through the back gate. Ducking down immediately behind a parked car, she checked down the road but could not see anything obvious that suggested she was being observed. Two streets away was a garage and inside that lock-up was an innocuous-looking little hatch-back. She waited for five minutes before unlocking the door to the garage, but there was no sign of anyone. She kept the car carefully maintained, never knowing when she might need it. It started first time. She backed out of the lock-up and pulled off without bothering to close the door again. There was nothing to steal in there and she suddenly did not want to run the risk of getting out of the car.

She drove out of the end of the street without anybody obviously following, and it *would* have been obvious this time of night. Of course, that didn't mean that surveillance couldn't have called ahead and there might be a car waiting to pick her up at the next junction. She didn't think so, but took a circuitous route just in case, changing lanes frequently on the dual carriageway leading out of town and circling back round on herself, taking almost an hour to do what was in fact only a ten-minute journey. She parked a street away from her destination and walked down a narrow cycle path between the houses to get to where she needed to be.

Again she waited. It was past ten o'clock at night. Everyone was inside in this quiet residential area. The faint sound of televisions leaking out through windows was the only thing that broke the silence.

Frankland's house was in darkness. She knew he had lived alone since his divorce a few years before. The house was a modest semi-detached with two bedrooms, but she knew it had a long garden and that she could get into the garden by climbing the next-door wall and going over the fence into his. She knew this because she'd done her reconnaissance. Her earlier military training had prepared her for the idea that she must always be ready, always know her ground. It was an attitude she had shared with Harry. She had liked him. Harry had always joked that she would be the one to get him killed. He would never have thought it would be his seventeen-year-old charge.

She was over the fence. Keeping in the shadow of the fence and then the privet hedge, she approached the house. No lights in the windows. No sound of television. No security light, even though she knew he had one that was sensitive enough to be triggered by next door's cat. He hadn't switched on his light this evening, then, as was his habit. Usually, once it started to get dark, the security lights were activated. Then the curtains were drawn, the doors were locked and he settled himself in for the evening. This is just what he did, unless he was working late elsewhere, in which case, he would switch his security system on before leaving and a timer would automatically deal with the lights.

He either wasn't there or something bad had happened.

She paused, listening. Someone in the adjoining house opened the back door and she heard a dustbin lid open and close again. Then the back door shut. She waited again and then turned on her torch, keeping the beam pointed down. It took her a little while to pick the lock but as soon as she entered the house, she knew that there was nothing living in there. It had that empty, soulless feeling that houses get when the occupants are gone. The curtains gaped open. And the smell of butcher's shop hanging in the air warned her of what she would find. She moved slowly from room to room, finishing in the spare bedroom that was the furthest away from the adjoining house.

It was there she found him. He was dead, as she had known he would be. He was lying on the spare bed, limbs stretched out and pulled taut by ropes that held them to the legs of the bed. The sheets and mattress were soaked with his blood, as was the carpet. She checked to make sure she hadn't trodden in any of it. She flashed the torch across his body to try and get some sense of his injuries. The body had been laid out as though on a mortuary table. Whatever information he had known, she reckoned, whoever had killed him knew it now. But how long had they known? How long had he been dead? And how specific had he been? Did they know about *her*?

Careful not to step in any of the blood, she approached the bed. His skin was still warm. From the look of the wounds all over his body, he'd taken a long time to die. Whoever had tortured him knew exactly how to prolong agony.

Reason told Petra that if they knew about her, someone would have come for her already. Chances were, then, that Gus Perrin now knew that there was an undercover within his operation but not specifically who.

She switched off her torch, went back the way she'd come and retreated just as carefully. Now was not the time to be stupid or to let panic rush her but she was relieved when she reached her car and drove away. It never entered her mind that she should go back to the house she shared with Billy. That life was gone now, her cover irrevocably blown.

In the boot of the car was a bag packed with essential clothes. Hidden in the lining of her camera bag was money. She drove out of town, stopping only when she needed to refill the tank with petrol. She called Clarke.

"My cover is blown. Frankland is dead. Tortured. Whoever did it to him, chances are they know everything by now. Maybe not *exactly* who I am, but certainly that there is a UC involved."

"I'm just about to text Lauren. I'm about half an hour away from the hotel," he told her. "Call me in an hour and we'll arrange a rendezvous."

She agreed. She smiled. She liked the fact that he was cautious enough not to suggest she come with them to the safe house. They must meet on neutral ground, somewhere he could check her out.

* * *

Clarke walked in through the lobby as though he knew where he was going, found the lifts and went up to the thirteenth floor. He walked along the corridor to Lauren's room, was startled to find that the door ajar. He pushed it open. The room was empty, stripped bare. Had she run? Had she panicked?

He went in, examined the wardrobe, the drawers, the bathroom. He could see the indentation in the quilt from where Lauren had been sitting on the bed watching television, but that was the only sign of the girl.

The door creaked open. He spun around. A dark-haired waif stood in the doorway. She had a gun in her hand and she looked as though she was prepared to use it.

CHAPTER 38

Carole answered the loud knock at the door. She opened it and was then pushed rudely aside by three of her father's men coming in. A fourth followed, dragging Marty with him. Marty's face was bruised.

"What the fuck?" Carole followed the men into her kitchen. "What is this? What the fuck is going on?"

"Where's Sam?"

Carole hesitated for the briefest moment, but then Sam herself appeared next to her in the doorway. She took in the scene, her face pale. "Marty! What happened? Have you had an accident?" One of the men laughed.

Carole took Sam's arm and held her back. "I want an explanation." These were three men she did not know well. They worked for her father but she had no real dealings with them. And that scared her more than anything. Her father had deliberately sent strangers into her home. She could see that one of them had blood on his shirt. Marty's blood, she assumed. This man came forward and grabbed Sam's other arm, pulling her away from Carole.

"You're coming with us."

"Oh no, she's not, Sam works for me. She's got nothing to do with you."

"The boss wants her, she comes with us."

Carole glanced across at Marty. He was clearly terrified and totally at a loss. "What's all this about? Sam is my assistant, that's all. Nothing she does has anything to do with you lot or my father."

The big man with blood on his shirt leaned in, his face practically touching hers. "And what if she's an undercover cop. What then?"

"What?" Carole could not believe what she was hearing. "Why the hell would he think that? He had her checked out when she came to work for me. She's clean, all the way back."

"Well, it would look like that, wouldn't it?" He pushed Carole away. Clearly, the fact that she was his boss's daughter cut no ice. She could see the anger in his gaze, and the bloodlust. She was suddenly terribly afraid. This was no longer absurd. This was dangerous.

"That's nonsense. We can sort this out. Where did you get this idea from, anyway?"

The man smiled, clearly enjoying this. She remembered his name now, Ben something or other. He was one of those who only came to the farm occasionally, when her dad needed extra muscle.

"Found out from the horse's mouth, didn't we? Old boy didn't want to tell, but he did in the end."

Carole's thoughts were racing now. They must have found out about an undercover from a police informant. She didn't like the sound of any of this. What had they done to that informant? Or had that informant sent them to interrogate someone else? She knew how this worked — undercover officers had a handler, so had they got to the handler? What had they done to him to make him tell?

"You attacked a police officer?" She looked from Sam to Marty and then back again. Sam looked petrified.

"I didn't do anything. I'm just your assistant. I don't have anything to do with the police." Sam was shaking, visibly trembling and she was crying now.

Carole found that she believed her. "Of course you didn't. This is all just so much stupidity."

So they must have gone to Sam's house and found Marty on his own there. He must have told them that Sam was working late here. And they'd dragged him here, just in case he phoned and gave warning. And, Carole realized now, she would have moved mountains to have got Sam out of this safely before they could get to her.

The men were moving towards the door now, hauling Sam with them. They'd lost interest in her partner. Marty rose, eager to follow, but Carole put a hand on his shoulder. "There's money in my bag, take it. Take my car and get out of here."

"You think I'd leave Sam?" He was furious, she could see that. Furious because he didn't want to leave Sam and furious with himself because he didn't know if he had the nerve to stay.

"Nothing you can do. I'll go. I don't believe she's undercover, I don't believe she's anything apart from what she says she is. I *will* sort this out. I will get her out of this. But in the meantime, we need one less person to worry about. So you get out of here. Now."

She didn't hang around to see if he was going to obey the instruction. She ran out after the three men who were now frogmarching Sam up to the main house.

As Carole stepped across the threshold of her father's home, two other cars arrived and two other accused — both women, she noted — were dragged past her and into the house. They weren't women she knew. So they were obviously associated with her father's business, but not high enough up in the pecking order for them to live at the farm.

The only one she was interested in the moment, though, was Sam. Another car pulled up. She recognized one of the guys getting out as Freddie, who ran one of her father's casinos.

She grabbed his sleeve as he stormed by. "Freddie, what the hell is going on?"

"Not now, love, not now." He paused and turned. "Carole, best thing for you now is to stay out of your dad's way."

"He's accused Sam of being an undercover officer. They just brought two other women in, as well. Freddie, I don't understand, what the fuck is happening?"

Freddie indicated that his companion should go ahead of him. "We went for Pat, but she's not there. House is in darkness, no sign of her. She went out the back way."

"Pat? No, no, no, not Pat." Pat was her friend. Pat and Sam had been her closest friends for the last three years. No, this was a nightmare.

Freddie hurried on, leaving her standing in the hallway, stunned. Out on the drive, she heard the familiar sound of her own car go by and knew Marty had at least followed her advice. She hoped they'd let him out through the gate and wondered if she should have told him to go to the police. But even now, that went against the grain. Besides, what would the consequences be? Carole may not care about her husband or her father, but she still had a son to think about, and that son was away at boarding school, away from either her protection or influence.

The sight that greeted her when she entered the main living room was surreal. The room was only used on special occasions or when her father had a lot of guests. Usually he settled himself in the small snug at the back of the house with his television and his comfortable chair. Sam had been watching the door, and Carole could see the slight relief in her eyes when she saw her come in. She went over to her friend and put an arm around her shoulders. The men who'd escorted her had moved aside, though were still within reach should Sam try to make a run for it. Freddie was telling Gus that they'd gone to get Pat, but that she wasn't there.

"Must have gone out the patio doors and through the back gate."

"No one saw her go?" Gus Perrin demanded.

"No one thought . . . I mean, she'd settled in for the night, and we all thought that was it. I mean—"

Gus Perrin held up a hand for silence. He looked at the three women who'd been brought before him. One had a black eye, the other was cradling an arm across her chest. From where Carole stood, she could see it was broken. They whimpered softly, leaning into one another for comfort. Carole held her breath. She could almost see the gears whirring in her father's head. Pat's guilt was not proved but it wasn't looking good.

She tightened her grip around Sam's shoulders. "It'll be all right," she whispered.

"Marty?" Sam said, in little more than a breath.

"I told him to take my car and get the fuck out of here."

"What's going to happen?"

Gus turned his head to stare at them both. Carole didn't reply. She hugged Sam tighter.

"Her, her and her." He pointed to the women, then turned his attention to one of the men who had brought them in. "Take them upstairs, put them in a guestroom, lock the door."

"That arm looks broken," Carole said. She released Sam and stepped forward. She knew that her father did sometimes listen to her. "She needs medical attention. Let me call the doctor."

A dark look crossed her father's face. But then he nodded and waved her away. "Get on with it, then."

Carole beckoned Sam and urged all three women out of the door before her father could change his mind. This could go one of two ways now. They could focus all their efforts on Pat, or they could decide that other people might be implicated and turn their attentions back to Sam and these other two poor unfortunates. The best chance she could give them was to get them out of her father's sight. One of the men had followed her out, and she was relieved to see that it was Freddie.

"Gus says they've got to be locked in," he told her.

Carole nodded. She herded the women upstairs and to the back of the house, where there was a twin-bedded guestroom. "Freddie, there's a first aid kit in the bathroom. Bring it, will you? And then give the doctor a call."

Freddie hesitated. Carole sighed. "Freddie, where the hell do you think we're going to run off to? The house is full of my father's thugs. Just get the medical kit, please, and get a doctor here."

She glanced at her watch. It was just past midnight. She found herself hoping that Pat was far away by now. And then she felt the tears begin at the thought that a friend had betrayed her. Impatiently, she wiped her eyes with the heels of her hands. Freddie returned with the first aid kit and she set it down on one of the beds. "Here," she said to Sam. "You clean up that eye, while I take a look at the arm."

She settled the injured woman in a chair. "What's your name?" she asked. "Don't be scared, no one's going to hurt you now, and the doctor will be here soon."

The woman, tears streaming down her face, just looked at her. *She thinks I'm mad*, Carole thought. *She could well be right.*

* * *

"You must be Lauren." Clarke tried to keep his voice steady. She was clearly scared, but she had a determined look in her eye and he realized that she would shoot him if she had to. He raised his hands slowly. "I'm here on my own. Your friend sent me, just like she said she would. I suggest we leave here now."

She came forward and placed the gun against his right temple. With her left hand she patted him down, checking for weapons, fingers delving into his pockets. He got the feeling that this was something she had *seen* done, but wasn't quite sure how to go about it. He stood still and did nothing threatening. Finally, she stepped back.

"Have you seen the news?" she said.

"News? Not recently. Why?"

"Because that bastard has reported me missing. It's gone out on the national news. My picture. So I've got my dad after me, I've got Gus Perrin after me, and now every fucker in the world after me."

Clarke absorbed that. "I'm a little surprised he didn't do that before," he said. "Your dad has a tendency to let other people do his work for him, so that would have been kind of logical."

For a moment, she glared at him and then she sighed, put the safety back on and put the gun back in her pocket. "Best be going then, hadn't we?" she said. She looked apologetic. "Sorry about that, I waited in the stairwell and watched. I wasn't sure you'd keep the promise to be alone. I needed to know, you understand that?"

"I understand that," he told her. "Look, maybe you'd better give me the gun."

She laughed. "Not going to happen."

Clarke knew he should press the point, but he also felt anxious about the fact that Kyle Sykes had reported her missing, had got the publicity that would activate social media, people in the street, hotel staff. This was bad news. "We'd best use the stairs," he said.

She nodded. She opened the door and checked the corridor before going out and scooping up the overnight bag that she had dropped in the doorway. She looped the strap over her shoulder, wearing it across her body so that she had both hands free, and headed towards the double doors at the end of the corridor. On the landing was a wheeled suitcase. Clarke reached for it.

"Leave it," she said. "It's empty and I wiped it down. I used hand cleaner, the alcohol's good at degrading DNA and fingerprints and I've been very careful. Everything I need's in my bag or my pockets. Where did you leave your car?"

He told her that it was in a side road a couple of streets from the hotel and she nodded approval. Clarke felt oddly pleased about that and then laughed at himself. He was a detective inspector, she was a seventeen-year-old girl on the run — why should he want her approval? But he found that he did. He could sense her nervousness, her underlying anxiety, and yet she was still keeping on, thinking clearly, making all the right moves.

They went down ten floors, and then she paused and pointed to a door. "If we go through there, then we can go out of the rear exit. There's a second set of doors into another stairwell and that avoids the lobby completely. It's a service entrance for the kitchen. And there are no CCTV cameras down that way. The only camera is on the loading bay, and we can avoid that one."

"You've really thought this through, haven't you?"

"I'd rather not die," she said calmly. "If I die, then it will be like letting Harry down, and I can't do that. You understand that, don't you?"

He nodded. "I understand that," he said. "You do know that Harry's—"

"Dead? Yes, I know. I went to the cottage, after my father's men had gone. I needed to know. If there was anything I could have done for Harry, I swear I would have done it. But he was dead. Really dead."

She led him down the corridor and out of the double doors at the end. She stood listening at the top, and only when she was satisfied did they begin to descend.

I should be taking the lead, Clarke thought. But then, she knew the route better than he did. She paused again at the bottom of the stairs, opening the door a crack and peering through. There was no one around. She ushered Clarke to the end of the short hallway, past storage cupboards and empty offices. It was dark down here, daytime staff having long gone, their route lit only by two small bulkhead lights that he guessed were operated on a separate system and left on in case of power cuts. At the end was a small door with a keypad. Without hesitation, she pressed four keys in sequence and opened the door.

"How do you know the code?"

"I watched. I hid behind the cleaning trolley and I watched. You always need to know your escape routes."

She led Clarke across the yard and out into the street, then turned left towards where he had parked his car. She paused frequently to glance back the way they'd come. She moved carefully from one area of dense shadow to the next, keeping back from the street lights. He had a strange feeling that she had probably been planning escape routes for a very long time, that this was not a new thing, probably not even something she'd learned from Harry. This was a kid who had grown up being scared, grown up not knowing when she would need to run, or hide, or simply disappear.

She halted and pulled him back into a shop doorway, her attention caught by something at the end of the narrow street.

"What?"

"Shh!" She pointed towards the end of the road, to the corner that would have brought them back round to the front of the hotel. *Was that a movement?* At first, he wasn't certain, but then a shape appeared briefly. A man, then a second. They stood on the corner looking down the street towards the shop doorway.

Clarke held his breath. He didn't recognize either of these man-shaped threats but he knew *what* they were. A chill ran the length of his spine as he realized that he must have been followed. Then came sudden, self-directed anger. Of course they'd kept tabs on him. Perrin's lot, or Sykes's, or maybe both. They'd have known when he went north, known when he turned back towards home, probably been puzzled as hell when he'd taken a detour and come to this city and this hotel.

"Fuck," Clarke breathed. Lauren grabbed his sleeve and pulled him into deeper cover.

For what felt like for ever, they stood in silence in the narrow doorway, Clarke running through scenarios should the men decide to walk on down the street. Did they know about the rear entrance? Did they know what was down this little road? The loading bay, the way into the kitchens?

Beside him, he realized that Lauren had already made her plans. Her weight shifted slightly as she reached into her pocket and withdrew the gun.

No, he wanted to tell her, *you can't shoot two people, not even two of your dad's thugs or whatever they are. Not here, not without consequences.* But he found himself wishing that he was also armed. Impatiently, he pushed that idea aside, risked a swift look back at the end of the street. "They seem to have gone," he whispered, and made to move.

"Wait!" she hissed at him. "That's what they'll want you to think. It's what they're trained to do."

Reluctantly, he stayed where he was, risking another look a moment or two later and discovered that she'd been right. The men had returned, standing backlit, like easy targets at the end of the street. For a moment, he was tempted to take her gun and shoot them himself. He shifted back into the shadows and tried not to breathe. His breath, his heartbeat, everything felt far too loud. His back was cramped with tension. He felt her lay a hand on his arm, as though she knew just how he was feeling and sympathized.

The sound of a car engine startled him. The grip on his arm tightened. "Keep really still," she whispered.

He heard the car pull up at the end of the road and then two doors open and slam closed. They were driving off. Clarke felt Lauren turn her face away, burying herself as deeply into the doorway as she could. He could sense her willing him to do the same. Clarke needed no persuasion. If the car came down their street . . . He risked a very swift glance. Three men, big vehicle.

He had never been so grateful for anything in the world as when the sound of the engine faded and the car took the other road, heading away from them.

Lauren grabbed his hand. "It's a one-way system — they'll circle back round," she said. "We don't have much time. We need to get to your car and then get out of sight. There's a multistorey open twenty-four hours. Come on, I'll give you directions."

"We should get right away from here."

"Yes, but we've got to do it the right way." She looked him full in the face. "You don't know them like I do. You don't know them from the inside, not like I do."

191

She's probably right, Clarke thought. Though it went against the grain, putting his trust in this kid.

More than anything, he was ashamed. He should have thought about them tracking him, not with Lauren as motivation but just as a matter of routine.

They reached his car and threw themselves in. "If they've been tracking you, they'll know your car," Lauren said, "so we have to be careful."

He nodded. "The multistorey you were talking about?"

"Take a left at the end of the road, then there's two turns that are one way, you take the third and it brings you round to the multistorey entrance. I wish I knew what they were driving."

"Some kind of four-by-four," Clarke told her. He had seen that much. "Dark green or black. Hard to say, under the street lights."

"Predictable," Lauren said.

"How come you know so much about the roads? You been here before?"

She shook her head. "There were tourist maps at the hotel. Harry said I should always know my ground."

"Good advice."

"Harry cared about me."

Not like anyone else was the implication. Clarke glanced sideways at her. She seemed calm, but he could feel the roiling anxiety just below the surface. He knew it was there because it was within him, too.

He came to the first of the one-way streets and, after a split second of hesitation, turned the wrong way down it.

"What are you doing?"

"Trust me. They're likely to catch up with us soon. And if *you've* thought about the multistorey, chances are they will have, too."

She looked doubtful but didn't argue. He could see her checking the wing mirrors for anything four-by-four-shaped on the road they'd just left.

Clarke spotted a gate part way down the one-way street. It was closed, but there was just enough of a space in front of it to allow him to turn around so that their car faced the right way. He manoeuvred quickly, then tucked the car between two others and switched off the lights. They slid down in their seats, looking towards the main road through the windscreen of the car in front.

They waited. *Time is doing its extending thing again*, Clarke thought.

"There!" he hissed. A dark four-by-four drove past, three men inside. They could be entirely innocent, of course, but Clarke was convinced it was the same car he had glimpsed before. Silently, he counted to fifty, then to one hundred, before he started the engine. He edged to the end of the street and turned right. Traffic was light, but they scanned it urgently.

"We need to get out of town," Clarke said.

Lauren pointed. "There's a sign for the motorway."

"Good as anything," Clarke agreed. His hands were shaking on the wheel. He gripped it tightly, trying to ease the tension from his shoulders. He'd nearly blown it. "Lauren, I . . ."

She waved a dismissive hand. "You don't know my dad," she said. "You don't know Gus Perrin. Oh yes, you might think you do, but you've been looking at them from the outside. Like they're some . . . I don't know . . . experiment you're doing, just to see what happens next. But you're looking at it all wrong. Men like my dad and Gus Perrin — they're not people you can understand just by looking at them from the outside, you've got to remember that. No one who really deals with men like that can stay on the outside. They get sucked in, so it's their whole life. It's like being in a cult or something. People on the inside, they forget what it's like on the outside. It's like it burrows into them. It's their whole life."

"I do get that, Lauren. I've been investigating people like your dad for years."

"No!" She slapped the dashboard in her impatience. "No, you don't. If you get fed up with your job, your house, your girlfriend, have a falling out with your boss, then you can just leave. You've got choices, choices that don't mean you end up dead. Those men who followed you. They gave up their choices a lifetime ago. You stand on the outside looking in and you think you get it. How can you get it?"

Clarke frowned, not too sure where the rage had come from. She didn't seem to be blaming him for almost bringing trouble down on their heads, so what point was she making? He could have understood her anger if it had been directed at his carelessness, but he felt this was about something else. "You feel sorry for them?"

"Not exactly." She looked uncomfortable. "I just know how easy it would be to give in. To be what my dad or Gus Perrin or whoever wants you to be, because being on the inside of something can make you feel safe. And it's not. Nowhere ever is."

CHAPTER 39

For a while Marty had driven, not knowing what to do or where to go. He had been waved through the gates as though nothing was wrong, even though he'd been driving Carole's car. Only one man had been on duty, which was in itself unusual. And he had been distracted by a car coming at speed the other way. Marty had had to swerve to get out of its path.

He decided to go home to the cottage at the edge of the farm, a house close enough to the village to be almost part of it, but still under Gus Perrin's gaze. The house was empty, though the lights were on. They'd left the front door open when they'd dragged him into their car. He summoned the courage to go inside, to pack some of his things, intending to head for a hotel for the night. He phoned Sam but it went straight to voicemail. Switched off. He tried hard to summon the nerve to go back for her, but he knew there was nothing he could do and that he must trust to Carole to work this out. A noise at the kitchen door made him jump and he turned to see the cat coming in through the cat flap and go to its food bowl. The cat was totally unconcerned.

Sighing, Marty filled the bowl and gave it fresh water, then left the house for the last time. Anything that was important to him was now in his suitcase and he suddenly realized that, with or without Sam, there was no way that he could go back to stay there ever again. He locked the door, got into the borrowed car and drove away.

The idea that he should go to the police formed very slowly. He'd been too shaken before and had never exactly judged the police as allies. Growing up in the city, a mixed-heritage kid in a diverse neighbourhood, he'd had several run-ins with the authorities. Nothing serious, but enough to reinforce his general suspicion of them. Now, however, it seemed like a good idea. He glanced in the rear-view mirror. The face that stared back was bruised, his eye blackened and his jaw turning an interesting shade of green. The local station wouldn't be open at night — it closed at six and didn't open till seven the following day — and so he drove into town to the divisional headquarters. With some trepidation, he approached the desk sergeant and told him that he needed to report a crime.

* * *

Carole glanced at her watch. It was almost three a.m. She'd heard the house phone ring two or three times, and had seen Kyle Sykes arrive and her father's solicitor shortly thereafter. She also knew that Billy and his cohort had been recalled and were now heading home. There was no sign of Pat and for that, at least, Carole was grateful.

The doctor had attended the two women and they now sat on the bed holding hands with a blanket wrapped around their shoulders and doing their best to ignore the daughter of the house. Carole knew that despite the fact she had tried to help them, she was still the enemy. She left them to it.

She'd put Sam in her own room. Sam Barker was scared. She had of course known what Gus Perrin was, but she'd hidden behind the notion that she was simply Carole's assistant and that none of it mattered. Ignorance, Carole thought, even manufactured ignorance, was certainly not bliss in this house. She found that she was annoyed, as much as anything else. Sam had been a fantastic assistant and was in her own right a gifted artist. Carole had allowed herself to feel that she had friends, that Pat and Sam really cared about her. Perhaps they did, but that didn't mean that either of them was going to be part of her life any longer. Not after this.

Carole's main concern now was to get Sam out of this in one piece. Pat, she decided, could take care of herself. If she really was an undercover police officer then no doubt she had her own prearranged escape routes and had had her own agenda all along. Carole was really hurt by that knowledge. That made her angry, too. She had long ago decided that she was beyond being hurt by anything like that.

She sat next to Sam on the bed and took the younger woman's hand. "It's going to be all right. He knows by now you've got nothing to do with any of this. By morning you'll be free to go, I guarantee it."

"It is morning." Sam's response was sullen and cold. She withdrew her hand from Carole's and hunched in on herself. "I really enjoyed my job, you know that. I really liked you, but you can't expect me to just forget about all of this."

Carole grabbed Sam by the shoulders and turned her so that she was looking directly into her eyes. "That's exactly what you're going to do. Look, I'll deposit money into your account, three months' pay, and if you need anything more, you just have to ask. I'll give you the most excellent references I can. You are going to walk away from this and you are never going to look back. But you are not going to talk about any of it, have you got that? Because if you do, my father will not forgive and he will not forget, and believe me, you do not want him remembering you."

Sam stared at her and then shook her off. Carole could see that she was pale and scared and that this was all beyond her comprehension. She had never played this kind of scenario through in her mind.

"Where do you think Marty will have gone?" Carole asked.

"Why should I care?"

"Don't blame him. I told him to go. There was nothing he could do here except get hurt. This is not his world, Sam, not yours either. Don't blame him for being scared."

"If he's got any sense, he'll have gone to the police," Sam was doing her best to sound defiant.

"You should hope to God he hasn't," Carole said.

"What do you mean?"

"My father has associates everywhere, including in the police. If he's gone to the police, Dad will know about it sooner rather than later."

* * *

Toby Clarke pulled off the motorway and into the services. Lauren was already looking round for a sign of Petra. Clarke had told her that Petra's cover had been blown, that her handler was dead and that she was now potentially in a lot of trouble.

It was decided that Lauren should stay in the car, in shadow. Her picture was now out there, on social media, news channels, newspapers. It would only take one person to spot her, only one report to give Kyle Sykes a clue to her whereabouts, and the danger would increase twentyfold. It was possible that whoever those men were, they would have shown Lauren's picture at the hotel. Someone was bound to recognize her.

Clarke had arranged to meet Petra in the main entrance of the service station restaurant and soon they came back together, carrying takeaway coffee and burgers. Petra got into the back of the car. Lauren found that she was overwhelmingly happy to see her.

Briefly, she filled them in on what had happened and what she had found when she had gone to Frankland's house. "My guess is they spent most of the day with him. That it probably started out as a straight interrogation, and then it got nasty. Which means that he wasn't prepared to tell them anything much and it also means they didn't know much to start with. So somebody must have tipped them off that there was a UC in the organization. I mean, they would have killed him anyway, but probably a bit quicker if he had told them something sooner."

"And by running, you've now confirmed what was told," Clarke observed.

"My cover was blown. I have no intention of ending up dead as well."

"You didn't know that. Most likely, they suspected a man." Clarke was not quite sure why he was playing devil's advocate — tiredness and irritation, probably. The truth was, he didn't blame her. It took a special kind of person to be an undercover officer and Clarke had long ago realized that he was not it.

Lauren was riled by his attitude. "Don't be so bloody stupid," she told him. "Of course she had to get out. There was no other sensible thing to do. You should know that — you lot lost two of your own when they were trying to infiltrate my dad's organization."

It was a fair point. Clarke apologized.

"So what now?" Petra wanted to know. "You've got a safe house organized, for Lauren I mean. I can take care of myself."

"No. You're coming with us," Lauren said.

Clarke began to argue. Lauren cut him off. "I owe Petra. You pay debts."

"I'll be all right," Petra told her. "I'll lie low till the fuss dies down, I have friends."

"Friends who lend you their dogs and their car." Lauren laughed.

Clarke looked puzzled, but it was pretty obvious that the two women were not going to explain.

"This safe house," Petra said. "Are you sure you can trust whoever set it up?"

"I believe so, yes. As you advised, I went outside of the division. I talked to my old boss. He's straight as a die and speaking of which, I really should report in. I went dark an hour before I collected Lauren, and I've not been in contact since." He reached for his phone.

Petra put a hand on his arm. "Use this one. It's clean, it's a new SIM. And tracking is switched off."

Clarke frowned but took the phone. "I've still got to switch mine on, I need to look up the number."

Lauren could see that Petra was annoyed by this. "Make it quick, phone on phone off. And then we move."

Clarke raised an eyebrow, but her anxiety was already infecting him and he didn't argue with her. The moment he turned on his phone, missed calls and text notifications buzzed and chimed.

Petra saw him hesitate, wanting to pick up the messages. "Find the number and get off the phone. Say the number out loud, that way we'll know it too."

A little reluctantly, Clarke did as instructed. He dialled the number into the new phone, noting that Lauren had scribbled it down in a small notebook. Petra did not seem to need such an aide-mémoire.

The voice on the other end of the call was impatient and angry. "Where the hell have you been? No one knows where you are. You call me and you asked me to set up a place of safety, and then you don't turn up. What the hell is going on, Clarke? I've spoken to your boss — no one knows where you are. I spoke to the gold commander of your division and he doesn't know where you are and has no idea why you would be wanting a safe house. Clarke, what have you got into?"

"I told you, I need a place of safety for a teenager. I told you the background, so you'll forgive me for not telling you more. There were complications, I got delayed."

"And would this teenager be Lauren Sykes? Half the country's looking for her. You're aware that her father reported her as a missing person?"

"I'm aware of that. I'm also aware that he's after her, and so is Gus Perrin. And I'm aware that both mean her harm. I'm also aware that she is an intelligence asset." He looked apologetically at Lauren when he said that. She shrugged. Of course she was.

There was a moment of silence on the other end of the phone. Then his contact said, "There have been developments you should know about. There's something going on at the Perrins place, reports of assaults and abduction. We've sent a couple of officers over. And you should also know that a serving officer has been murdered. DCI Frankland was found dead at his home earlier this morning. And it's a nasty business, Clarke. It looks like they tortured him to death."

It was Clarke's turn to hesitate. He looked at Petra. How much should he admit to knowing? "I thought Frankland was retired?" he said.

"Officially, yes. Unofficially, no. Clarke, you know as well as I do that a handler can't just walk away from his undercover officers."

Clarke decided he should keep quiet about Petra for the moment. "What do you think they wanted from him? Does he have any connection to the Perrin or the Sykes OCGs? If so, this makes it even more important to keep the girl safe."

"It does. OK, Clarke, I'm guessing you have more of an overview of this than you're letting on. I'm going to trust you. I'm going to let you call the play on this—"

"You're telling me the safe house maybe isn't safe?" Clarke said.

"I'm telling you I don't know. I'm telling you there are rumours that I don't like."

Petra had taken Lauren's notebook. *Ask him about Henderson*, she scribbled.

Clarke was puzzled but complied. "Are any of those rumours about DCI Henderson?"

Silence on the other end of the call was the only confirmation he needed.

"Right, so we really are out in the cold then?"

Clarke did not wait for a response. He hung up the phone and then switched it off. "Why Henderson?"

"Because I saw him at Billy Hunter's house. You know he gambles beyond his means, don't you?"

"I didn't, no."

"So what do we do?" Lauren asked.

Her eyes looked very large and dark in the dim of the car, Clarke thought. "You go with Petra, you find yourselves a cheap hotel somewhere, or whatever Petra thinks is best and you hold in there. I'll give you the address of the safe house, in case you need a backup plan. But I'm not sure how much we can trust it. I'll try and work something else out in the meantime. Have you got money?" he asked.

Both women nodded. "Enough for now," Petra said.

"And I still have my gun," Lauren told him. He saw a flash of humour in her eyes, unexpected but oddly welcome.

"I don't want to know about your gun," he said. "By rights, I should have taken it off you the moment I saw it."

She laughed. "Like you could have done," she taunted. Then she grew more serious. "Where are you going? You're going to confront Henderson, aren't you?"

"If he is a traitor, then we need to know."

"And you think he'll tell you?"

"I have to try and find out what's going on. And for that, I need to go back home, scout around, see what I can find out."

Lauren looked at Petra, who nodded. "I'll send a message to the new phone. I'm not going to tell you where we are, just that we're OK. Call me back on that number, but only when you're sure it's safe to do so. Here." Petra handed him a small, tissue-wrapped bundle. "Three more SIMs. Be careful."

"Did *you* report the body?" Clarke wanted to know.

"Frankland was my friend," she told him. "I wasn't going to just leave him to the flies."

Lauren grabbed her bag and Clarke watched as the two women walked away, keeping to the shadows.

CHAPTER 40

Freddie knocked on Carole's door. When she opened it, he said, "You've got to bring her back down again. Something's happened."

Carole glanced back at Sam, who was still sitting on the bed, then looked at Freddie with renewed terror in her eyes. "*What* has happened?"

Freddie shrugged. "It seems the boyfriend was stupid enough to go to the police. You lent him your car — he should have just kept on going. But no, the idiot had to report an assault. Had to claim a kidnapping. There are two uniformed officers downstairs now waiting for Sam to come down and tell them everything is fine. That it's all been one big misunderstanding."

Sam stood up. She looked hopeful. "I can leave with them," she said.

Carole sighed. "Sam, the cavalry's not arrived, so don't push it. Now you just go downstairs, and you tell them it's a big fuss over nothing."

"And if I don't? What if I ask to leave with them?"

"Well, you can ask," Freddie told her. "But believe me, girl, they won't welcome it. They just want to get out of here. They're just going through the motions, like their boss told them to."

"I suppose *they* work for him as well, do they?" Sam practically spat the words at Carole.

"Probably not," Carole said. "Ask yourself, would you want to walk into a house like this? Knowing what you do about my father? And remember, there's only two of them, and if Gus Perrin chooses to say that they walked away, got in their car and drove off, how are you going to prove otherwise?"

"Won't they have radioed in, or something? Won't they have told their colleagues where they are?"

"I'm sure they would have done," Freddie told her. "But just because they were somewhere at one moment, does not mean they're going to be there the next. And if a dozen witnesses say that they drove off, and we don't know where the hell they are, how could you prove different? Now get your arse downstairs."

Carole led the way, with Freddie bringing up the rear. She knew that Freddie was exaggerating, but probably only a little bit. She knew that Kyle Sykes made people disappear on a regular basis. Sykes certainly didn't care which side of the law they were on. She suspected her father shared the same views. She certainly wasn't going to risk anything at the moment. All Sam had to do was agree that everything was fine and they could go away.

The two officers, both looking very young and very vulnerable, stood in the middle of the large living room. It surprised Carole at first that the police had not sent anyone more senior to deal with Gus Perrin. *Someone's just ticking boxes*, Carole thought. Marty's claims had to be followed up, but someone was making certain nothing would be made of them.

She didn't know who was in her father's pocket. Had never wanted to know. But evidently, in diverting just a routine patrol to check up on Marty's statement, they were both covering their backs and sending the message to Gus that this was not going to be logged as anything resembling a priority call-out.

These two have probably never seen so many smartly suited and heavy-set men in one place at one time, she thought.

Her father sat, centre stage, his face expressionless. Carole felt the chill of that look. Knew how angry he really was. She extended her hand ready to shake and approached the nearest police officer. "I'm Carole Josephs," she said, "and this is my assistant, Sam. Sam Barker. I understand you want a word with her."

"There's been a report. A man came in to report an assault on himself, and to say that this young lady was being detained against her will." The officer eyed Carole and then turned his attention to Sam. "So if you'd like to come with us and make a statement . . ." he trailed off.

Carole sighed impatiently. "Let me guess, it was Marty who called at the police station, and Marty who made the complaint. He and Sam had a set-to earlier this evening and, well, I'm afraid I intervened. He was getting rough with Sam, so I clouted him. If you want me to come and make a statement to that effect, I'll do so in the morning, but it's pretty late. I'm sure we all just want to get to bed."

As if the officer realized for the first time that she and Sam were still fully dressed at four in the morning, the young policeman frowned.

Carole read the look. "We've been having a bit of a family celebration," she told him. "I have a new exhibition — I'm an artist. Sam has been so tremendously helpful in setting it up, and she's practically family, so of course, she joined us." She was aware that nobody else in the room had spoken or even moved since she'd come in. That it must seem very strange to these two observers. They must have realized that the atmosphere was anything but celebratory, but she just wanted them out of here, just wanted Sam safely back upstairs, and her father to calm down. Suddenly she felt extremely weary. She couldn't go on like this, it was just all too stupid.

"And is this true, Miss Barker? That you and your partner had a disagreement and—"

"I'm fine," Sam said flatly. "Please go away. It was just an argument, just a misunderstanding."

She couldn't have been more unconvincing, Carole thought and the two police officers evidently thought so, too. She could feel the mood in the room shift and guessed that so could they. One of them moved towards the door. "Miss Barker, if you'd like to go and make a statement in the morning, and you too, Mrs Josephs? So we can just clear this up once and for all."

"I'll see you out," Carole said, and before anyone could object, she had opened the living-room door and led the way into the hall.

She watched them go down the steps to get into their car, silently urging them just to disappear into the night and go back to the business of giving out speeding tickets or picking up drunks. She was profoundly relieved when they pulled away. She didn't think her father would have been stupid enough to do anything drastic, but you never could tell, and as she had told Sam, there were plenty of witnesses to back up any story he chose to create afterwards.

She leaned against the closed doors for a moment, wishing that she could have gone with them and taken Sam with her. But she still felt a responsibility to the two other women upstairs and anyway, even if she'd tried, she really didn't think her father would have allowed them to leave. Her moment of calm was interrupted by screams coming from the living room.

Carole ran across the hall and flung the door open. "What the hell?"

No one else had moved, but Sam now knelt at Gus Perrin's feet, one hand wrapped around the other. She was sobbing. Tears of pain ran down her cheeks.

Gus Perrin looked across at his daughter. "And if I catch up with that boyfriend of hers, it won't just be the fingers that get broken. Make sure she understands that."

Carole hurried to Sam's side, lifted the younger woman to her feet and half carried her from the room. Somehow, she got her upstairs and back onto the bed. Two fingers of the left hand were broken and crooked and already black with bruises.

"I'm sorry," Carole said. "I am so, so sorry."

* * *

Marty had made a statement, then been left alone in the interview room while the police officer went to make calls. It seemed as though he'd been gone for a very long time. Marty tried again to call Sam, but her phone was still switched off. He had Carole's number, so he tried that. Nothing.

Almost an hour had gone by since the officer had left. Marty got up and tried the interview room door. To his horror, it was locked. He tried the handle, twisting and turning. There was nothing happening.

Marty began hammering on the door, shouting at the top of his voice. It seemed like an eternity before somebody answered from the other side. "You all right? Hang on a minute, the door's jammed. These old latches, sometimes they stick."

Marty stepped back from the door, watching as the handle was jiggled and the door itself tugged back and forth in the frame. Eventually, something clicked and the door opened. The uniformed officer that he remembered from the front office stood there. He looked apologetic.

Marty pushed past him, heading down the corridor towards the front office. He was terrified that the man might try and stop him. The officer just shouted after him, something like "Are you all right, Mr Baines?" but Marty was already out of the door. He went to where he had parked Carole's car, but it was no longer there. Marty swore.

He began to walk to where he remembered there was a taxi rank. The streets were empty, but he could not shake the feeling that someone was watching his every move.

CHAPTER 41

Toby Clarke desperately wanted to go home to shower and change and maybe get some sleep, but as he drove back into town, he was aware that the morning briefing would have begun and he should really be there.

DCI Henderson glanced across as he opened the door. On realizing who it was, his expression changed up a degree or so from his usual mild annoyance. He didn't like to be kept out of the loop, Clarke realized, and he had been out of communication since the previous evening. Henderson would not be pleased about that. He would especially not be happy that his old divisional commander had raised the alarm, had even contacted the gold command of this division, trying to track Clarke down. Henderson would have taken that as a personal slight.

Not that Clarke cared about any of that. Henderson was now a suspect in his eyes. Possibly a dirty cop.

He perched against a table at the back of the room, aware that all eyes had swivelled towards him and as quickly swivelled away, focusing with unnatural concentration on their boss. Hopkins was sitting at the back and passed him a collection of briefing documents, earning herself a share of Henderson's silent irritation. Clarke glanced through the sheets she'd given to him and then he too turned his attention back to his boss.

It seemed little progress had been made on the murder of the three men found on the waste ground. Crime scene photographs, names and addresses and intelligence summaries now covered a large board, but this had been moved off to the side of the room. The space behind Henderson was now occupied by images of the late DCI Frankland. Petra had described the crime scene to Clarke but even so he was taken aback — not by the fury and ferocity with which the man had been attacked, but by what had obviously been a slow, methodical and excruciatingly painful process. He had seen people who had been tortured before, but not like this. Frankland's body was covered in short but deep cuts. Three of his fingers had been removed. And finally, presumably when they were done with him, he'd been carved open from throat to pubic bone like some horrible parody of a medical post-mortem.

"Fucking hell," Clarke muttered. He saw Hopkins stiffen and then nod slightly. If all they'd got out of him after all that was that there was an undercover officer within Perrin's organization, Frankland must have had more courage and endurance than Clarke even wanted to imagine.

At the front of the room, Henderson was listing the injuries in the order in which the post-mortem had revealed they probably happened. Time of death was barely an hour before Petra had found him, Clarke realized. She had been bloody lucky. Had she chosen to stay at home that night and not gone to find out why her handler hadn't been responding to her ever more urgent requests for contact, she would have been scooped up by Perrin's men and probably have become yet another corpse for the police to puzzle over.

Knowing that he had to tell what he knew, or at least part of it, Clarke raised his hand. *Like being back in school*, he thought. Henderson paused mid-flow and then said with the heaviest of sarcasm, "It seems that our prodigal has something to say. Should we listen to him, boys and girls, or should we make him wait his turn?"

Clarke couldn't be bothered with all this. Henderson might be annoyed now, but there would be worse to come. And besides, what Clarke now knew about his boss meant that he didn't particularly care what the hell he thought any more. He made his way to the front of the room, aware again that every eye was upon him and that you could now hear the proverbial pin drop.

He placed the briefing papers on the desk and turned towards his colleagues. "I've been in contact with the UC that Frankland was protecting," he said. "We believe she is currently in a place of safety. And for the record, I don't know where that is, but DCI Frankland died protecting her." He pointed at the board, gesturing angrily. "I couldn't have withstood that and I don't think anyone here could have done. The Perrins know who she is now, but that wasn't through Frankland — that was through their own process of elimination. So we now have Gus Perrin realizing that for the last three years, he's had an undercover officer very close to him. We also have Kyle Sykes knowing that his daughter was responsible for Charlie Perrin's death. So we have two very dangerous men who now feel personally slighted."

A ripple of disbelief made its way around the room. Henderson began to speak but Clarke got in first. "Be assured, I know this from Lauren Sykes herself. She shot Charlie with his own gun. Which explains the forensic anomaly I talked about in the post-mortem report."

"And what, Perrin had him shot in the head with his own shotgun just to cover it up?" a disbelieving voice demanded.

"I'm assuming something of the sort," Clarke confirmed.

"So, where's the girl now?" Hopkins asked.

"Lauren Sykes is still alive, and safe. We know that she was on the run with Harry Prentice, who is now dead. From evidence found so far, and a dying declaration made by Joe Messenger, Sykes found him but the girl had already gone. The Perrin and the Sykes OCGs were due to be, shall we say, joined in unholy matrimony, but the girl put paid to that, and for the record, it was because Charlie Perrin tried to rape her. Before we look into that particular killing, we need to protect her from being murdered herself. As you are aware, her father has now declared Lauren Sykes to be a missing person, so her picture is all over the newspapers, all over social media, all over the television. We now have two women to protect. Lauren Sykes, and one of our own." He tapped one of the photographs on the board. "And if nothing else, we owe it to DCI Frankland to catch the bastards that did this."

A murmur of approval. This is what they wanted right now. They were getting more fired up by the moment — and so was Henderson.

"My office. Now."

* * *

Clarke had barely closed the door when Henderson turned on him. "What the fuck do you mean, turning up like this? You've been off the radar for thirteen hours and yet you waltz in here as though nothing's happened."

Clarke leaned back against the door. "Billy Hunter," Clarke said. "Gambling debts. Ring any bells?"

Henderson began to bluster but even Clarke could see he didn't have the heart for it. "That has nothing to do with anything that happened here. I settled those debts."

"With what?"

"Fuck you, Clarke. I paid them fair and square."

"The Perrins don't do fair and square. You know that. You've handed them your head on a plate. Gus Perrin won't back off, even if you have paid the *money* back." Another thought occurred to Clarke. Something about Henderson's wording rang alarm bells. "You borrowed from them?"

Henderson went red, then pale. "Frankland was my friend and my long-term colleague. If you think . . ."

"I think you're compromised," Clarke told him. "You've opened yourself up to pressure from the Perrins. I know for a fact that you went to Billy Hunter's house in company with

211

Freddie Benson, because you were seen. How can anyone know what you might have told—"

Henderson began to protest. Clarke raised his hands. "OK, I don't doubt that you never meant to tell them anything. You know as well as I do the harm of wrong words in the wrong place. You knew there was a UC in the Perrins's organization."

"I didn't know who. Only Frankland knew who it was."

"And you never dropped even the slightest hint, you never had pressure put on you to reveal even the slightest bit of information, I suppose? The Perrins just patted you on the back and told you to go on your way? You gambled in their casinos, you lost money hand over fist, then borrowed more to pay it back. Who do you think you borrowed it from?"

Henderson closed his eyes. "Not the Perrins."

"Who, then? Please say it was a bank or you put it on your credit card. Or are they maxed out, too?"

Henderson closed his eyes. Behind Clarke, the door was shoved open. Clarke moved aside. Superintendent Eric Craig stood in the doorway looking at the two men. Henderson opened his eyes but Clarke ignored the newcomer. Suddenly he knew what else his boss was hiding. "You borrowed the money from Kyle Sykes, didn't you?"

"I didn't know that's who I was dealing with. I didn't . . ."

"What's going on here?" Craig wanted to know. His tone was calm, but Clarke could see that he was anything but. He realized, slightly belatedly, that their voices must've carried all the way down the corridor, back to the briefing room. Only thin partition walls separated Henderson's office from their colleagues. Frankly, Clarke didn't care.

"Ask him," Clarke said and walked out of Henderson's office.

* * *

Petra had continued on the motorway for a little over an hour and then taken a slip road and an A-road through a small town and a few small villages. Finally, she pulled into a layby to consult a map. She and Lauren had then discussed where to go to next. Lauren favoured somewhere busy, one of the chain hotels like the one she'd just left. At least they could disappear into the background there. The fact that her picture was all over the place was worrying her immensely.

Petra had been inclined to agree but she, too, was concerned. "Look," she said. "I'm bloody knackered. Let's find somewhere to stay for today and probably tonight as well, then we'll leave early in the morning. Clarke might have got back to us by then, told us what the state of play is and then we can make a more informed decision."

They headed for the next decent-sized town, and then changed their minds again when they found a motorway services that also had a motel. Lauren waited in the car while Petra booked them in. Petra saw Lauren into the twin room, then went off to find them both some breakfast. When she came back a little later with a selection of fast food, she found Lauren skimming through her phone looking at the news sites.

"Free Wi-Fi," Lauren said. "So I don't have to think about running out of credit."

"Find anything interesting?"

"Well, my dad has really gone to town on this publicity stuff. You'd think he actually liked me from the sound of it. I just wonder who suggested it to him — it's not the kind of thing he'd have thought about himself."

No, Petra thought, it wasn't the kind of thing Kyle Sykes would have come up with. Unlike the Perrins. Gus employed a web designer, and a couple of freelance bods to keep things up to date. Gus Perrin's public business profile was slick and corporate. He even had a Twitter account.

"I've been thinking," Lauren said, putting her phone down and opening a paper-wrapped burger. "God, I've eaten so much junk food this last week. Anyway, I've been thinking, what about asking those friends of yours? The one you borrowed the car and the dogs from."

Petra shook her head. "I don't want to involve anybody else if we can help it."

"I didn't mean involve them in anything dangerous; I mean maybe swap cars, that sort of stuff. If anybody figures out what you're driving, and if you're right about my dad having police informants, or even the Perrins having police informants, then all they'd have to do is look at the ANPR cameras. We've done a lot of miles on the motorway."

She's right, Petra thought. Nobody should be able to connect the little car she was driving at the moment to either Petra Merrow or Pat, but that didn't mean it couldn't happen. And she knew the Perrins had access to the ANPR network — though not exactly how.

"I'll give it some thought," she said. Involving those particular friends brought a whole load of complications with it. But if she had to . . .

"So, what does the news say?" she asked Lauren again.

"There's an interview on one of the news sites with Kristy Young's mother. She cried almost all the way through it, said he'd been a good boy, that he'd just fallen in with a bad crowd but that he had had a good job." Lauren scoffed. "A good job employed by my father. Except, as he always tells everybody, he doesn't employ anybody. They're all 'freelancers'. So Kristy actually worked for an agency that my dad owns."

"That your dad owns?"

"That a shell company my dad's involved with — owns," Lauren clarified. "God, it's so complicated, I've written as much of it down as I can remember, but now I don't know what to do with it."

"Written it down? Can I see?"

For the first time, Lauren looked at her with something like suspicion in her eyes. "How did you actually get to know Harry?" she said. "You still haven't told me that."

No, I haven't, have I? Petra thought. She took another bite of her own burger, aware that Lauren was watching her closely.

"It's not that difficult a question," Lauren told her. "So stop playing for time and just give me an answer. I'm only trusting you because Harry said I should. Because Harry thought you were worth his while trusting, and there aren't many people Harry thought that about."

"No, I don't suppose there were. OK, so a few years ago, just after Jean died, Harry went off for a bit. You know that. What you don't know is that Harry contacted someone. A colleague of mine, and said he wanted out. Harry had had enough. And then I think he wished he'd made the move sooner."

"Harry would never have left me." Lauren looked stricken for a moment. "Oh my God, he didn't leave me, did he? He hung around because of me. Was it because of me?"

Petra hesitated. "Mostly," she said gently. She watched the emotions flit across the girl's face. "Harry and Jean loved you very much. They were terribly worried about what the future held for you, I know that. Harry had seen too many good people taken down by your father's ambition. After your mother was . . . murdered . . . Harry realized just how crazy Kyle Sykes was. I think that was a real wake-up call for him. Then Jean died, and I think he felt he had very little left to lose. He agreed, under some duress, you have to understand, to quietly pass bits and pieces of information our way."

Lauren's eyes widened, but Petra had the impression that she had just confirmed what the girl had already suspected. She watched as Lauren consciously squared her shoulders, bracing herself as though for another blow.

"And were you involved in this, this coercion, this decision-making? Did you put pressure on Harry? Didn't you know what risks he was taking? That your lot lost two undercovers who my father knew about? I heard him boasting about it, how he found out *and* how they disposed of the rubbish."

Interesting, Petra thought. "And have you written about that in your notebook?" she asked.

Again, the slight look of suspicion crossed Lauren's face. "You know what, I'm not sure if I can trust you with whatever is in my notebook, or what's in my head, or anything else. Yes, you've proved yourself so far, but maybe you're also doing this because it's a way of getting advancement, or because you've got some kind of moral notion of the right thing to do, or because it's your job, and I know you think that Harry made a lot of bad decisions, but you know what? He made them for all the right reasons. He wasn't doing it because it was a job, or because somebody told him to, or even because somebody paid him." She looked closely at Petra, and then added, "I suppose you lot did pay. I suppose he was trying to serve two masters. Poor old Harry, you lot just used him the same as my father always used him. But you know what, Harry did what he did because he loved me, because he cared, because he was a good man at heart. I'm not sure if you're a good person, I haven't decided that yet."

"That's OK," Petra said, "because just lately, I'm not sure either. But the way I see it, we're both in trouble. We don't want your dad or any of the Perrins catching up with us and right now, I'm not sure who to trust inside the police, either. Somebody told somebody about Frankland, that despite the fact that he was supposed to be retired, he was still running at least one undercover operation. For all I know, I might not have been the only one. Now Frankland is dead and as it happens, he was also a friend of mine. Someone I valued. Look, you've got a right to be pissed off and you've got a right to be mistrustful and you've got a right to be angry and all of the other things you're feeling at the moment. But the way I figure it is, so do I. So let's stop talking about motives and let's stop talking about who can be trusted, because right now, you and I have to work together if we're going to get through this alive. Agreed?"

Petra could see the girl considering this carefully. She found herself wondering if Lauren had ever done anything spontaneous in her entire life until she had killed Charlie Perrin. She guessed that Lauren had spent her life standing on the sidelines, weighing the odds before making any decision. She found herself warming to the girl.

"OK," Lauren said. "But if we're going to get out of this, we need information. We need the full picture. So you and

I, we're going to talk, and we're going to pool our resources. I'll tell you what I know and you tell me what you know and we'll see if we can figure out how far my dad's web spreads. Who might help us and who will give us away in a heartbeat." She reached for a cardboard carton of chips. They were pretty cold now, but they were salty and well-seasoned so she didn't really care.

It was Petra's turn to consider. Finally, she nodded. "Toby Clarke," she said. "I know absolutely nothing about him that makes me doubt his word, or his honesty. I think he'll do his best but what I don't know is what pressure can be brought to bear on him from above. You and I right now, we're kind of freelance, but Toby's got to obey the rules."

Lauren laughed at that. "Freelance what?" she asked. "Freelance fugitives? Not much of a job description, is it?"

CHAPTER 42

Billy Hunter had rarely been invited into his boss's inner sanctum, the little room at the back that the family always referred to as "the snug". His companions had been left waiting for him in a large living room and the atmosphere was not good, Billy thought. *Definitely not good.*

He was alone with his boss and his boss's son. Billy had always thought of John as something of an administrator. The Perrins hired in all the bodies they needed for the rough stuff, but looking at John now, standing stony-faced next to his father, Billy was not so sure the Perrins needed anyone else. In his day, Gus Perrin would have taken care of employees who displeased him with his own bare hands. Wheelchair-bound as he was, Billy knew that his upper body strength was still as impressive as it had ever been.

"You've got to believe me, I knew nothing about this. She had me fooled, all down the line, she had me fooled." He paused, a moment of regret seeping through. "Are we sure about this? I mean I know she's gone off somewhere, but maybe she's gone off taking pictures. Are we sure about this?"

"Sure as can be," Perrin said. His tone was casual. They might have been discussing the weather or what bet to place. Both Billy and Perrin liked the horses and had spent time together perusing the odds. Billy had been sure that his employer actually liked him, but now none of that mattered.

"So how did you find out? When did you find out?" It must have been a recent discovery, Billy thought, otherwise they'd never have sent him and the others up north on that wild goose chase after the Sykes girl. He noticed that Kyle Sykes had been left sitting in Perrin's living room looking very uncomfortable. It occurred to Billy that Kyle Sykes was probably in as much trouble as he was. Sykes's own men had been nowhere in evidence.

"A little birdie dropped the name in our direction. Trying to keep himself out of trouble, he was. We pressured him for some more information, finally got it yesterday. Our little bird couldn't make a payment, so we traded. He let on that they'd got someone inside our business. Said he knew the name of the cop who was still handling the undercover."

Perrin leaned forward in his chair. There was nothing casual about him now.

"But you had her checked out." Billy had taken an anxious step backwards. "Pat was clean, you said, so you said . . ."

"Seems I was wrong," Perrin said. "And you know how I hate to be proved wrong. Three sodding years, Billy. Three sodding years she's been sharing your bed and God knows what pillow talk. Who the fuck knows what you've told her in all that time."

"Nothing! I've told her nothing. I told to keep her nose out. She took pictures, that was all. I know how to keep business separate, Gus. You always tell us that. Business and pleasure got to be kept separate."

Billy was thinking furiously. What little bird? Who had been talking to Freddie? Then he suddenly realized, remembering the visit to his house Pat had asked him about. Freddie Benson's late-night visit with that cop. "Henderson. Henderson told Freddie. You trust fucking Henderson?"

"No, we trust what the fucking handler told us by the time Freddie and our boys had finished with him." Perrin chuckled. It was not an encouraging kind of laugh. Billy quailed. "Apparently, he was a tough old bird, took a long time for them to get anything out of him, but he finally let slip that the undercover was a woman. Which narrowed down our options nicely."

Billy seized on the one small fragment of information that gave him some hope. "Then you don't know it was Pat, it could have been any number of women."

"It was Pat," Perrin said, with a cold finality that weakened Billy's legs and had his bowels turning over.

"Gus. Boss." He looked over at John, hoping for an ally there. The door behind Billy opened. Two men walked in and seized him by the arms. John took a gun from his father's desk drawer.

"Make it quick," Gus told him. "Billy might be a fool, but he's been a good boy. However, when we catch up with that bitch . . ."

"Gus, please—"

He'd seen men plead with Gus before, and the good it did them. But something primal had taken over and to his shame, he just couldn't stop himself.

They marched him out into the corridor and down towards the kitchen, out through the back door and into the gardens beyond.

CHAPTER 43

Frankland's house was cordoned off and a small knot of journalists stood at the end of the road. They parted reluctantly as Clarke's car nosed its way through. A reporter from one of the regionals recognized him and he heard a shouted question. He parked in front of the scientific support van and made his way into the house, pausing only to sign himself in and ask the constable on duty who was the officer in charge. He was told that DC Denise Allwood was managing the scene and that she was upstairs. *She must've left just before I went to confront Henderson,* Clarke thought. He imagined she'd be expecting him to arrive with his tail between his legs, having been reprimanded for his attitude in the briefing room. But Clarke had forgotten that gossip travels faster than pizza delivery and when she met him at the top of the stairs, it was pretty obvious that she'd been brought up to speed on his confrontation with Henderson and probably on the arrival of the superintendent.

"What the hell is going on?" Allwood wanted to know. "I mean—"

"Truthfully? I don't fucking know," Clarke told her. "What do we have here? He was found due to an anonymous tip-off, is that right?"

Denise sighed but nodded, and they both took refuge in the minutiae and discipline of process. "I'm guessing you know who made that phone call," she said. "But yes, anonymous phone call came at 11.25 p.m. First officer attending arrived ten minutes after that, found the patio door open and came inside. The call came from a burner phone, which has now presumably been disposed of, or at least, the SIM changed. Though you probably know about that, too."

Clarke held up a hand to stop her. "And then what?"

She cast him a sour, impatient look but continued. "The woman who made the call told us exactly what to expect in terms of where to find the body. First officer on scene came up and looked, went back down, puked in the garden. His colleague came up and looked and—"

"I get the picture. And time of the death is estimated to be somewhere between nine and ten? That's precise."

"Based on ambient temperature, and liver temp. The liver was — well, as you could see from the photographs, the liver was exposed. The doctor arrived just after our people did." She glanced towards the bedroom where Frankland had been found. "He was supposed to have retired, you know that? He shouldn't have even been involved in this. They managed to swing it by calling him a consultant or some rubbish?"

"I know that. But running an undercover is the kind of job you can't just hand over. The more people in the loop the more dangerous it is. And this one was in deep cover, had been for a while."

"Yes, but I mean, a woman? Whose stupid idea was that?"

"I thought you believed in equal opportunities?" Clarke's attempt at levity fell flat.

She glared at him. "It's nothing to do with that. A male undercover officer would have a choice about what kind of role they played in that kind of organization. You know what attitudes they have towards women, both the Perrins and the Sykeses of this world. Anybody that gets involved in that, they would have to be in a relationship with someone. Would have to get involved, and I mean *really* involved. I know there's legislation that says undercovers are not supposed to do that. A man may have managed to keep things separate, but a woman couldn't. Think about it. A woman who wants to get anywhere near anybody in an organization like that, they've got to get themselves a boyfriend, a lover. It's all men at the top, there's no space for a woman to infiltrate — they've got to be totally involved. So they'd have to be sleeping with the bastard, otherwise they'd stick out like a sore whatsit and their cover would be blown in no time. If she's been in deep cover for three years, she's been involved with somebody."

Clarke suddenly realized that he'd not actually thought much about that side of things. He knew that Petra had been living with Billy Hunter, but he'd been thinking about it on the level of her being a police officer, not on the level of her being a woman. It was not lost on him that there'd been a number of court cases in recent years when male undercover officers had had to face up to their actions and responsibilities. In the seventies and eighties and probably later in some cases, they had gone undercover to gather intelligence within various political organizations, and several had started serious relationships with women within those organizations, some had even had children. The story, when it had broken, had had major ramifications that had been felt throughout the police force. But he'd never given the reverse position any thought, and he really should have done. Petra — "Pat", as Billy Hunter had known her — had given three years of her life to this, lived in Billy's house, slept in his bed, been emotionally involved with him . . . The thought of someone like Petra being emotionally entangled with Billy Hunter seemed laughable. But then again, how well did he actually know her? The answer to that was, not at all.

Was Lauren really safe with Petra? He still didn't know exactly what the connection had been between Petra Merrow and Harry Prentice. Lauren had told him about the phone number and that Petra had known Harry. "*Not quite a friend*" was how she said Harry had described her.

"No," he said. "You've got a point. I hadn't thought of it that way."

Allwood looked slightly mollified. "You want to go into the room?" she asked. She stood aside and Clarke moved into the doorway and surveyed the scene, comparing the photographs he had so recently studied. He had not known Frankland well, but this still affected him deeply.

"I liked him a lot," Allwood said. "His door was always open if you wanted to talk, and he was always kind of quiet, not showy. He never put anyone down. He was just confident in his own abilities, and I liked that."

"Has there been any progress made on the other three? I skimmed the notes, but maybe you can bring me up to speed." Clarke could feel her need to tell him that those other three didn't matter, that one of their own was dead and he should be focusing on that, as Henderson obviously had been doing. "It's all linked," Clarke told her. "And we're not going to be able to stop it until we can see the bigger picture."

She gestured impatiently. "Interviews with family suggest that each one of them received a phone call about an hour before leaving home. Another one just before they headed out the door. Phil Stern and his son drove off together. Somebody in a black car came and collected Kristy Young, but the family won't speculate as to who might have been driving or if they'd seen the car before. All three left home at around eight p.m. The families assumed they were going out for a drink because that's what they'd been told."

"And they were the last sightings?"

"Looks like it, yes. None of the family has said that the three men seemed worried, or anxious. They just got themselves ready like they were going to the pub and that was the last anyone saw of them."

"And I'm assuming Kyle Sykes is alibied."

"Half a dozen witnesses, from about seven in the evening to about the same time the following morning. No forensics, no DNA, no weapon and no witnesses to a vehicle dumping bodies in the early hours of the morning. There aren't any houses down that way, not even student flats. It's all up for redevelopment."

"Convenient. Not even any rough sleepers?"

"Not since last year. It's so damn exposed, even the rough sleepers avoid it. They prefer to be closer to town."

Clarke nodded. There had been two deaths last winter, when the weather had been exceptionally cold. Two men sharing an improvised shelter had frozen to death. Word was, it was now seen as an unlucky place. Clarke had seen kids riding dirt bikes on the rough ground, and he knew that syringes were regularly found there by dog walkers coming up off the canal bank. They often complained about it to the police. There was no shelter anywhere, no one living nearby, no industry where people might be working late. Which, no doubt, was why it had been chosen as the dumping ground.

He glanced back at the blood-soaked bed and, though he really didn't want to have the idea put in his mind, he knew he still had to ask. "How long do they think . . ."

"They tortured him for?" She shrugged but he could see the tears threaten. "Hours, they think. His hands and ankles had been tied to the legs of the bed. He twisted and fought so much, the rope cut through to the bone. Can you imagine that? I mean, can you just imagine?"

I can now, Clarke thought. Some vague memory surfaced about Special Forces being taught to fight one type of pain with another, one they could control. But he had no notion if that was just myth and hype or if it was something Frankland might have done deliberately. He found himself hoping so, hoping what had been a very brave man had maintained some small modicum of control.

His phone rang. It was Superintendent Craig ordering his return.

CHAPTER 44

Clarke arrived back to find his colleagues in a frenzy of moving desks, tech support knee-deep in additional terminals and people he didn't know vying for territory in the inadequate space. A lot seemed to have changed since he'd left to go to Frankland's house. He glanced at his watch and noted that he'd only been gone a couple of hours.

"Toby." Hopkins sidled over. She handed him a welcome mug of coffee.

"What the hell's going on?"

"Henderson's gone, MIT is moving in. I mean, that was bound to happen, but . . ."

This is happening in a big hurry, Clarke thought, finishing where she had trailed off.

"Craig's waiting for you in his office. With someone called Crenshaw. He's gold commander for—"

"I know Crenshaw," he told her. Was this a good thing? At this particular moment, Clarke was no longer certain. He didn't have long to think about it, because Craig must have heard his voice. He stuck his round, grey head round the door of his office and called Clarke inside.

"Good luck," Hopkins told him.

"Yeah. Right."

Shaking hands with his old boss, he held up the coffee Hopkins had given him by way of declining the offer for more coffee. Taking a seat on one of the uncomfortable, barely padded chairs, he waited for the inevitable, not sure just how much trouble he might be in. He decided to take the initiative. "So, DCI Henderson—"

"Had some leave due to him and is taking a break. No doubt he'll be signed off due to stress."

"So he'll be signed off sick and offered an early retirement package," Clarke said. "Henderson should be—"

"Not your decision. Henderson will be dealt with through the proper channels and is no longer your problem. Now, I suggest if you want to avoid or at least mitigate those same channels, you bring us up to speed. Putting it simply, Clarke, what the fuck is happening here? No omissions, no fudging."

"First things first," Crenshaw said, taking over from Craig. "The girl and the UC. What's their status?"

"Safe, for now," Clarke told him. "But, sir, I don't know exactly where they are and, given developments, neither do I think I should—"

"We may well be a bit beyond that consideration," Crenshaw told him. He handed two newspapers and a folder of other material to Clarke. "Someone will spot them and someone will call that number." He tapped at a hotline number printed just below the newspaper headline that screamed *Missing Girl, Undercover Officer in Kidnap Scandal*. "So far, the families are several steps ahead of us and it's not yet midday."

Clarke skimmed the material he'd been given. It was an incredibly mixed bag. It was as though a gaggle of tabloid headline writers had brainstormed variations on the kidnap, corruption and undercover scandal and thrown every possible angle onto the page. On television and the internet, too, he noted, judging by the screengrabs and printouts in the folder.

Rumour and misinformation. People trafficking the idea that Lauren might have been kidnapped by a disgruntled employee. That the police had no interest in the teenage daughter of a man they regarded to be a known criminal. That she had been with her fiancé on the night she disappeared and the possibility he might have been killed defending her.

Other stories suggested that the police, apparently working on false intelligence, had embedded an undercover officer within a perfectly legitimate business corporation — with photos of "Pat".

There was an interview with friends of Pat (a gallery owner, and a female wedding photographer). Claims that the police, despite recent high-profile prosecutions, were back to their "old tricks". The words "*honeytrap*" and "*setup*" came up a number of times, along with the observation that Pat was a very attractive woman with "obvious charms". The use of a female undercover clearly added a level of titillation to proceedings. There were screengrabs taken of several internet sites of claims that Billy Hunter, who had lived with Pat for three years, had now taken his own life.

"Is he dead?" Clarke wanted to know.

"Found an hour ago. Single bullet wound. It *could* have been self-inflicted, but—" Craig shrugged. "Essentially, they've just thrown everything out there and are waiting to see what sticks.

"We've got a press conference scheduled for late afternoon and our media liaison are working flat out to try and control this, but we need to get those two women off the streets and into safe custody. And we need to do that now. It will only be a matter of time before someone spots them. It will also only be a matter of time before someone recognizes Pat and comes up with her real identity and who knows what further shit will hit the fan then." Craig dropped down into a chair as though the entire business was suddenly too exhausting.

This is bad, Clarke thought. He was also taken aback by how fast this had all moved. "How have they managed to do this so quickly? How deep does this all go? I mean, Henderson—"

"Our media experts believe much of this to be pure speculation. Putting two and two together and spinning it to make fourteen. Not much of it stands up to analysis, but that's not going to stop the speculation, and it's not going to stop these stories from getting bigger. You can imagine, this is network gold."

"But they've moved so fast."

"Gus Perrin is a major shareholder in the Radcliff media group," Crenshaw told him.

Clarke hadn't known that. Looking at the two senior officers, he didn't think they had, either. "Through yet another shell company?"

Crenshaw laughed bitterly. "No, all open and above board. His name is on the register at Companies House, alongside fully registered interests in his hotels and golf courses. He started off as a minor shareholder and he's been building his interest incrementally over the past decade. Up until now, the only crossover we've ever been aware of happens when the local papers in the group turn up to celebrate yet another Gus Perrin gift to the poor and needy."

Clarke turned to his old boss. "What do you want from me now, then?"

Craig's reply was urgent. "We need to get Lauren and the officer properly protected and you need to share, Clarke. Tell us what the fuck you've got yourself mixed up in so we can start to make some sense of it and start the counter-attack."

* * *

Petra set her notebook down and stretched, crunching her back. She and Lauren had spent the morning exchanging intelligence and consolidating what they knew. She had been surprised at just how much the younger woman understood was going on and how much more she had guessed.

The USB drive that had been sent to Petra by Frankland was still in the lining of her coat and she wished she had a means to look at it, but they had no computer access so she knew that would have to wait. There was no doubt as to its importance. But this left her with two questions. Frankland had evidently copied this intel from his own files, probably from his own computer. Who else now had that information? More importantly, he had obviously been fearful of exposure — hers and presumably his own — and that fear had been justified. Petra wondered if he had feared for his life when he'd sent her the drive, or whether he had just been afraid that her operation had been compromised. It would be typical of Frankland that his strategy was to give her the intel, then leave it up to her to decide what action should be taken to keep herself safe. Frankland was no fool. Surely had he suspected that someone might break into his house, torture him, kill him, he would have sought sanctuary elsewhere.

No, she decided. He had been wary, had wanted her to have the USB drive as insurance. *"Forewarned is forearmed"* had always been Frankland's motto. So he had known that something was wrong, that intelligence was leaking from somewhere to the wrong people, but he had not yet been *so* anxious that he'd felt personally threatened or even that he should tell her to withdraw immediately.

So what had changed?

"Henderson," Petra said aloud.

Henderson had let something slip, something that allowed the Perrins to put everything together. *Led them straight to Frankland and straight to me.*

Lauren looked up when she had spoken. She had been studying the notes that now spread across both beds. She glanced at her watch. "News time soon," she said. She slid off the bed and went to look out of the window. The view was a line of bushes and a corner of the car park. And rain, really heavy rain. "You think he'll call this afternoon?"

Clarke. She meant Clarke, of course. *She's scared and she's bored*, Petra thought, that odd combination of feelings that after a time became unbearable. That often caused individuals who should have known better to precipitate action, just so they could feel more in control. Petra glared at her phone, willing it to do something. She'd seen it happen in her military days. She was impressed by how much self-control Lauren was actually exhibiting.

The phone rang. Petra snatched it up and answered on the second ring. Across the room, she could see Lauren tense. Then she came over to listen to the call. Clarke rang off moments later and Lauren and Petra immediately logged on to the internet, scanning news sites.

"Fuck," Lauren said.

"Pack all our notes, fold them small so they fit in your bag, coat lining, any non-obvious place and then we're out of here."

"Should we wait for him?" Lauren asked, but she was already sorting their possessions ready for departure. She too would rather be on the move.

"We need to get off the motorway, get away from prying eyes, then I'll let him know where he can collect us from. We'll follow him. I'm not losing the car."

Lauren nodded. She was stuffing papers into her bag. She stopped. She shoved one of the beds aside and studied the floor beneath.

"Concrete floor," Petra said. But Lauren's impulse was right. The notes they had made, the information they had pooled, they should protect that. Petra was willing to believe that Clarke was trustworthy, but beyond that . . .

The beds had a divan base lifted from the floor by small pads. Lauren slid her fingers beneath the bed. The underside had fabric stretched across the framework and stapled into place. Using the end of the car key, she worked one of the staples loose and created a gap through which everything could be posted. Then she moved the bed back into place. She pulled on her coat, checked the pockets, the lining. Money, phone, gun, all in place. Thank the lord for padded coats and all that could be concealed in them. Then they were back in Petra's little hatchback and on their way.

CHAPTER 45

The newly arranged safe house was on the edge of a modern, part-built estate, set apart from the rest and concealed behind a high fence at the end of a cul-de-sac. They could see as they drove up that it backed onto an abandoned industrial space. Cranes and demolition equipment were parked beside what looked like old factory. Eventually this house would be at the heart of the site but for now, it felt almost isolated.

A few families had moved into the houses on the other side of the estate, close to the show homes and the main road, but deeper in, the roads had not yet been made up and the next batch of homes scheduled for sale was not due on the market until well into the new year.

It was late enough in the afternoon for dusk to be closing in as Clarke drove onto the muddy patch that would eventually be the driveway. Petra, spotting that there was room for her to get down the other side of the house, drove round to the back of the property and turned the car back to face the road again.

"Just in case," she told Lauren.

Lauren nodded. "Not a place I'd have chosen," she said. They got out of the car and watched as Clarke walked round to join them. "I wish there was more light. I want to see what's out there."

A third car had driven in and parked in the unmade road. Three men got out. "Armed police," Petra said.

"Better to be safe," Clarke told her.

"If you say so."

"Shall we go inside?"

They followed him through the back door. The armed officers had spread out. Lauren was envious of their torches. She stood in the doorway, watching closely as they examined the perimeter, noting that there was a wheelie bin outside the back door which, placed on its side, would just about allow her to scramble over the fence.

"There's food," Clarke said. "Gas for the cooker hasn't been connected yet, but there's an electric hotplate and a microwave."

One of the armed officers had come through into the kitchen. "This is . . . Pete. He'll be staying in the house tonight. One of the other two will be stationed in their vehicle and the third will alternate with him on patrol. By tomorrow, we should have a clearer picture of what's happening. It's going to be OK, Lauren."

"Is it?" She studied "Pete" carefully. A tall, heavily built man with a sharp haircut, he looked to Lauren as though he might be ex-military. She knew the type. Her dad employed enough of them.

She left the kitchen and went off to familiarize herself with the rest of the house. Beds had been made up in two of the rooms. The windows had been locked and Lauren could find no keys. The landing window wasn't designed to be opened. *Rats in a trap*, Lauren thought.

She went back downstairs to find that "Pete" was loitering in the hall, evidently waiting for her to reappear. She ignored him, examined the downstairs rooms. TV, sofa, a stack of books and magazines. The room had obviously been hastily arranged and she wondered vaguely if they had taken the couch from one of the show homes. It had that "for show, not for comfort" look to it that she associated with posh lounges.

The other two rooms were empty. One, she supposed, would be a dining room and the other a study or home office. On the windowsill of this room, she spotted what she had been searching for. A key to the window lock. Lauren breathed a sigh of relief and pocketed it.

She returned to the kitchen. Petra was preparing sandwiches and listening as Clarke updated her. Lauren watched her face as he told her about Billy Hunter's death. Petra didn't give much away, but Lauren noted the slight tightening around her mouth that spoke volumes.

"Did you like him?"

"Like him? No, not really. But he was better than most."

"And he's dead because of you."

"Lauren!" Clarke was shocked. "You don't have to be—"

"No, she's right," Petra told him.

"It's no good dressing it up," Lauren returned. "People are dead because of what we've done and we have to live with that. Deal with it."

She turned on her heel and went off to inspect the house once again.

Clarke watched her go. "And how is *she* dealing with all this?"

"Better than I'd expect." Petra sighed. "Look, we should all eat something. What about Pete and his friends?"

"Just feed Pete for now. I'll make sure the other two are sorted before I go."

Petra nodded and returned to her sandwich-making, taking refuge in what Lauren called her "normal".

Clarke went to see what Lauren was up to. He found her upstairs, stripping the two single beds. She glanced up at him. "Can you give me a hand?"

"Sure, with what?"

"I want to bring the mattresses down. I'm not sleeping up here."

"OK, and why's that?"

"The windows don't open, so there's no way out. Downstairs, there's at least the two doors."

"Lauren, you don't need to do this. You don't need to worry—"

She glared at him.

"OK, I'll help you. Grab that end and I'll go backwards."

By the time they'd got the first mattress downstairs, food was ready. Pete sat down at the kitchen table with them and for the most part, they ate in silence. Clarke announced that he'd give Lauren a hand with the second mattress and then he'd better be off.

"We're sleeping downstairs?" Petra asked.

"Windows are locked. Double-glazing's hard enough to break and this place is triple-glazed."

"Fair enough," Petra told her. "I've told Pete to lock the doors but leave the keys in place."

Lauren glanced over at the back door and nodded her approval. Clarke went a little later, leaving Petra and Lauren busy making up the beds in the living room. He checked in with the other two officers and called Superintendent Craig to update him, then drove away, knowing there was nothing more he could do but unable to shake the feeling that he should be doing more.

Belatedly, he wondered if Lauren still had her gun. He should have taken it from her, should at least have insisted that Petra take charge of it. *No, what I should have done is disarm her back when we first met.* So why hadn't he? And why hadn't he even mentioned to his bosses that the girl had a gun?

The answer to that was easy. Lauren's paranoia had infected him, thoroughly and absolutely. *And anyway,* he reflected, *was it really paranoia when the world really was out to get you?*

CHAPTER 46

The next day seemed almost unreasonably calm. Clarke had finally managed a few hours' sleep and a decent breakfast. More importantly, he turned up for work having showered and changed his clothes. He arrived to find his usual desk space had been divided between three newcomers and their computer equipment, and that Hopkins had jealously guarded a portion of her own workspace for his use.

Clarke surveyed the room, attempted to count the bodies and gave up, speculating that they'd almost certainly exceeded fire regulations, packing so many into such a small space.

There was a memo waiting for him on his bit of Hopkins desk, from the CPS, asking him to call a Miss Johnson about Miss Sykes's case. It took him a moment and two readings of the note to realize that this was about Lauren Sykes's possible involvement in Charlie Perrin's death and yet another reading to realize that this was about Lauren being a possible *witness* to Charlie's death. *So which was it?*

Hopkins grinned at him. "Looks like the CPS are taking their lead from the tabloids. Fiancée kidnapped, husband-to-be shot trying to defend her honour or some such. What happens when they find out what really happened, do you think? Will she be charged, seeing as she actually did shoot him?"

"It was self-defence," Clarke said. "But for now, we go along with whatever the CPS think it is."

Hopkins looked amused. "It's all getting a bit complicated, boss." Then she glanced around the room and asked quietly, "What did Henderson actually do? I mean, we all heard you yelling at him, but—"

"DCI Henderson is currently on leave," he told her. "Just now, that's all there is to it. I'd better give this Miss Johnson a ring."

Hopkins looked disappointed. "People are talking," she said.

"The rumour mill is always churning."

"But they're saying that Henderson might be in deeper than . . . That there might be someone else implicated. You know, working for one of the OCGs."

Clarke frowned. "Who told you that?"

She shook her head, looked embarrassed. "Just something I heard." He waited, but she seemed reluctant to say any more about it. "You'd better make your phone call," she told him. She plucked a folder from her desk and walked off with it.

She looks uneasy, Clarke thought.

Half an hour later, the Lauren Sykes problem still as tangled as ever, he was reporting to Craig.

"Crenshaw's organized the shift change at the house. His people. Ours will return this evening," Craig told him.

"Is that wise? I mean, the fewer people involved the better."

"You can't leave the same officers on permanent deployment."

"And this way you get to share the overtime with another division," Clarke commented.

"Don't you take that tone. If you'd handled this by the book, the girl would have been taken into protective custody long since. Formal statements would have been taken and arrests probably made. As it is—"

"You're not thinking of bringing her here?"

"At some point, she's going to have to be interviewed under caution and our undercover officer is going to have to answer for her part in all of this."

"But you can't bring them here. Not yet."

"I wasn't planning on bringing them here. Crenshaw's organizing that end of things. The plan is that later on today, or possibly tomorrow morning, they'll be taken to your old divisional headquarters and the initial interviews will take place there. We need leverage, Clarke. Time and tide are against us and we need their statements."

"I want to be present. Lauren and . . . Pat, they trust me."

"And apparently, you don't trust us." Craig let the statement hang. "Pat," he said, "the undercover, is one of our own. I fail to understand your reluctance to reveal her identity. It's only a matter of time before the whole world knows. You must be aware of that."

"Frankland didn't tell you," Clarke said. "I'm not going to be the one who does."

"I could have you suspended."

"And what good would that do?" He could see how angry Craig was becoming but all he felt right now was weary. True, Petra's identity would soon be revealed and, he had to ask himself, did any of that matter now? Probably not, but as he'd just told Craig, he wasn't going to give anyone anything they didn't actually need. "I want to be there," he emphasized.

Craig looked as though he was about to object. Then he nodded. "Contact Crenshaw, make the arrangements."

* * *

Back at the safe house, Lauren had watched the shift change closely. She'd not spoken to the other two and not had much to say to Pete. Their new Pete was a sandy-haired man whereas the first Pete's hair had been brown but that apart, they seemed to have been poured into the same mould. She was restless, impatient, watching the news obsessively, channel-hopping until Petra eventually took the remote away and found a film. "God, look what I've found," Petra said. Bruce Willis doing his thing yet again.

They sat together on the uncomfortable, show house sofa and watched in silence as inside the Nakatomi tower Bruce Willis, stripped down to his vest, pulled shards of glass from his bare feet.

"You OK?" Petra asked.

Lauren lifted her hands to her face and wiped away the tears. "Yeah, I'm fine," she said.

CHAPTER 47

Sam Barker had been given her instructions. *Go to the police station, as you agreed you would and tell the police officers that it was absolutely nothing. That nothing untoward had happened. That you had an argument with Marty, Carole intervened and whacked him in the face but that it's all fine now.*

Sam had managed to get a couple of hours sleep after the doctor had given her painkillers and strapped her fingers up. She'd not intended to go to sleep, but sheer exhaustion had won and she'd been woken up just before nine by a young woman she vaguely recognized as being one of the kitchen staff. She had been sleeping on Carole's bed in what had been Carole's old room, but of Carole there was absolutely no sign. The girl who brought breakfast on a tray said that Mrs Josephs had left a couple of hours before and that Mr Perrin wanted to see her. "Mr John Perrin," she had elaborated.

Sam hadn't wanted anything to eat, but she'd drunk the coffee gratefully. Before going downstairs for her meeting with John, she had padded along the corridor to the guestroom to see if the two women were still there. She'd found the same girl who'd brought her breakfast making the beds and she didn't know anything about the two other women, only that the "guests" had left with Mrs Josephs that morning.

So why hadn't Carole woken her before she'd gone? Sam felt thoroughly hung-over and realized that the doctor must've given her something to make her sleep as well as something to kill the pain. She had found a little pack with some pills in it on the bedside table, her own name written on the label. They had been marked codeine, but feeling suspicious of this she had left them where they were. Her hand was throbbing now.

Downstairs one of the men hanging around in the hallway had directed her to where John was waiting. He, too, had been having a late breakfast. Of Gus Perrin, there had been no sign. She had stood in the doorway and waited to be told what to do next, then had noticed that a suitcase, evidently taken from the house she had shared with Marty, had been placed on a chair alongside her handbag. She'd completely forgotten about her bag, but then remembered that she must have left it at Carole's cottage.

John had finally glanced up from the newspaper. From where she'd been standing, Sam had seen a picture of Lauren Sykes and the woman Sam had known as Pat on the front page. John had tossed it across the table towards her.

"Make no mistake," he'd told her. "They'll be found and dealt with. Now, my sister has a soft spot for you and, as it turns out, we're prepared to draw a line. Carole promised you money — that's been transferred into your account in lieu of notice, and there's a phone number for you to ring if you need more. Like I say, my sister has a soft spot for you. Marty's fucked off, so you can forget about him. So what you're going to do now is you're going to go down to the police station, like you promised you would last night, and tell them nothing was wrong. And then you're going to piss off. Don't care where. You understand."

Sam had nodded. She understood all right. "Where's Carole?"

"Gone away for a bit of a holiday. Not that it's any of your business now."

And at that, she had been dismissed. A car had been waiting and she had been frightened for a moment about

241

where it was going to take her. But it had simply driven her to the police station, stopped outside and the driver had told her to get out. And so here she was, sitting in an interview room, ready to give her account of what was supposed to have happened the night before.

The problem was, Sam was not about to do that. Her hand was still throbbing and she used that pain to give herself courage.

"I was supposed to come here this morning and tell you that it's all fine. That nothing happened last night, just a misunderstanding. But that bastard broke my fingers. That fucking bastard broke my fingers. So if he thinks I'm going to do what he tells me . . ."

There were two offices in the room with her and one was DS Hopkins. Hopkins excused herself for the tape, left the room and called Clarke, wanting to know what the hell she should do next.

Clarke was on his way to visit Petra and Lauren. He debated about turning around and following her into the interview room. "Take a statement, I'll sort it out when I get back," he decided.

CHAPTER 48

Clarke called on them and told them about the interviews under caution. "Craig wanted them to happen today," he said, "but events have run a bit ahead of us, so they'll begin first thing tomorrow."

"What events?"

"Sam Barker type events. You remember her?"

"Carole's assistant. Yes, of course. Is she OK?"

"She's more or less fine, I suppose, seeing as how our definitions of 'fine' are a bit flexible at the moment. She walked into the police station this morning, said she'd come to make a statement about an alleged domestic we'd attended last night. She has two badly broken fingers on her left hand and was dropped off at the police station in a car registered to one of Perrin's employment agencies. It's likely Gus Perrin intended this as just more mud in the water. She's being statemented as we speak, but I'm not sure she's going to stay on message." He relayed what little Hopkins had told him. "The same night you disappeared, her boyfriend, Marty, walked into divisional HQ and made a statement to the effect that Perrin had sent men to beat him up and take Sam away. The officers sent to the Perrin place were persuaded there was nothing amiss. I'm guessing

Sam was sent in to corroborate the Perrins' story, but she's tougher than they thought."

"She always struck me as independently minded. What about Marty? Is he OK?"

"Not a clue. He left divisional headquarters, got a taxi to the railway station, and we're hoping CCTV will give us some idea where he went after that."

"As far away as possible, if he's got any sense." She frowned. "It's going to be tough on him, though. He had a job he loved and a relationship that kept him happy."

"And a boss capable of turning violent at the drop of a hat, though when I spoke to him, he'd seemed to be almost enjoying the fact."

"Anything about my dad?" Lauren hadn't spoken until now.

"Last seen at the Perrins' farm."

Lauren nodded as though that made sense. "Dad wanted me to marry Charlie," she said. "But the thing is, he saw that as a way of keeping control. Keeping something, at least. Gus Perrin had been putting a whole load of pressure on. Buying up shares in Dad's legitimate businesses, moving in on his territories . . . It had taken Dad a while to realize, I think. He thought it was new people moving in, but eventually he realized it was the Perrins."

"So he figured better to be married to the mob than eradicated by them," said Clarke. That made sense of a lot of things. "And how did the Perrins feel about this arrangement?"

She shrugged. "Charlie seemed happy enough. Look, no one told me any of this. I'm just very good at listening at doors and going through my dad's desk when he's not there. I've pieced stuff together and, talking to Petra, I've figured out more of it."

"So, what now?" Petra asked.

"Today, we see what these new developments throw up and then tomorrow I come and collect you, take you over to my old stomping ground and we get you statemented."

"Might take some time." Lauren rolled her eyes.

Clarke got up, ready to go. Lauren laid a hand on his arm. "Wait a minute, there's something else." She exchanged a glance with Petra, who nodded. From a pocket, Petra took the stick drive and handed it over to Clarke.

"What's this?"

"Frankland managed to get it to me, the day before he was killed. I've not had a proper look at it yet, but from what I've seen, he collated the intelligence I'd given him and . . ." She shrugged. "Like I say, I haven't had a proper look at it yet. But it might help you put together a real case against the Perrins."

"And you didn't think to mention this before?"

The look in Petra's eyes hardened. "I hardly know you," she said. "But I've decided to take a chance. This information, maybe it got Frankland killed, maybe it was just that Henderson gave something away, I don't know. But please be careful."

Clarke stared at the innocuous black stick sitting in the palm of his hand and then tucked it in his pocket. "It's going to be all right," he said.

Lauren laughed. "I'm sorry," she told him, "but I don't think you're in charge of deciding that. I'm not sure any of us are."

CHAPTER 49

By the time Clarke returned to the station, Sam Barker was leaving with one of Crenshaw's people and Clarke, unable to be everywhere at once, had to hope that would be all right. He made a beeline for his computer and examined the contents of the stick drive that Petra had entrusted to him. He was shocked by how much intelligence she'd managed to pass on over the three years. How many connections Frankland had made both to open cases and to business arrangements that looked legitimate but that clearly Frankland had had suspicions about.

There were pages of what looked like photocopies of accounts, which were just so many numbers, but what numbers? *Telephone numbers*, Clarke thought, then realized that the figures represented investments, cash and bonds and shares. And there was intelligence concerning Kyle Sykes. It looked like the Perrins had been planning a takeover for quite some time. Sykes's manoeuvrings to unite his family with theirs had probably been too little, too late. Clarke took the time and the precaution of transferring this information onto his own computer and then, as a further precaution, created a file and uploaded the whole lot onto the cloud. While it mapped over, he brought himself up to speed on

Sam Barker's statement and the activity of the major enquiry team. Warrants were being applied for. Clarke had the impression that much of what he'd been involved in was now slipping out of his hands.

Finally, when he was sure everything had been copied, he went to see Superintendent Craig and laid the stick drive on the desk in front of him.

"What's this?" Craig asked, much as Clarke had done himself a few hours earlier.

"Frankland's records. The intelligence he gathered from the undercover, collated with his own enquiries. Truthfully, I don't understand half of it. There are what looks like accounts, lots of figures, lots of speculation, I think, but . . ."

Craig stuck his head out the door and barked out four names. Before Clarke had time to catch up with what was going on, Craig had assembled a team to analyse the data.

He called Lauren and Petra at about eight o'clock. There'd been another shift change, yet another "Pete" was now eating sandwiches at their table. Petra sounded flat and depressed. Lauren just seemed anxious. Clarke gathered that she did not like the new Pete.

"I'll come over first thing in the morning," he promised her. "Things are moving at this end. This will soon be over, Lauren. I promise."

"Promises you can't keep are not worth the breath," she told him. Then she sighed and apologized, "Look, I know you're doing your best, I'm just finding it hard and so is Petra."

Hopkins was calling his name and so he rang off. She pointed to the television in the corner of the incident room. A familiar face. Petra's face, and the information scrolling across the bottom of the screen that told him that she had been identified. DS Petra Merrow, the undercover known as Pat, the one now implicated in the disappearance of Lauren Sykes.

"Great," Clarke muttered. "That's just great."

CHAPTER 50

Smoke. The smell of smoke. It broke through her doze. Lauren jumped up. The room was full of it. It was snaking its way under the small gap beneath the door into the room where Lauren and Petra had been watching the television.

She shook Petra. "Wake up, wake up!"

Petra opened her eyes, blinking at Lauren. "What the hell?" Then she realized what was wrong. "Oh my God."

Lauren went to the living-room door and placed her hands on it. The surface of the door was hot. She glanced at Petra and then took a chance. She opened the door just a crack before slamming it closed again. The hall carpet was fully ablaze, as was the front door. There was no way they could get out that way. "Someone's poured accelerant through the letterbox."

Where are the police that are supposed to be guarding us?

Swiftly, she told Petra what she had seen.

Petra was peering out through the gap in the side of the curtains. The police car was still parked in the cul-de-sac. One man lay on the ground beside it, blood pooling around a head wound. She thought she saw shadows moving towards the side of the house, but she could not be sure.

Lauren grabbed her coat and threw Petra her jacket. "We can't go out the front," she said. "We need to get to the car, or over the back fence, so we're going to have to go out through the hall and into the kitchen."

Petra knew she was right — there was no other way. True, Lauren had the window key. They could unlock the front window and they could climb out and hope not to be seen. Was that likely?

No, Petra thought.

"OK, that's what we have to do," she agreed, but she didn't think she had ever felt so scared. Then a gunshot rang out. *Was that from inside or outside of the house?* Petra found she was unable to guess.

CHAPTER 51

It was after ten when Clarke finally headed back to his flat. He opened the front door, dumped his coat in the hall and suddenly realized that there was a light on in his living room. Then the door to his kitchen opened and he was confronted by a large, suit-clad body who seized him by the arm and propelled him through into the living room at the front of the flat.

Kyle Sykes was seated in a chair facing the door and he had a gun in his right hand.

"So, where's my bitch of a daughter?"

"How the hell should I know?"

Kyle Sykes laughed. "You've met Freddie," he said. "I've borrowed him, you might say, from Gus Perrin, because of his talents at persuasion. Your ex-DCI Frankland was equally certain that he knew nothing. Freddie persuaded him otherwise." Kyle Sykes began to laugh. "Not that it matters. I know where she is. Her and that fucking bitch, Pat or Petra, or whatever her real name is. But I might let Freddie play anyway, just for the sheer hell of it. How about that?"

Freddie tightened his hold on Clarke's arms. Steel fingers bit into muscle and threatened bone. Clarke remembered what they had done to Frankland. And did they really know the location of the safe house or was this a bluff?

"Can't tell you what I don't know," Clarke said. "Out of my hands now, Kyle. Your daughter's being protected, but no one's going to tell me where she is. That's way above my pay grade."

Had he been followed again? Clarke thought not. He'd been almost fanatical in the care he'd taken when he'd come and gone from the safe house.

"You're not a good liar, DI Clarke," Kyle Sykes told him. "You've known where she is since you picked her up from that hotel." He tutted. "Now, you really were careless over that. My men followed you all the way up there and all the way back down again. Imagine how surprised they were when you took your little detour."

"I lost them though, didn't I, Kyle? But as for your daughter, I handed her over, she's safe. Nothing more I can tell you."

Kyle Sykes laughed and Clarke knew suddenly beyond doubt that not only did Kyle not believe him, but that he already knew where Lauren and Petra currently were. He didn't need Clarke to tell him.

So who had leaked that information?

"You'll know it's all over by the shouting, Kyle. We're coming for you. Frankland may be dead, but what he knew hasn't died, and it's now being acted upon."

Kyle Sykes shrugged. "Pity you won't be around to see the outcome, then." He nodded to Freddie and Clarke felt one hand move down onto his wrists and clamp tightly and painfully around both. The grip was so fierce that he could feel the bones moving. Sykes shifted suddenly, getting up out of the chair and leaning in towards Clarke. "I can't tell you how much I've been looking forward to this," he said.

* * *

Clarke knew he was going to die. He knew his colleagues would find him, bound and dead and mutilated, and that if Sykes and Freddie had their way, he'd take an impossibly long time to die. The image of Frankland swam into his head. As Sykes leaned in towards him, Clarke lurched forward, and brought the full force of his skull up under Sykes's chin. The man went down like he'd been shot and Clarke, dazed from the blow, twisted his body, hoping against hope that the shock of what he had done would loosen Freddie's grip.

Freddie lost hold and then grabbed at Clarke's arm. The violence of Clarke's struggle threw the pair of them off balance. Clarke kicked out, made contact — but with something hard that felt like bone. Numbness spread upward through his leg, calf to knee. Freddie grunted, it seemed more in surprise than pain. Clarke threw himself backwards as hard as he could, taking advantage of the fact that neither of them were on solid footing. Freddie's grip loosened again, just for a split second, and Clarke kicked out again, screaming at the pain that shot through his leg. Out of the corner of his eye, he saw Kyle Sykes twitch and knew he had to fix things now, while the odds were shifted even slightly in his favour. He'd not fool Sykes again.

With a massive effort, Clarke threw himself backwards, dropping his full weight to the floor. Then, as Freddie put out a hand to break his own fall, he rolled free. He scrambled to his feet, heading for the door. Freddie lurched, grabbed at him. Missed, but not by much. Now Sykes was on his knees and had retrieved his gun.

He fired, hitting the wall close to Freddie's head. Clarke heard Freddie shout, saw him turn angrily on Sykes. Sykes seemed beyond worrying about hitting his own man, intent on getting Clarke.

The moment of discord bought Clarke precious seconds and he dived for the front door, hit the stairs and ran.

CHAPTER 52

"Ready?" Petra asked. Lauren nodded. Time seemed to have stretched since Lauren had last opened the door, but Petra knew it had been only seconds. The door handle was hot now. Lauren had grabbed the quilts from their makeshift beds. "Synthetic," she said. "They'll probably melt, but it's better than nothing."

She wrapped the duvet round the handle, flung the door open, then, flinging the quilt around her, charged out through the hall and into the kitchen. Petra realized that she was screaming. Despite the smoke that cut visibility to little more than a hand's breadth in front of her, that choked the air from her lungs, she couldn't help herself. She felt Lauren give her a shove and heard the kitchen door slam, shutting out the blaze in the hall. Then fresh air as the back door was flung open . . . and a gunshot ripping through the smoke.

* * *

A door opened on the next landing. "Call the police," Clarke yelled. Freddie was closing on him, the big man thundering down the stairs. Sykes fired again and Freddie bellowed at him. Clarke heard the woman who'd just open her door begin to scream. "Just call the bloody police!"

His lungs were burning with fear, with the effort of running. He gripped the banister rail and swung himself round the next bend in the stairs and felt the impact as something hit him in the upper arm. Realizing he'd been shot, he fell the rest of the way down the flight of stairs.

Another door opened, another face appeared and then disappeared inside. Neither Sykes nor Freddie seemed to care what amount of noise they were creating now. Clarke took small solace from that as he struggled to his feet and almost threw himself down the next flight of stairs, his feet flailing on the steps, his hands scrabbling for purchase on the rail. His left hand, slick with blood, slid as he tried to hold on. He was on the final flight now, could see the doors ahead of him. Freddie reached for him again, grabbing his arm where the bullet had already ripped through. Clarke screamed in pain. He felt the pressure of Freddie's gun against his skull, wondered, through the confusion of anger and pain, why Freddie didn't just pull the trigger. He was dimly aware that he could hear Sykes yelling and another voice, that of a woman shouting from upstairs, but he could not make out the words. The pain in his arm was almost overwhelming and Clarke's legs collapsed beneath him. A gunshot echoed in his head.

* * *

Lauren returned fire. She could not see where the shot had come from. They had no option but to keep going forward. There was shouting and more gunshots. In the confusion, it was impossible to tell what was going on. She wondered if one of the armed police was still out there, still alive, and shooting back at the intruders. Certainly from the sound of it, there seemed to be something of a battle going on. But they did not have time to stop and work it out.

"Can we get to the car?" It was only a few feet from the door, but they'd still have to start the engine, drive off and hope they didn't get killed in a hail of gunfire on their way out.

"It's either that or go over the fence," Petra muttered. She had the car keys in hand and a flash of light told Lauren that the car doors were now open. They dived inside. At that moment, they caught a glimpse of the armed officer. He was crouching beside the fence and returning fire. Lauren opened the window. "Get in the back," she yelled.

Petra blessed the little car as the engine fired the first time and they surged forward. The officer grabbed the door and hurled himself onto the back seat. "Stay down," Petra shouted. Foot to the floor, they swung out onto the unmade road. Someone bounced off the wing of the car and crashed to the ground. The officer was firing out of the window now. Petra just pointed the car and tried to keep it in a straight line on the filthy, slick road.

She didn't slow down until they were on the main road and something like a mile away. She pulled into a bus stop and looked around wide-eyed at the other two. "Anyone hurt?" The windscreen was a mosaic of cracks spreading from two round holes. There was blood on her face, from flying glass.

"I'm OK," Lauren said.

"I will be, but I think I need an ambulance." The police officer was deathly pale. His vest had saved his life, but his face was bloodied and one arm hung limp at his side. His other hand was pressed tight against a hole in his leg, just above his knee.

"First aid kit in the glove compartment," Petra told Lauren. "Then you'd better phone an ambulance. I'm not sure where we are, though."

She opened the rear door and began to examine the officer, deciding that the wound in the leg was probably the worst, but that he was right, he would be OK as long as he got medical help. But he was in a lot of pain and was still losing blood.

"I've got GPS on my phone," Lauren told her. "I'll sort out what to tell the ambulance. I'll be as quick as I can."

Petra nodded and set about trying to patch up the police officer. She was scared he would go into shock. She could hear Lauren talking into the phone now. But she was having a hard time convincing the ambulance controller that yes, she really did mean a gunshot wound.

Petra sighed. She took the phone from Lauren.

"My name is DS Petra Merrow," she said. "And I need immediate assistance. We have an officer down and our current location is?" She looked at Lauren, who provided the GPS coordinates.

"Right," Petra said as she hung up, reflecting that this was the first time in three years that she had used her rank and proper name to an outsider. "Looks like I'm getting my own normal back, doesn't it?"

CHAPTER 53

Toby Clarke woke surrounded by bright lights, and wondered where the hell he was. His head hurt abominably, as did his arm and leg, and it slowly dawned on him that he wasn't dead and he was probably in a hospital bed somewhere.

He moved and Hopkins's face suddenly swam into view. "What happened?"

"As far as we can make out," she told him, "Kyle Sykes was waiting for you in your flat along with one of Perrin's thugs. Somehow or other, you managed to get away and fortunately you made enough noise that one of your neighbours called us."

"Ah," Clarke said. He dimly remembered a woman shouting, and he remembered falling, and he remembered the pain in his head. He lifted a hand and found that his head was in fact bandaged. And so was his arm. So he had been shot. That memory at least was real. He winced. Everything hurt.

"You got a nice groove in your skull. The doctor says you'll always have a little bald patch there that might be quite cute, but fortunately for you, you have a thick skull. The bullet only grazed it."

Clarke remembered how he'd dropped to the ground and, rolling beneath Freddie's momentum, had felt the big man fall. *Sykes*, Clarke thought. Sykes must have fired after that. Had it been Freddie, Clarke knew he would not have survived, not at such close range.

"Sykes?" he asked.

"In a cell. They found Freddie Benson at the foot of the stairs. Concussion."

Clarke blinked, absorbing that, trying to get his thoughts in order and remembered suddenly what Kyle Sykes had said about knowing where Lauren and Petra were. He started up, trying to sit, but the pain stabbed through his head once more. Nausea overwhelmed him and he thought that he might be sick or pass out, or maybe both together. *Lauren and Petra*. He wasn't sure he had managed to say the words out loud, but he must have done, because Hopkins responded.

"Someone set fire to the house. Two officers killed, one badly injured. Lauren and Petra are OK, but I don't know much more than that right now. But it's not your problem. Your problem is getting better."

Clarke told her that he was happy to oblige, or at least, he thought that's what he said, before he slipped back into unconsciousness.

CHAPTER 54

Lauren watched as the police officer was loaded into the back of the ambulance. She was standing beside the car while Petra did her best to explain the situation to the anxious paramedics. Police officers were on their way, they'd been told, but there was an incident about a mile up the road that seemed to take priority. The paramedic looked expectantly at Petra, as though expecting her to fill in the gaps for him. It was pretty obvious that these two things were related, the injured police officer and whatever had happened at the new housing estate.

While they had waited for the ambulance to arrive Lauren had taken Petra aside. "They are never going to give up, are they?"

"Arrests will be made," Petra had told her. "The information I gave Clarke—"

"Like going to jail is going to stop them," Lauren had said. "You know as well as I do that my dad or Gus Perrin or any of them will be just as capable of running their little empires from inside as they are from the comfort of their own homes."

Petra had opened her mouth to object and then closed it again. She'd known Lauren was right and there was no arguing with that. Lauren had wondered if Petra would ever feel safe again. Being a police officer might improve her security, if she was lucky, but Lauren had no such protection.

"The only way they'll stop is if I'm dead," Lauren had said.

Now, as the ambulance prepared to leave, Lauren seized her chance. She knew that the police would be here very soon and, once they arrived, there would be no further opportunity. She knew the car was a wreck, and that she'd be pulled over if anyone saw it with a broken windscreen and the bullet holes in the side, but it was still dark — it was still night — she had a few hours to put distance between herself and Petra. Herself and everybody else. Seconds later, she was in the car and gone.

When the patrol car finally arrived, they found Petra sitting alone on the kerb, looking utterly lost.

CHAPTER 55

It was a cold and blustery morning when Emily Cairns and her dog took their usual route along the top of the cliff at Burness Head. They walked in all weathers, staying in only when the winds were strong enough to make Emily feel that she might be blown off the cliff at any moment. There was a seat right at the top of the head that looked out across the bay and Emily always paused there, sitting for a few minutes to enjoy the sight of the waves and the occasional seal. Today, there was something on the seat. A backpack and a note, weighed down with stones.

Emily's heart skipped a beat. *Oh, no*, she thought. *Surely not*. She read the note. It was brief and to the point. *I'm sorry, but this is best for everybody*. It was signed, *Lauren*. Hesitantly, Emily went to the edge of the cliff and looked down. There was a car among the rocks at the foot of the cliff, its wheels in the air and fierce waves breaking over it, threatening to drag it further into the sea.

The news reports later spoke of a young woman hounded by the police, running from her father, caught up in a situation that she could not handle. A tragic life cut short. The story would be picked over in the days that followed as the media chased the arrests that had been made, the revelations about men killed in the cottage by the coast, the undercover officer who had now been suspended from duty pending enquiries and the funerals of the police officers killed in the line of duty, and skirted past the OCGs that the police claimed had been smashed — but which seemed very much intact, to those in the know.

* * *

From his hospital bed, Toby Clarke read the papers. Watched the news, talked to those colleagues who visited him. Tried to make some sense of it all.

Kyle Sykes had been arrested. Other arrests had been made, based on Frankland's USB drive and as far as Clarke could tell, the strategy of the task force was to sweep up anyone mentioned and then figure out what could be made to stick.

No one seemed to know how Kyle Sykes had found the safe house. Clarke had begun a list of those who might possibly have known. Craig and Crenshaw, the armed police . . . who else? Theoretically, anyone on the team could have found out. Frustrated, he had put his list aside.

"We'll find out who it was," Crenshaw told him when he came to visit.

"It could have been you," Clarke said.

"Or you. They followed you once. We checked, there was no tracker on your car, but . . ." Crenshaw shrugged. "We'll find out, you can be sure of that."

"And in the meantime?"

"Gus Perrin has slid smoothly into Sykes's territory, taken on most of his employees—"

"He didn't have employees," Clarke objected. "They were all responsible for their own tax and National Insurance."

Crenshaw gave him a puzzled look.

"A joke," Clarke told him. "Probably not a very good one. What happened to Sam Barker and her boyfriend? The statement she made—"

"Will be held back for the moment until the Crown Prosecution Service has finished faffing about. Sykes will be charged with your attempted murder and we're confident we can put him at the scene when Harry Prentice was killed. Joe Messenger's statement has been entered into evidence. The wife is willing to testify if it comes to it, but as she can't tell the court more than that Kyle Sykes came to collect her husband, it's likely she'll be spared the trouble. The CPS will push for charges that can be made to stick. We'll have to settle for what we can get, Clarke."

Clarke nodded, angry but not surprised. "And Sam Barker?"

"So far as Gus Perrin is concerned, Sam Barker delivered the message he told her to deliver. That she'd had an argument with her boyfriend and that was that. She's out of the way. If she's needed, then we'll bring her back, but there's no sense endangering yet another life. As for her boyfriend, he's turned up at his parents' place. My guess is he'll be left alone, so long as he keeps his head down. Perrin won't make waves he doesn't have to make. He's not as impetuous as Kyle Sykes."

"Impetuous. Is that what you call it?"

Crenshaw ignored the sarcasm. "Carole Josephs, incidentally, is at a relative's place down on the south coast. I'm told the publicity has done her career no harm at all. The exhibition is practically a sell-out."

Clarke laughed, but there was no humour in it.

"The great shame is, we lost Lauren Sykes," Crenshaw said. "That's the most tragic thing of all."

CHAPTER 56

Petra Merrow and Toby Clarke had attended Harry Prentice's funeral together. They had slipped in, after the service had started, and sat silently at the rear of the crematorium. There were not many people in attendance. Most of the people who had known Harry were awaiting trial, or simply didn't want to be connected with the man who had been killed by the wrath of Kyle Sykes.

Ruby Messenger was there, and she glanced around and nodded to Clarke as he came in. Then she turned away.

Earlier, Merrow and Clarke had gone to the motorway services, to the little motel where Lauren and Petra had stayed before going to the safe house that had proved not quite so safe. They had retrieved the notes that Lauren had hidden beneath the divan. These had now been entered into evidence. Petra herself was still on suspension and Clarke was officially on sick leave. Neither was sure what was going to happen next or if they still had careers in the police force.

They had brought flowers for Harry, on behalf of Lauren, and on behalf of themselves. Petra certainly felt that she had learned to know Harry through Lauren's descriptions of him. Harry had truly loved her.

"So what *actually* happened to her?" Clarke asked, as they placed their own floral tributes among the others in the garden of remembrance.

"I'm not sure what you mean," Petra said.

"She'd never have driven off that cliff."

"She needed to be dead," Petra told him. "What else could she do?"

CHAPTER 57

On the day that Emily Cairns had discovered the backpack and note on the bench, Lauren had watched as the car tumbled down into the sea and crashed on the rocks. She felt sorry for the little car — it had taken them a long way. She checked the pebbles, that there were enough to hold down the note and she looked anxiously at the sky, hoping that it wouldn't rain and soak the note through before it was found. But the dawn was clear and cold, and she thought she would be lucky. Sooner or later, somebody would find the backpack anyway, and she'd left enough evidence inside to make it clear who it had belonged to. She murmured an apology for any shock she might cause to the finder, but it couldn't be helped now.

She made her way slowly back to the road. It was about a mile and by the time she got there, her feet were frozen and soaked by the wet grass. There was a single car parked in the car park. The driver was a dark-haired young man and, when Lauren got into the car, two dogs yipped excitedly. There was a bag in the foot well with a flask of coffee, some sandwiches and a warm blanket. Chocolate in the glove compartment.

"Your car and your dogs?"

He grinned at her. "Borrowed car and borrowed dogs."

"So," she said, "I suppose I'd better decide who I want to be now."

He nodded. "Names are like tattoos, you've got to feel comfortable with them on your skin. So take your time."

The car was warm. Lauren wrapped a blanket around her legs and sipped her coffee. She had no idea where they were going or where she'd end up but, for the first time she could remember, Lauren Sykes actually felt safe.

THE END

FREE KINDLE BOOKS

12275494R00159